Reluctant Siege

Clay Warrior Stories

J. Clifton Slater

This is a work of fiction. While some characters are historical figures, the majority are fictional. Any resemblance to persons living or dead is purely coincidental.

Reluctant Siege takes place in late 265 B.C. to early 264 B.C. when Rome was a Republic and before the Imperial Roman Empire conquered the world. While I have attempted to stay true to the era, I am not an historian. If you are a true aficionado of the times, I apologize in advance.

I'd like to thank my editor Hollis Jones for her work in correcting my rambling sentences and overly flowery prose.

Now… Forget your car, your television, your computer, and smart phone - it's time to journey back to when making clay bricks and steel were the height of technology.

J. Clifton Slater

Website: www.JcliftonSlater.com

E-Mail: GalacticCouncilRealm@gmail.com

FB: facebook.com/Galactic Council Realm & Clay Warrior Stories

Reluctant Siege

Act 1

The Republic organized its army in regional garrisons. When faced with a rebellion, or threats from tribes or barbarians, the Senate approved a Legion for that specific enemy. One of the two Consuls assembled the Legion and assumed the title of General. Most of these Legions were victorious, some were not. Most of these politicians turned General listened to their military leaders, others did not.

In 265 BC, Consul Quintus Fabius Gurges marched his Legion north to put down an Etruscan rebellion. The Etruscan city of Volsinii sat atop a fortified plateau in what today is the Tuscany region. Volsinii's defenders were prepared for the Legion. As a result, General Gurges' campaign was not a success.

Chapter 1 – The Slopes of Volsinii

The Legion's reinforced camp sat a mile to the east. Not far from where the Tiber river slashed through the wide valley. Three days ago, General Gurges marched his army up from the Capital and constructed the camp. Bypassing the hills and peaks lying to the town's south and west, Gurges, for once, followed the recommendations of his officers. They had suggested an attack from the north. However, they had also recommended placing the Legion camp on the plain and not adjacent to the Tiber river.

The tilted plain on the north started at the base of the steep slope leading up to Volsinii. It spread out to cover half the width of the plateaued city and, unlike the other sides where the slopes resembled near vertical walls, the plain faced a climbable grade. Although not perfect, the plain allowed for staging and maneuvering of the maniples' ranks that made up the Legion's assaulting force.

His staff did caution, the drawbacks to the plain were the foothills ending at the southwest flowing Tiber. Besides the ability for an enemy force to hide in the hills, the riverbank could act as a road for any tribesmen coming from the north. The other issue was the distance to the sturdy walls of the camp where the pack animals and Legion's heavy weapons were stored. But this was an assault not a siege. The ballistae, or bolt throwers, shouldn't be needed.

Consul Gurges who had raised the Legion, named it after himself, and took the mantle of General, discounted the warnings. As he explained after sacrificing a bull to Victoria, "The Goddess of Victory will grant us a swift end to this affair."

Many Legionaries commented about the General's failure to also sacrifice to Victoria's siblings – Kratos, Bia, and Zelus asking for Strength, Force and Zeal. The views were whispered among the ranks of Legionnaires. One didn't openly voice an opinion about a nobleman's actions. Seeing as Gurges was a Consul serving the last weeks of his one-year term as a Co-Consul of the Republic, and their General, all ranks were below Quintus Fabius Gurges.

***

The skirmishers raced through the ranks of the maniples and launched javelins. Many of the Etruscī and Insubri rebels held tribal shields. By shifting them, they avoided the iron heads of the Legionaries' weapons as the deadly tips rose to the height of the rebel lines. Four of the rebel warriors standing on the plateau fell back and out of sight.

When their supply of javelins was exhausted, the Velites drew gladii and scrambled up the steep slope. In a hail of stones, arrows, and spears, the skirmishers forfeited their lives to test the resolve of the rebels. Before the skirmishers were completely decimated, trumpets sounded the recall. Now released from their assault on the heights, the Velites raced down the hill and filtered back through the lines of the maniples.

"It appears the rebels will not easily surrender the high ground," General Gurges stated to the mounted Tribunes crowded around his horse. None of the young noblemen expected the rebels to give up. The Centurion and his escort, sent yesterday to demand the surrender of Volsinii, had returned filled with Etruscan arrows and knife slashes. Neither survived their injuries.

"I guess, we do this the hard way," Gurges announced then waved a dismissive hand at his Tribunes. "Go prepare your sections and report back here when you've completed your tasks. Trumpeter, prepare to sound the advance for the first rank."

Off to the side of the General, Colonel Pholus sat on his horse surrounded by four of the Legion's senior Centurions. Although he could hear the General, his eyes weren't on Gurges. They were fixed on the bodies of the Velites left behind when the skirmishers retreated. Most lay still, but every so often, a few of the bodies came to life and attempted to crawl or roll down the hill. This movement attracted arrows, rocks, and spears from the rebels. Soon, all the bodies of the Legion's skirmishers were dead.

"Butcher," whispered a Centurion.

Pholus ripped his eyes from the bloody slope and snapped his head around.

"Yes. We will have an officers' meeting this evening to discuss lessons learned from the assault, Centurion," the Legion's Colonel announced as if the Centurion had asked a question. "Until then, get to your Centuries and buck up your NCOs."

The four senior Centurions kicked their horses into motion heading for their sectors.

"They are obstinate, don't you think, Colonel Pholus?" Gurges called across the gap between the two leaders of the Legion. Pholus swallowed hard and his stomach turned before he noticed the General was pointing at the heights of Volsinii.

"Yes, Sir. It'll be costly to remove the rebels," Pholus replied. As a professional military leader, he referred to the lives and limbs lost by Legionaries needed to pacify the town.

"Not to worry Pholus. I should more than break even once I sell the spoils of war and fill my slave pens," Gurges explained using a different definition of cost. "And best of all, I'll be a hero of the citizens. That will serve me well when my term as Consul ends and I resume my seat in the Senate. Nothing holds sway in politics like being a hero of the people. Wouldn't you agree?"

"Yes, General. Maybe you can hold a parade?" suggested Pholus with a hint of sarcasm.

"A grand idea, Colonel," Gurges exclaimed. "It'll cut into my profits but, the people do love to cheer a hero of the Republic."

***

All Consuls when they organized a Legion to engage a large threat were arrogant. Most however, listened to their experienced core of military leaders who ran the army. Gurges had little to say until he looked at a map of Volsinii during the march north. Then, he announced his battle plan and how he would disperse the Legion.

"Two days tops to put the rebels to death," the Consul, with no military experience, announced. "We'll use the skirmishers to clear the heights and the infantry can dance into the town. I imagine a cavalry charge will be thrilling to watch. Great sport, don't you think?"

At the time, Colonel Pholus and the officers from Planning and Strategies had stood with eyes downcast as the

General moved blocks of colored wood around the map. As if the troops, represented by the blocks, were skating on a flat icy pond rather than attacking up the face of a defended slope. Even later, when Pholus explained the small numbers on the map denoted elevations, the General refused to change his plan. Then, Gurges reminded Pholus that the General was a Consul of the Republic, and the Colonel was from a farming family. Thusly, the Colonel should be cautious when contradicting his betters. The attack would go just as the General planned.

***

Pholus was ignored as the gang of Tribunes returned from alerting their sections along the lines of Legionaries. Each had raced to a Century's Centurion, shouted at the officer before kneeing their mount on to the next Century. Once they finished, the young noblemen raced back to the General as if this was a game. Pholus glanced at the bodies on the hillside and back at the converging Tribunes. They hadn't stopped to consider the cost in lives so far, or the lives of those preparing for the actual assault. Just one Tribune seemed to even acknowledge the deaths.

Tribune Peregrinus' horse was trotting rather than galloping back to the command staff. He was the youngest of the noblemen on the General's personal staff. After alerting his sections, Peregrinus took time to stare at the bodies on the hillside as his horse closed with the crowd surrounding the General.

"I have a change," announced Gurges to his Tribunes while he glared at Colonel Pholus. "Remember this lads, flexibility in negotiations is important to winning. Not giving in to every weak idea from your secretaries, but being cognizant of areas where you can improve your position while seeming to give in. That will prove valuable to you later in life."

Tribune Peregrinus rode up as the General finished his political sermon.

"Mister Peregrinus. Did you have a nice stroll among the common soldiers?" demanded the General. Then he continued without waiting for an answer, "I'll sound the advance for second rank when the first maniple is halfway up. However, I want the cavalry repositioned. I was going to wait until they had a path to charge but, as I can see now, they'll be more valuable on the line. Split them in half and place the cavalry on either end of the third maniple. We'll get the rebels in a pincer movement. Go, alert your sections."

Once again, the Tribunes raced away while Colonel Pholus almost puked. They had little enough cavalry, and now the mounted units were being split and committed to the fight. Worst of all, the battle was just beginning, and the General had left no units guarding the Legion's rear.

***

The three ranks of Legionaries launched javelins. A few Etruscī and Insubri warriors died but most of the javelins fell short. With the first maniple moving, the rebels had to come off their hill and engage. If they didn't, the line of Legionaries would reach the top and it would become a shield wall fight for the town. Ambush and open field fighting were the tribesmen's preferred strategies. Shield to shield, close in carnage, belonged to the Legionaries. The first maniple was six paces into the assault when the rebels committed.

A Legion's heavy infantry was divided into three lines of the maniples. The third line composed of hardened veterans. In front of them, the line consisted of experienced Legionaries. Out front on the first line, were rookies and inexperienced Legionaries. The idea was to get the newest Legionaries combat experience and to toughen them up by allowing them first blood.

From the top of the hill town, tribesmen poured over the crest and ran, in mass, down the steep hill. Colonel Pholus watched as the first line locked shields and braced for the onslaught. The General hadn't ordered the second line forward. Mostly because the Legionaries hadn't gone far enough up the slope to suit his plan. By the time the wave of rebels reached the first maniple, they were sprinting to stay on their feet. They hit the Legionaries like a herd of stampeding Aurochs. In spots, the line held. At other places, the tribesmen pounded through the shields.

Their momentum broken from hitting the shields, the rebels easily reversed course and attacked the Legionaries from behind.

***

"We're sending up the second line. Go lads," the General announced in a voice that spoke of controlled confidence. Probably the voice he uses while debating in the Senate, assumed Pholus. As the Tribunes kneed their horses into motion, Gurges spoke to the trumpeter, "Stand by to advance the second line."

Colonel Pholus wanted to gallop his horse at the General and run the old wind bag over. While Gurges waited for everyone to be in place, the first maniple fought for their lives in a melee with the tribesmen.

Along the busted line, rebels and Legionaries hacked, blocked, and stabbed each other. Murder and death being just a breath or a misstep away. In front of and behind them, and sometimes beside them, the rookie Legionaries blocked and stabbed trying to make sense of their broken line. Their training had prepared them to hold a line, use a shield and a gladius in unison with fellow Legionaries. And to maintain alignment while maneuvering. In other words, they were trained very well, but for combat in ranks, not as pit fighters.

Grunts, cries of madness and pain accompanied drops and splatters of blood soaring around the combatants. Soon, no one could tell if the red stains were theirs, a comrade's, or the blood of an enemy. About a third of the inexperienced Legionaries of the front line were down when the trumpets sounded.

The experienced Legionaries from the second maniple stepped forward and joined in the gladii fighting. When possible, a Legionary would reach out and pull a rookie out of the fight and thrust him behind the line. As more and more of the surviving first line were pulled out of combat, Corporals began shoving javelins into their hands and forming them up as a second rank. Their training fit this type of fighting and they began stabbing over the shoulders of the second maniple.

***

Being proficient with the javelin and protecting the man in front of you was important for three reasons. If you kept the enemy from taking down the man in front, you wouldn't have to be in a belly-to-belly sword fight. Also, staying with your maniple increased your chances of survival. When the skills of Legionaries on either side were equal to yours, and you knew the men, you had confidence that no stray spear or sword point would slip in from the side. And finally, there was pride in being part of a maniple. After the battle, you would share tales of heroics and stupidity by the rank in front of you. If you entered the front line, you'd be teased about your weak javelin work, or your maniple would mourn your death. So, keeping the enemy off the man in front of you was indeed important.

The second maniple with help from the survivors of the first maniple, began to gain ground. As the experienced Legionaries hacked down the rebels in front of them, they used the space to take half steps forward. Soon, they were a full third of the way up the steep hill.

Behind them, the hardened veterans waited. Their chance would come at the top of the slope where the fighting would be the most vicious.

***

The Tribunes sat their mounts in a loose formation around the General. Everyone relaxed a little as the Legionaries took back control of the battle.

"Just as I planned," bragged General Gurges. "We've pulled the majority of the rebels out of their merda-hole and brought them to the tip of our gladii."

A fire on the summit flared to life. When an amphora of olive oil was tossed on the flames, a column of black smoke rose high into the cloudless sky. Then, an Etruscī horn blared. The deep resonance floated over the struggling warriors and Legionaries.

The beating of swords and gladii against armor and flesh continued. What changed was the addition of professional soldiers to the rebel forces. Ranks of ordered Etruscans crested the hill and marched down the steep slope to join the battle.

***

After years of fighting and vicious engagements, the Etruscan civilization had been forced to sign treaties with the Republic. For two decades, they had supplied warriors to the Republic's army. Now, some of those trained by Legionaries were turning the skills and weaponry against their teachers.

The arrival of disciplined troops went unseen by the rookies and the experienced Legionaries. They were living and dying in a narrow world of pain and sweat. Their survival counted in heartbeats left no spare moment to take their eyes off the next screaming barbarian.

Several hundred of the twelve hundred twenty hardened veterans of the third maniple noticed the soldiers. But, without a signal from the General, the best fighters of the

Legion couldn't move up. Although the addition of armored Etruscan soldiers was seen, the information was useless.

To the rear of the battle line, one person did notice the nine hundred Etruscan soldiers. General Gurges waved his Tribune corps into a horse mounted huddle.

Chapter 2 - Unexpected Rebel Formation

"I'm moving up the third maniple," General Gurges explained. "Wait for the trumpets. Then we'll see how those traitorous barbarians fare against our best."

"General. The horn, I understand," commented Tribune Peregrinus. "But why did the rebels light a signal fire."

Pollenius Armenius Peregrinus was sixteen and the eldest son of a wealthy family with political connections. His assignment to Consul Gurges' staff was only a way to give the lad military experience. Years from now, Pollenius could use his Legion time to further his political ambitions. When General Gurges brought the Legion together to crush the Etruscan uprising, it presented an opportunity. An easy win and useful experience, his father boasted as he packed his son off to war.

General Gurges studied his youngest and least experienced Tribune. If time permitted, he'd counsel the youth on not interrupting when his elders were speaking. But, Gurges was busy. Instead, he decided to remove the lad from the battlefield.

"Tribune Peregrinus. Take charge of the reserve Centuries. And watch. Maybe you'll learn something," General Gurges ordered. Then returning his attention to the other Tribunes, he directed, "Prepare the cavalry to turn the barbarian line. I want this over by nightfall."

The plan was for the mounted Legionaries to roll the ends of the Etruscan line inward. Once constrained, the enemy front would shorten allowing the heavy infantry to concentrate the fight on a narrower front. On an open plain or even in the foothills, it was a superb use of cavalry. However, the steep slopes of Volsinii were not ideal for the Legion's cavalry.

"Signalman. Standby to advance the third maniple," Gurges ordered the trumpeter as the Tribunes rode off to alert their segments of the battle line. "Then we'll let the cavalry have a bit of joy."

"On your command, Sir," the trumpeter assured his General.

Gurges sat comfortably on his horse turning his head from side to side. He was pleased with the speed of his Tribunes. They raced from Centurion to Centurion and soon the last two Tribunes reached the cavalry units. His seventy-five mounted Legionaries on either end of the battlefield received his orders and the Tribunes waved their arms. The motion was picked up by the other Tribunes. Like a ripple in a pond, the wave rolled from the far ends of the Legion's line until they converged on the General. With all of his units ready, he glanced down at the trumpeter.

"Sound the advance for third maniple," Gurges ordered. He waited patiently for the trumpets down the line to repeat the signal. Once the veteran infantrymen shifted forward to enter the battle, the General added, "Signal the cavalry!"

***

For the leading edge of the Etruscī and Insubri warriors, meeting the third maniple was shocking. One moment they were battling well trained but average Legionaries. Then, spaces opened between the Legionaries and a different kind of human stepped into the gaps. The experienced, and what was left of the rookie Legionaries, stepped back. Suddenly, the tribesmen faced a many clawed monster.

The harden veterans of the third maniple advanced. Their gladii pumping as if churning butter and their shields thrusting forward in bone breaking rhythm. By the time the trained ranks of Etruscan soldiers pushed aside their tribesmen brothers and reached the front line, the third maniple was warmed up and ready for them.

***

The General wasn't a fan of horsemen, especially for a short excursion into the foothills along the Tiber river. He couldn't justify the expense but, to satisfy the Senate, he allotted for one hundred fifty when he presented his plan to the Senate. A few Senators with military experience voiced concerns, but in the end, the plan was approved. The Senate allowed the formation of Gurges Legion.

Mounted troops did serve one purpose. The cost of maintaining his mounts and those of his Tribunes got distributed through the cavalry budget. Not only would he make a fortune on slaves and bounty from putting down the Volsinii rebellion, he would do it under budget. Although the citizens didn't care about such things, the Senate did. Certainly, he could use it as an example when he surrendered the Consulship in a couple of weeks and resumed his place in the Senate.

Every time a would-be hero of the Republic came forward asking for gold to finance a Legion, Quintus Fabius Gurges would stand and, with the assurance of a successful General, he'd cut the adventurer's budget. The General laughed at his own cleverness as his understrength cavalry units nudged their mounts forward.

***

Foot soldiers responded to enemy cavalry because it was hard to defend against moving mounts. Huge numbers of fast-moving hooves and long swords chopping down from on high as the horsemen passed were devastating. If the infantrymen were in formation, the ends of their lines were the most vulnerable. In an open field and out of formation, the cavalry was an infantrymen's worst nightmare. But on steep terrain, the mounts couldn't get speed or maneuver with any authority.

Rather than turning a few Etruscī and Insubri inward, the mounted Legionaries confronted massed warriors. The introduction of organized Etruscan soldiers to the center of the line allowed the tribesmen to push reinforcements to both ends. There, they lowered their spears and long swords and engaged the cavalry. The Legion mounts struggled up the slope and approached in columns. Instead of a cavalry charge, it became a series of slow-moving horseback sword fights. The mounted troops climbed to the fight, swung their swords a few times, then came about and descended the hill. At the bottom, they got back in the column and prepared to do another circuit.

On the other end of the Legion line, that cavalry unit also got bogged down in a chain of passing flourishes. As the battle for Volsinii progressed, the barbarian line remained fully extended. This prevented the Legion's infantry from forming into three ranks where they could rotate men off the shield wall and give the veterans a rest.

Chapter 3 – Reserve Status

Tribune Peregrinus trotted his horse away from General Gurges and the Tribunes. Although the spirited horse moved with its head held high, hooves flashing and bristling with energy, its rider displayed none of those attributes.

Peregrinus' cheeks flushed and burned hot at the shame of being dismissed from the battlefield. He slumped on the neck of his horse and sulked. Somewhere in the young Tribune's misery, he began to worry.

What would he tell his father? While the other Tribunes were riding back and forth coordinating the Legion, Pollenius Armenius Peregrinus was exiled to the Legion camp as a spectator.

And the reserve units? A ragged collection from the Central and Eastern Legions. No doubt misfits sent by their Centurions to rid their units of problems.

They didn't even qualify for a maniple. He'd watched them drill. The reserve Centuries practiced squad tactics and two-line attack formations. Compared to the power of the three-line maniples, it was almost sad to watch them. Maybe they were valuable in garrisons but, here on a true battlefield, they were only fit for reserve status.

***

Peregrinus jerked his horse to a stop and eyed the reserves. There should be four hundred and eighty Legionaries and officers. Yet he could only see about a third of that number. The rest were probably in the fortified camp sleeping, or off hiding, and drinking cheap wine.

An old Centurion marched up to him and, after a cross chest salute, asked, "Orders, Tribune?"

"Just watch. Maybe you'll learn something," Peregrinus spit out.

"Yes, sir," the Centurion replied calmly before walking away.

Peregrinus wanted to dismount and pace, or stomp the ground, to release his frustration. But he was of the Patrician class, and it would be unseemly for common citizens, let alone Legionaries, to witness his fit of temper.

"The General committed his cavalry too soon," announced a voice in the crowd of reserve Legionaries.

Peregrinus' head snapped around and he shouted, "Who said that?"

"I did, Tribune," admitted one of the reserve Legionaries.

The man was just a few years older than Peregrinus but carried scars on the crown of his head, on both arms and on his thigh. Although he had a pleasant face, the scars made him look like a brawler, which only confirmed the young Tribune's opinion of the reserve units.

"Name?" Peregrinus demanded.

"Lance Corporal Alerio Sisera," the Legionary replied.

"Sisera. Keep your mouth shut," Peregrinus ordered. "When General Gurges wants your opinion, I'm sure he'll ask for it."

"Yes, Tribune," the Legionary replied.

***

As soon as the young Tribune turned around, another Legionary bristled, stood straighter, and opened his mouth. Before the hot-headed Legionary could say anything, Alerio jabbed him in the ribs with his elbow. The Legionary gasped but, the elbow worked, he didn't say anything to the Tribune.

"Private Drustanus. Lance Corporal Sisera. A word if you please," called out a Sergeant.

Drustanus and Sisera picked up their three javelins and their shields and walked over to the Century's Sergeant.

"In times of battle, our nerves are on edge," Sergeant Meleager advised them. "Our blood gets up and we're ready to lash out verbally or fight. Now, a wise man saves his ire and energy for the barbarians. As the Tribune pointed out, watch and maybe you'll learn something. Understand?"

"Yes, Sergeant," Alerio answered.

While the talk was aimed at the Legionaries, Tribune Peregrinus couldn't help but overhear the comments. However, he didn't see Sergeant Meleager and old Centurion Seneca exchange nods.

***

From the Legion camp, the men fighting on the hill at Volsinii were small, almost finger sized figures. But the lines were clear as the Legionaries fought, and the horsemen tried again and again to turn the barbarians.

One simple fact of a shield wall was both sides grew exhausted. Commanders needed to feed fresh bodies into the fray to maintain momentum. Without the relief, even the ablest veteran soon wore out. And while the third maniple had been hammering the Etruscī and Insubri warriors, the failure of the cavalry to shorten the barbarian's line required them to stay in the extended rank. When the Legion's NCOs managed to send the newest and the experienced Legionaries back into rotation, the moves resulted in the Legion line falling back a few steps. Both sides were slowing down in their ferocity except the tight ranks of the Etruscan soldiers. They were maintaining a cycle of rotation, keeping fresh troops in the fight. The truth of a shield wall was rested troops won the battle.

The other truth of a shield wall was an outside force could change the outcome of a conflict. Unfortunately, the force wasn't from the Republic.

***

Tribune Peregrinus sat transfixed as the Legion began back stepping. Fighting uphill against the press of bodies from above prevented the Legionaries from shoving the barbarians to make room for advancing. Plus, the extended line stunted a regular rotation. Those issues, in combination with the number of rebel tribesmen and the organized Etruscan soldiers, resulted in the Legion giving ground.

A whistle sounded from the far-right corner of the fortified Legion camp. Peregrinus hesitated a moment before turning to look in the direction of the whistle.

More than half the reserve Centuries were running in that direction. Behind him, three squads sprinted for the left corner of the camp.

"Centurion. What's going on?" demanded the young Tribune.

"Barbarian cavalry coming from the north," Seneca replied as calmly as if it was a parade ground exercise. "It'll do the men good to have a Tribune present."

"Shouldn't we go reinforce the General?" stammered Peregrinus.

"No sir. The Legion will do a fighting retreat," Seneca advised. "They need a place to retreat to more than a few extra gladii."

"Yes, of course," Peregrinus declared as he turned his horse. "I'll go review our positions."

"A fine idea, Tribune," Centurion Seneca stated as the young man kicked his horse into action. Then over his shoulder, he shouted, "Sergeant Meleager. Who do you want guarding the gate?"

"Seventh Squad, sir," the Sergeant replied.

"Isn't that Sisera's squad?" Seneca asked. "Why him?"

"I have friends in the Southern Legion," replied the Sergeant. "If you're going to be outnumbered, Lance Corporal Sisera is the man you want at your side."

"Alright, give him thirty extra bodies," Seneca suggested. "Now I wish we'd selected a new Corporal for the Century."

"I agree, sir," Sergeant Meleager answered by holding up an ink-stained right hand. Without a Corporal to act as the Century's treasurer, the reports and accounting fell to the Sergeant. He wasn't sure what he disliked the most. The ink from writing, or the long hours of administrative work done, after a day of training his men.

Chapter 4 – Ravine Mayhem

"We'll wedge it," announced Lance Corporal Sisera.

"Wouldn't a straight-line formation work better?" asked another Lance Corporal.

"For guarding the entrance, yes," Alerio admitted. "But as the Legion comes in, they'll break your integrity. Remember, we have to let our guys in and keep the barbarians out."

"My squad will take the north side of the wedge," the Lance Corporal stated. "Because that's the direction the barbarian horsemen are coming from."

Alerio nodded his approval before looking at his Left and Right-Side Pivot men.

"Cimon. Drustanus. Where do you want the squad to be?" he inquired. "It'll be safest at the stockade wall."

"Where will you be Lance Corporal?" Cimon asked.

"Seeing as Sergeant Meleager put me in charge of this detail," Alerio stated. "I'll be at the head of the wedge."

"Then I'll be on your right," announced Drustanus.

"And I'll be on your left," Cimon reported.

Moments later, Sergeant Meleager of the Forty-seventh Century, Gurges Legion jogged from the south end of the Legion's fortified camp. As he approached the gate, he slowed to look over the defensive formation.

Sisera stood at the tip of a wedge with three javelins jammed into the ground at his side. Private Cimon was on his left side two Legionaries back from the Lance Corporal. Private Drustanus stood in the same position on the other side. A double line of Legionaries on each side of the wedge stretched back in a vee-formation to the stockade's gate posts.

The Sergeant nodded his approval continued jogging passed the wedge towards the northern defensive position. He believed in giving good men a chance and letting them do their job. Alerio Sisera was a good candidate for the Corporal position. But he was only here for the rebellion.

Once the fighting was over, the Lance Corporal would take leave to visit his family's farm before reporting back to the Southern Legion.

***

Tribune Peregrinus found three hundred seventy Legionaries on the north side of the camp. They were in a double line stretching from the bank of the Tiber river to the foothills. The formation was situated to block the approaching barbarians' line of march. Instead of a straight gallop at the Legion, or the camp, the horsemen needed to go into the foothills or through the Legionaries.

A senior Centurion marched up to his horse and asked, "Orders, Tribune?"

Peregrinus realized, for the first time in his life, he was in charge of something important. His chest swelled with pride, and he no longer worried about what to tell his father.

"How did you know about the barbarian cavalry?" Peregrinus asked.

"The signal smoke from Volsinii," explained the Centurion. "It couldn't be for the local fighters. Centurion Seneca decided they must be sending a message to another force. He ordered the formation."

"What do you need, Centurion?" Peregrinus inquired while letting his eyes drift over the Legion lines.

"A ballista or two would be nice, Tribune," the officer replied in jest.

"Let me see what I can do," Peregrinus announced as he reined his horse around and kneed it towards the gate.

The Centurion was shocked. He was only teasing the young Tribune.

***

Peregrinus rode towards the stockade, guided the horse in an arc, and approached the gate from the west. His eyes on the Tiber river to his left, he didn't look around until the steed was galloping straight for the gate.

When he looked forward, to his horror, his horse was bearing down on a wedge of Legionaries. The reins just began to tighten when the wedge parted as would a gate. Looking back, he watched as the wedge closed behind him. Then he was through the gate and driving his horse towards the transport wagons.

"First Engineer! First Engineer," he yelled as he vaulted to the dirt.

"Tribune. What can I do for you?" the engineer asked.

"Do you have ballistae in those wagons?" he demanded.

"Why yes. But this is an assault, not a siege," remarked the Legion's First Engineer.

"Not anymore. The Legion is engaged almost a mile from here and we have mounted barbarians coming from upriver," Peregrinus explained. "We have one chance to slow them down and give the Legion a chance. We need artillery."

"In the field?" the Engineer asked, his eyes widening in disbelief.

Peregrinus looked at the log walls the Legionaries had constructed just a day ago. From the piled dirt to the trenches in case the walls were breached to the top of the logs.

"No, First Engineer. From in here," Peregrinus stated. "Over the walls. Can you do it? And I mean fast."

"Well, yes. But I need authorization from command staff," the engineer stated.

"The command staff is about to be overrun. They are out in the field fighting for their lives. If I had time, I would go and get one for you," Peregrinus said before stopping and realizing he was whining as he did when he was a little lad. He straightened his shoulders, locked eyes with the engineer and announced, "I am Pollenius Armenius Peregrinus, a Tribune for the Legion of Consul Quintus Gurges. By my authority, you will bring your ballistae to bear on the enemy. Or, I shall execute you right here by my own hand with my own gladius."

Peregrinus hadn't realized he'd rested his hand on the pummel of his weapon. The Legion's First Engineer had, and he reacted to the threat.

"Right away, Tribune," he shouted as he turned to the mule drivers, material handlers and his artillery staff. "That wagon and that wagon, to the north wall. You other men pull the tarps and unwrap the bolt throwers."

"The barbarians are coming, First Engineer," Peregrinus challenged as he jumped onto his horse. "And the Legion is depending on you."

He wheeled around and urged the horse towards the gate. As the steed galloped for the gate posts, he shouted a warning.

"Coming through," he yelled. The wedge parted and he shot through, rolled right, and raced for the Legionaries blocking the northern approach.

***

The Insubri were superb horsemen. Many tales sang the lie of charging to battle on a pony stretched out in full flight. But the northern tribesmen knew better. Men would be there to kill if you ran at them or took half a day to walk the distance. An Insubri warrior would only rush the last twelve inches and that was to stab you through the heart. They would never mistreat a fine mountain pony by wearing it out before a battle.

And so, it was for the fifteen hundred warriors coming down the bank of the Tiber river. They walked, slow and steady, as if stalking prey.

***

As Peregrinus rode around the corner of the camp, he saw a cluster of Centurions. Standing in the center was old Centurion Seneca. Every time he spoke, the other officers responded in the positive by word or body language.

"Tribune Peregrinus," Seneca announced in greeting as Peregrinus dismounted. "Care to inspect the formation?"

"Centurion. I'd like to inspect the formation," admitted Peregrinus. "If you'll teach me about the why-of-it as we walk."

A sharp whistle interrupted their conversation. Seneca raised his hand to his brow and searched beyond the lines of Legionaries.

"That lecture will have to wait, Tribune," Seneca explained. "And don't sit your horse. Those are Insubri warriors. They grew up shooting birds on the wing. I wouldn't think a Tribune on a horse would be much of a challenge for them."

"What do I do, Centurion?" Peregrinus asked and realized it came out odd because his teeth were chattering.

"You walk behind the line. Every fifth man, you slap him on the shoulder and tell him to kill one for your father," stated Seneca. "At the next legionary, ask him to kill one for your mother. When you run out of blood thirsty relatives, invent a few more. Work your way up and down the line."

"It doesn't seem like enough," pleaded Peregrinus.

"When you face death or take a life, it's nice to know you're doing it for an officer who cares," explained Seneca. "That's really all it takes. Be a Tribune, who cares."

Chapter 5 – The Northern Approach

The Insubri gathered just out of javelin distance. Sitting astride their ponies, they pointed out the shields and made a point of counting the number of Legionaries standing across the trail.

They could have turned, ridden up the hill and circled around but, the Legionaries seemed to tickle the northern tribesmen. The Legionaries, on the other hand, found the situation anything but humorous.

Peregrinus glanced down the line and noted the Centurions casually speaking with the men. He swallowed his fear and stepped towards the back of the closest Legionary.

"Kill one for my father," he mumbled.

The Private turned his head and asked, "Pardon, Tribune. Did you need something?"

Peregrinus hesitated. His experience with common Legionaries had been passing on an order or during an inspection with the General's staff. He really had no idea how to approach one or how to motivate the men. Then he lifted his eyes to the Etruscī warriors and swallowed.

"Yes, kill that cūlus on the brown pony for me," Peregrinus instructed.

"That one on the right?" the Legionary asked while pointing with his javelin. Three other helmets turned to listen.

"Yes, him. And if you can manage it, the one beside him," Peregrinus said.

"We can do that for you, sir," another Legionary assured him.

"How about the one on the other side?" a Legionary chimed in.

"Look, I don't mean to over tax your unit, but yes," Peregrinus stated. "I don't like his looks. He's too ugly to live."

Then Tribune Peregrinus walked away and counted off five Legionaries. Before he could say anything to the new group, one of the original Legionaries shouted to the men in front of him.

"Ask the Tribune which ones to kill," the man roared. "Seems the Insubri are offensive to the Tribune's sense of beauty. Ask him which ones are too ugly to live!"

"They're all ugly, sir. Which ones are particularly offensive?" a Legionary asked.

"The one on the red pony," Peregrinus replied.

"Too ugly to live?" the Legionary asked.

"Absolutely. Can you kill him for me?"

"Yes, sir. It'll be our pleasure."

When Seneca passed Peregrinus, the Tribune working his way up the ranks and the Centurion down the ranks, the Centurion slammed a fist to his chest in a cross-chest salute.

"Too ugly to live, Tribune?" Seneca asked.

"It's all I could think of to inspire the men," admitted Peregrinus. "Sometimes, it takes a cultured eye to recognize true grossness."

"Indeed, it does, Tribune Peregrinus," Seneca stated as he moved to approach another section of Legionaries. It took him a moment to replace the grin with his war face.

***

By the time the Insubri notched and unleashed the first volley of arrows, the Legionaries were calling and challenging the warriors. But it got serious when fifteen hundred mounted men kneed their ponies and pulled their swords.

The Legionaries threw javelin after javelin but still the riders came at the double line. Bravado faded as the ground began to shake and rumble from hooves pounding the earth. Over their shields and from under their helmets, the Legionaries' vista went from a riverbank with green hills beyond, to heaving chests of men and ponies.

"Brace, brace, brace," cried out the Centurions so they could be heard above the roar.

Just as the first rank of ponies struck the Legion line, three loud, sharp twangs cut the air. Followed by long bolts that each tore through three riders before burying itself in a fourth's pony. Combined with the injuries from the javelins, the gladii strikes, and the additional twelve warriors to fall from the bolts, the Insubri veered off and circled around to their original location. Big mistake as the ballistae sang out again and more Insubri fell to the riverbank.

***

The mounted warriors jerked their ponies around and further up the riverbank, they nudged their mounts onto the side of a hill.

"Who ordered the artillery?" a Sergeant asked.

Centurion Seneca walked up and in a loud voice announced, "That would be Tribune Peregrinus who saved your ugly hides. Now, if you don't have any more questions, we need to get to the Legion."

Insubri warriors were cresting the hill. In a short while, they would reach the battlefield and have a straight run at the Legion's back.

"I thought we didn't have enough men to be effective on the field?" commented Peregrinus.

"We don't. What we'll do is set up a catch line," Seneca instructed. "An island of strength for retreating units. It'll be a rally point and a safe zone for the wounded."

"Then we should get going," Peregrinus stated.

"No Tribune. We're going. You're needed here," advised Seneca. "The survivors will be staggering in with no direction and a broken command structure. As a staff officer, you have the authority to keep the gates clear and assign work details. Until the General and his staff arrive, you're in command of the camp."

Peregrinus stood watching as the Legionaries jogged to the west. For a moment, he fumed at being left behind. Then a thought crossed his mind. Would his father believe he was in command of a Legion fortification? Even if only for a little while? Grabbing the reins, he jumped onto the horse's back and urged the animal towards the main gate of his Legion's camp.

***

Alerio Sisera leaned on a javelin and watched the small figures in the distance. Because of the long sloping plain and the steep grade leading up to Volsinii, he had an excellent view of the fighting.

The maniples were attempting to break contact. But the long lines of Legionaries were breaking down as the Etruscī and their allies concentrated on weak sections. In spots, the tribesmen poured through gaps, circled around, and attacked the Legionaries from the rear. Each break created pockets of small units that were soon surrounded. Almost as if the Legion were a giant centipede being chopped into pieces, each segment that separated from the main body struggled to survive.

Although the ends and some flanking elements fought individual battles, the center lines of the Legion were fighting as a unit. In another twenty paces, the Legionaries would reach relatively flat ground and could form a defensive fighting square. The moveable formation would allow them to fight their way back to the camp.

Alerio was so focused on the fighting, he didn't hear or see the horse line up with the gate. When he did, he shouted to alert the Legionaries behind him and stepped out of the way. As he moved, his eyes noticed the line of Insubri ponies snaking down a far hillside. The race between the Legion getting off the slope, and the Insubri warriors joining the fight, played out in his mind repeatedly. Sometimes the Legion reached the plain and formed up. Other times, the Insubri reached the Legion while it was still strung out and vulnerable.

"Lance Corporal Sisera. Right?" a voice demanded.

Alerio broke from his trance and turned to find himself looking at the side of a horse. Shifting his gaze up, he recognized the rider.

"Yes, sir," Alerio replied to the angry young Tribune.

"What do you need to hold this gate?" Peregrinus inquired.

"I'd like to have time to partially bury a wagon on either side of the gate to protect my men," Alerio answered. He indicated spots a few yards outside the rows of Legionaries leading back to the gate posts.

Peregrinus studied the gate and the approaches to the opening in the stockade wall.

"The ground's too hard to get them deep enough," the Tribune commented. "Let me see what I can do."

With those words, Tribune Peregrinus kneed his horse and trotted into the camp. Alerio watched the young nobleman leap from his horse while shouting at the mule handlers and wagon drivers. Then, the Lance Corporal spun back to the battlefield.

The back two maniples broke off the battle line and ran down the slope. From this distance, Alerio couldn't tell which maniples broke contact, or which was left on the front line alone to fight the Etruscī. He was of two minds. If the veterans were left on the line, then the rookies and experienced Legionaries would form the square. But the powerful veterans, the core of the Legion, would be decimated during the fighting retreat. If either the newest or experienced Legionaries were left behind, most would die but, the defensive square would be stronger. It became a null subject when the mounted Insubri warriors hit the retreating legionaries from the rear.

Three horses broke from the mess of the battle. As they drew closer, Alerio relaxed, the riders wore Legion armor. The one in front, its rider kneeing the flanks hard, pulled ahead of the other two. Behind the lead horse, the riders slumped, and it seemed the horses were following the first horse rather than being guided by the Legionaries. A mounted Tribune reached the wedge. Without slowing, he rode by Alerio and disappeared into the camp.

The other two horses slowed as they approached the gate detail. Both riders were from the cavalry, and both had wounds. Alerio called two Legionaries over and had them lead the horses into the camp.

"Nice of the Tribune to help the cavalrymen," Drustanus said out of the side of his mouth.

"Stow it, Private," warned Alerio. "We don't know if he was carrying orders."

"Or running from a fight," Cimon added.

Noises behind Alerio drew his attention and he spun to see what caused the racket.

***

Two wagons came through the gate being pushed by mule handlers and wagon drivers. Behind them, Tribune Peregrinus marched out holding two torches.

"One wagon on each flank," he directed while pointing with the torches. "Leave space between the stockade wall and the back of the wagons. We don't want to burn down the camp."

As the wagons were pushed into position, Peregrinus smiled at Alerio.

"No time to dig," the Tribune announced as he tossed one torch into a wagon. The bed flared up in bright blue flames. "So, we'll use fire to keep them off your flanks." With that, he tossed the second torch into the other wagon.

"Pretty flames, Tribune," commented Alerio. "What did you use?"

"Goat grease. The Legion will be short of lubricant, but this seemed to be the more pressing issue."

"Yes, sir. And just in time," Alerio said as he raised a javelin and shouted to his detail. "We are here for one reason. Protect the gate."

Before the Legionaries could respond, Alerio whirled around and launched the javelin. It shot high into the air before arching over and diving towards the ground. Before it touched dirt, the iron tip pierced the chest of the leading Insubri warrior. He toppled off the pony and was trampled by the hundred horsemen following him towards the gate.

In a flash, the sky was filled with javelins. As the shafts fell, mounted warriors pierced through chests, arms, or shoulders, fell with them. But there weren't enough javelins. And the ponies continued to rush forward.

In a typical cavalry charge, the mounted warriors favored attacking from the side and chipping away at an armored formation. Gallantly charging through the enemy's lines in a rush of glory was the ultimate goal. But, plowing into the heart of an enemy's formation was a quick death for a horseman and his mount. With the burning wagons preventing a side attack, and the obvious suicide offered by the deep wedge formation, the Insubri warriors dismounted and charged the gate on foot.

Under his helmet and with his face hidden from the tribesmen by his shield, Lance Corporal Alerio Sisera smiled. On the backs of their ponies, the Insubri posed serious problems for the infantryman. On the ground, the warriors entered his arena. Alerio's smile reflected the anticipation of them entering his kill zone.

Chapter 6 – Battle for the Gate

"Cimon! Drustanus! Back four and hold," Alerio shouted. "We'll bring them to you."

Behind Alerio, the two pivot men shifted and stepped back. They moved into positions on the outside shoulders of the fourth Legionaries in the wedge.

The fastest warriors crashed into Alerio. He applied only enough resistance to prevent them from passing his shield. While they shoved and attempted to reach him with their long swords, Alerio stepped back. Their blades hacking at the moving shield.

On the fourth pace, the shields from the next two Legionaries in the wedge joined Alerio's. They used the shields to hold the Insubri at bay. Three stepped back and on the fourth pace, two additional shields locked into position. The five Legionaries continued the controlled retreat.

In the eyes of the charging tribesmen, it appeared the Legionaries were collapsing and trying to reach their camp. They bunched up and shoved forward. Every one of the Insubri wanted to be the first to break through the withdrawing Republic's soldiers. Being this close to the gates fueled their fury and thirst for glory. However, it also made them overconfident.

The five Legionaries increased their speed and the eighty remaining Insubri roared as they rushed forward. Eight rapid steps back and four more shields joined the Legion line.

"Brace, brace," Alerio yelled. "Set!"

Where the shields had been moving away from the tribesmen, suddenly they stopped and solidified. The charging Insubri on the front edge were trapped between the Legionaries' shields and their tribesmen crowding and shoving from behind. With too little room to wield their long swords, they attempted to claw at unmoving shields.

"Advance!" Alerio ordered.

At the ends of the battle line, Cimon and Drustanus repeated his order.

Nine shields pressed forward but, there were too many bodies stacked in front to allow movement. Nevertheless, the shields parted slightly, and nine steel gladii thrust into the trapped bodies.

"Step back, back, back," Alerio shouted.

Again, his orders were repeated by the pivot men. As the nine Legionaries gave way, the Insubri stumbled forward tripping over the bodies of their dead.

"Kill them," instructed Alerio and his words echoed from the ends of the line.

Each of the nine Legionaries leaned forward and sliced into two or three of the off balanced warriors. Quickly, they stood upright and reset their shields. From behind, a voice cried out to form a second rank.

Now, with two ranks of Legionaries in place, Alerio ordered, "Advance. Advance. Advance!"

With support from javelins stabbing over their shoulders, Alerio's squad thrust their shields forward. As the shields pulled back, their gladii drove into the Insubri. The long swords of the tribesmen were caught between the tightly packed bodies or, were held overhead. Both rendering the heavy weapons useless for close-order combat. The Legion gladius, on the other hand, required only enough room to swing forward and back to deliver killing strikes.

"Advance, stomp, advance stomp," shouted Alerio.

Cimon and Drustanus repeated his words. And, all eighteen of the Legionaries in the two ranks heard the orders clearly. Clearly enough for the shields to power forward and hammer the Insubri. The short blades followed closely behind. As the lines moved, each Legionary stomped any warrior on the ground. If they weren't dead already, by the time the ranks passed over them, the wounded were crushed by the Legion stomp.

***

Alerio was pushing with his shield and stabbing with his gladius when he heard familiar words. Somehow over the yelling and screaming, the Insubri also heard the words.

"Advance. Advance," shouted a new voice from the rear of the warriors.

Realizing they were trapped between two Legion forces, the Insubri turned sideways and ran. At first a trickle, then a full-fledged flight as all of them dashed for their ponies. Once the ground in front of the gate cleared, Alerio saw the other unit.

Twelve wounded Legionaries carried, or supported, seven more. It was hardly a terrifying force although those with a free handheld a gladius. The first survivors from the battlefield staggered forward moving around the dead or wounded Insubri.

"Cimon. Drustanus. Make sure they don't cause any more trouble," ordered Alerio. As his pivot men ran forward to dispatch the wounded tribesmen, Alerio turned to the Legionaries beside him and those behind. "Clear the debris and reform the wedge. This isn't over yet."

The wounded Legionaries struggled down the bloody lines of the wedge. Now safe from marauding bands of horsemen and with the camp in sight, they stood a little straighter and moved more quickly.

A Sergeant with shattered pieces of armor hanging off his shoulders broke from the group and limped to Alerio.

"What's your name Legionary?" the NCO demanded.

"Lance Corporal Alerio Sisera, Seventh Squad of the Forty Seventh," Alerio reported.

"Thank you, Sisera," he replied before his knees gave out and the Sergeant fell to the dirt.

Four mule handlers with a stretcher ran through the gate heading for the Sergeant. They plucked him from the ground and rushed back to the camp. As they approached, Tribune Peregrinus appeared between the gate posts.

"Sisera. What's his rank?" shouted the Tribune.

"He's a Sergeant," Alerio yelled back.

"NCO treatment area, over there," Peregrinus directed the stretcher bearers. Then he glanced at Alerio. "Sisera. Do you need anything?"

"We could use an amphora of vino. And an afternoon off to enjoy it," Alerio called back.

The other Legionaries guarding the gate laughed and nodded their agreement.

"Not today, Lance Corporal," replied Peregrinus. He pointed towards the battlefield before disappearing back into the camp.

Alerio spun around. A quarter of a mile away, a running battle was moving slowly across the plain. While horsemen circled and fired arrows, other Insubri warriors battered the Legion shields with their long swords. In the middle of the melee, Legionaries in a fighting square traveled directly towards the defensive wedge, the gate, and the safety of the camp.

Chapter 7 – One Man Is Indispensable

"Seventh Squad. Fall in on me," Alerio directed. He studied the burning wagons and the space between the flames and the gate. Then he addressed the remaining Legionaries in the wedge formation, "Put four men on each gap and another two watching their flanks."

"Where are we going?" Cimon inquired as he and the rest of Alerio's squad moved up.

"We're forming a blocking force so the horsemen can't cut off that unit," Alerio replied as he pointed to the Legionaries fighting their way towards the camp.

"One squad to block cavalry?" asked Drustanus.

"Is that a problem, Private Drustanus?" Alerio demanded.

"Just to be clear. You do understand what trampled means?" asked the Private.

"Tell you what. If you get trampled to death, I'll sacrifice a bull to the Gods for you," promised Alerio.

"A lot of good that will do me," complained Drustanus. "I'll be dead."

"I'm sorry you'll miss the feast, Drustanus," Cimon commented. "It should be a grand affair seeing as we'll have an entire bull."

Alerio wiped the blade of his gladius on the sleeve of the tunic he wore under his armor. Once clean, he sheathed it and walked to a burning wagon. His squad watched as their Lance Corporal disappeared behind the wagon. Shortly after, the wagon cantered over as if a wheel had come off and Alerio emerged carrying four burning pieces of wheel.

"By columns of twos, follow me," announced Alerio as he swung the burning hardwood pieces while jogging away from the gate.

The nine members of Seventh Squad, Forty Seventh Century, broke into two columns and raced to keep up with their Lance Corporal.

***

Further out, the fighting square moved slowly towards the camp. Waves of Insubri riders raced across the front of the square. In their wake, Legionaries dropped out of the ranks either wounded or dead. After each pass, the leading ranks of the square thinned until Legionaries from the sides were moved to fill in for the missing men. With the sides thinning, Insubri warriors breached the formation in spots. Now small battles broke out inside the square.

Between the fighting outside, the hand-to-hand struggles inside, and the addition of more wounded, the fighting square faltered. It slowed as attrition took a toll on the Legionaries and boosted the spirits of the Insubri.

Colonel Pholus ran across the square and slashed a warrior who was about to behead a wounded Legionary. The Legionary struggled to his feet.

"Can you fight?" asked the Colonel. When the man saluted and nodded his head, obviously too exhausted and weak from his wounds to speak, Pholus ordered, "Then get back in the fight."

With those words, the Colonel looked around for a Centurion. Not finding any, he sprinted to where a Sergeant and six men clashed with ten warriors. He took a place in the line and added his gladius to the Legion strikes. After a flurry of blade stabs and slashes, the ten warriors lay dead.

"Sergeant. Get your men to the General," Pholus ordered. "He's wounded and his only protection are a couple of Tribunes."

"Yes, sir. What about you?" the Sergeant inquired.

"I'll be fine. I need to check on the…" an arrow shaft appeared in the Colonel's throat. His eyes rolled up and a hand reached to towards the arrow. The Legion's second in command toppled over, falling heavily to the churned-up dirt.

***

Lance Corporal Alerio Sisera jogged until he determined the squad was halfway between the gate defenders and the fighting square.

"Fall in on a single line," he instructed.

"The camp is behind us," stated Private Drustanus. "And the Insubri are between us and the Legion formation. What are we going to do?"

"Drustanus you are at the head of the column," Alerio said. His swinging of the wooden pieces had ignited flames that leaped and smokes. "Cimon. You are at the rear of the column."

Then Alerio walked to the center and shoved the middle Legionaries apart. Once there was a wide gap separating the column into two distinct parts, he stepped back.

"You men in the center are fixed. Pivots, watch for my signal," shouted Alerio so the entire squad could hear. "When I give the word, each half swings out until we have two parallel lines facing the Insubri cavalry."

He motioned with the burning torches indicating the formation he wanted.

"Then what do we do?" Drustanus asked from his position.

"You kill Insubri," Alerio said with a smile.

"And how do we reach them?" Drustanus demanded.

"They'll come to you. Watch for my signal," Alerio said.

He spun around and ran ten paces. Then he stopped and waved the burning boards in the air.

The Insubri horsemen noticed the lone Legionary standing and waving at them. Behind the mad man, a broadly spaced single line of Legionaries stood as if inviting the warriors to come and slaughter them. With the fighting square hunkered down behind their shields and not moving, the mounted tribesmen decided to shift to easier prey.

Ponies wheeled around and the warriors shouted with delight. One pass through the exposed Legionaries and then they could get back to the bigger group. One glorious charge to brag about that night around the campfires. They kneed their ponies and galloped towards the Seventh Squad, Forty-Seventh Century, Gurges Legion.

***

Alerio waited to be sure the Insubri were heading towards him. Turning to face the squad, he waved the boards and shouted, "Pivots! Wheelback!"

The strength of the Legions was the ability to hold a line while maneuvering. With Cimon and Drustanus moving and directing the movement, the squad smoothly and quickly transformed from a single line facing north to two side by side files. While the squad shifted, Alerio ran back and stopped three paces from the center men, now heading the files.

Alerio positioned himself in front of the opening between the files and turned. Bearing down on him was a horde of mountain ponies and sword waving warriors.

All the squad's Legionaries bent their heads around watching their squad leader calmly standing and not looking up at the charging cavalry, but down at the burning boards. He lifted his wine skin and took a mouthful of vino. No one could fault him for wanting a last drink before he died. Then, their Lance Corporal spewed the mouthful of wine on the burning boards. The flames, hot and roaring on the hardwood, didn't totally extinguish from the moisture. Where they did go out heavy smoke began to pour off the boards.

Their squad leader waved the boards in a circle which left a cloud of smoke in the still air. Not enough to hide him but, certainly enough so every member of the squad could smell the smoke.

***

Mountain ponies, while loyal to their riders, were still wild at heart. Their survival instinct strong as they were always on alert and ready to run from predators, lightning storms, and fire. As they raced forward at the urging of their riders, they saw a swirling cloud. In the center of the cloud were four flames whirling around. When the smoke entered their nostrils, a primitive message streaked through their equine brains. Fire!

Ancient impulses took over. The seven ponies headed for Alerio broke stride and charged to the sides. The shoulders of the panicked ponies slammed into mounts in full gallop. Like domino tiles falling, the ponies toppled over, and soon, the ground was covered by downed ponies and riders. Because all the Insubri wanted the glory of an all-out charge, those following ran into the wreckage and they toppled into the mess of ponies and warriors.

"Seventh Squad. Forward on the double," Alerio shouted.

His order was echoed by Cimon and Drustanus.

The two-files surged into the pileup reaching out with their javelins to kill and maim dazed warriors. As they moved deeper into the carnage, Alerio kept an eye on the unaffected Insubri. When the horde began to collect themselves, he shouted, "Seventh Squad. Turnabout and disengage."

Again, Cimon and Drustanus repeated the order and the men spun around. The files were soon out from among the ponies and wounded and dead warriors.

"Nice trick," Drustanus said as he passed Alerio. "What do you do for an encore?"

Alerio, dropped the burning boards and jogged with the files.

"I don't have one, but I don't need one," Alerio stated while pointing at the fighting square.

When Seventh Squad drew off the horsemen, the fighting square began to move again. They still fought dismounted warriors but, without the cavalry hindering them, the front line found heart and marched forward.

Another squad from the gate joined the Seventh. The combined squads jogged to the formation and formed another front line. By the time the Insubri horseman collected themselves, the leading edge of the fighting square reached the gate defenders.

Alerio peeled away and stood to the side. His squad joined him, and they watched as the wounded were carried through the gate. One of the injured stood out. Although surrounded by a half squad and a Sergeant, Alerio could clearly see the gold inlay of the General's armor as he was carried through the gate.

Chapter 8 – Siege of the Legion

As the sun sank lower in the western sky, Alerio caught sight of Tribune Peregrinus. He appeared briefly between the gate posts. From an angry lad, the Tribune had aged and changed. For the time he was in view of the gate defenders, the Tribune moved nonstop. With arms waving and orders pouring from his mouth, the young nobleman directed Legionaries and handlers before strutting out of view.

"That Tribune is favored by Zelus," commented Drustanus.

"He does seem to have an endless supply of energy," added Cimon. "Obviously touched by the God."

"Don't you two have anything better to do?" asked Alerio.

"As a matter of fact, Lance Corporal Sisera, we haven't," Drustanus replied. "You see, we've been on gate duty all day."

"And how do you find that?" Alerio inquired.

"Boring for the most part. If you don't count the times our squad leader tried to kill us," Drustanus related.

Before Alerio could defend himself and his actions, Cimon spoke up.

"In coming," announced the Legionary. "Looks to be about a hundred or so Legionaries."

"Wedge people," Alerio shouted as he lifted his shield and marched to the point of the vee-formation. "Looks like they have wounded. Someone alert the medics."

The Legionaries were still far away but moving unmolested towards the gate. Everyone on the gate detail scanned the plain searching for any sign of the Insubri. Over the last part of the day, small groups, or pairs of Legionaries, had limped in from different parts of the sloping plain.

Shortly after the fighting square dissolved at the gate, the tribesmen had trotted off towards Volsinii. It didn't mean they wouldn't be back, it just meant they hadn't been around to interfere with retrieving stragglers.

"Seems as if the tribesmen have had enough for the day," Peregrinus suggested.

Alerio was surprised by the voice as he'd been concentrating on looking for an attack on the group. He turned to find the Tribune standing beside him. The young nobleman's armor was caked in dried sweat, blood and covered in a layer of dirt that stuck to the liquids before they dried.

"You look like a member of third maniple, Tribune," Alerio observed as he indicated the grime and dirt. "Come out for a breath of fresh air?"

Peregrinus inhaled and coughed on the lingering smoke from the wagons, the copper smell from the blood spilled, and the stink of dried sweat on the Legionaries.

"I inspected the latrines earlier, I believe the air was fresher there," Peregrinus commented. "I want to inform you that I'm organizing a relief for your detail. It's a little muddled right now, but you should be off by sunset."

"Not that it's within my rank to ask, but what's the problem?" inquired Alerio.

Peregrinus inhaled and hesitated as if he wasn't going to reply. Then, he shook his head to clear it and looked at Alerio.

"The General is barely hanging on, apparently the Colonel is dead somewhere out there," the Tribune reported while pointing beyond the group moving towards the gate. "We've lost most of our officer corps, command staff and senior NCOs. I seem to be the fourth or fifth ranking officer left in the Legion. And apparently, the only one unwounded. I never knew the thousand and one details required to run a Legion camp."

"Are the wounded being tended to? And the men fed?" Alerio asked.

"Yes, I have the medics working on the wounded," responded Peregrinus. "And I have the General's cooks making stew and baking bread."

"And the gate is secure," Alerio reported. "You've covered the basics. What about the Tribune that came in earlier? He seemed fit."

"What Tribune?" demanded Peregrinus.

"Before you brought out the wagons and burned them, a Tribune rode in," explained Alerio. "He seemed older, but I wouldn't trust him. He left two wounded cavalrymen in his dust. Sorry, sir. I didn't mean to speak out of line."

"All this time, there was another staff officer in the camp?" Peregrinus growled. "Excuse me Lance Corporal Sisera. I have a pair of cōleī to kick."

"Yes, sir, I understand completely," Alerio said.

But the words were spoken to the Tribune's back. The young nobleman was stalking towards the gate with his shoulder set hard and his fist balled up.

***

The group came close enough for Alerio to recognize Sergeant Meleager and Centurion

Seneca. Around them were over a hundred men with another seventy or so carrying about thirty-five wounded.

"Report, Sisera," Meleager demanded as he stepped away from the formation.

They were separated as the units marched by. Once the last Legionary had passed, Alerio stepped across to his Sergeant.

"The gate is secure, Sergeant," Alerio stated while holding out his arms to indicate the Legionaries, the open gate, and the burned wagons.

As an experienced NCO, Meleager had a sharp eye for details. The first thing he noticed was the dried blood on Sisera and his squad. While the rest of the detail had a few traces, it was obvious Seventh Squad had done some hard fighting.

"Explain those," Meleager stated while pointing at the burned wagons.

"The ground was too hard, and we didn't have time to dig. So, Tribune Peregrinus burned them," Alerio explained. "It worked as you can see, no tribesmen breached our gate defenses."

"The young Tribune?" asked the Sergeant.

"He's been running the camp single handedly," Alerio said. "From what I can see and the response from inside, he's done a good job organizing the returning Legionaries."

"Alright, let me see about getting your detail relieved," the Sergeant said as he turned towards the gate.

Suddenly, two columns of Legionaries appeared. At first glance, there seemed to be two full Centuries stacked, loaded down with gear, and ready to march. Behind them, two raised voices quarreled.

"I'm taking the Centuries and going to get help," a man exclaimed. "As the senior Tribune, it's my decision."

"You can't take healthy Legionaries out of the camp," Tribune Peregrinus argued back. "We have too many wounded. I need those men to guard the camp."

The two noblemen walked through the gate. One leading a horse and Peregrinus walking along looking up at a taller and older Tribune.

"Look Peregrinus, you are a nice lad, but I know what I'm doing," the other Tribune said with a condescending tone. "You can stay here and play Legionary. As for me, I'm marching out of here right now."

"I will not allow it," Peregrinus insisted.

"Who is going to stop me? You?" the Tribune challenged then he shouted. "Centuries, stand by. Forward march."

The Centuries stomped once and took two steps. Centurion Seneca appeared behind the two Tribunes.

"Centuries, halt!" shouted the senior Centurion. "Sorry sirs. But marching out at dusk into enemy held territory is suicide. I cannot allow it."

"And who are you?" asked the Tribune.

"I'm senior Centurion Seneca formerly of the Forty-Seventh Century," he explained.

"Formerly? What does that mean?" asked the Tribune sourly.

"It means I've assumed the responsibility as senior Centurion of the Legion," Seneca stated. "And for your information, I've polled the Legion, and in the absence of a staff officer, we've elected a temporary commander."

"I am the senior staff officer," the Tribune insisted. "As such, I am marching out of here with these Legionaries."

"No sir. Not without the authority of the camp commander," stated Seneca.

"And who would that be?" demanded the Tribune.

"Tribune Peregrinus. Based on his heroic efforts to care for our wounded and to see to the comfort of his Legionaries, the Centuries have voted him our Commander," Seneca announced. Then the old Centurion turned to Peregrinus and asked, "Orders, sir?"

"Stand these Centuries down and organize a relief for the gate detail," Peregrinus directed. "We'll need to go over each Century for fitness and set a guard rotation. There's a town of rebels a mile from here and a force of mounted Insubri nearby."

Before anyone could react, the older Tribune leaped on his horse and kneed it into a gallop. The move so shocked everyone that they stood watching as he rode down the bank of the Tiber river. At the foothills south of Volsinii, fifteen Insubri ponies raced onto the riverbank and the Tribune was hacked from his horse.

"Nearer than he thought," Drustanus whispered.

"Senior Centurion Seneca. I believe we'll need to rethink our guard strength," Peregrinus pondered. "What does the Legion call a situation like this?"

"A siege, Tribune," Seneca replied.

Act 2

Chapter 9 – The Better Pantry

Alerio and Seventh Squad were huddled around their campfire. Since their relief, the sun had set, the stars vanished behind heavy clouds, and the temperature dropped. The entire squad was tired and cold. There was a bright spot, the hot food.

"Why are we out here when it's going to snow?" inquired Cimon as he broke off a piece of bread and dipped it in his bowl of stew. After chewing off the tasty piece, he declared, "This stew is almost as good as mine."

"We've served together for five years, Cimon," observed Drustanus. "And never have you made anything as delicious as the stew from the General's cook."

"Well, the cook has a pantry with better supplies," protested Cimon. "What do you expect me to do with cornmeal, salt, flour and the occasional piece of greasy meat and a few wilted vegetables. Tell you what. The next time it's my day to cook, use my iron pan and see what you can make."

"I don't cook. I hunt and trade for the squad's wine," explained Drustanus.

He reached down and refilled his clay mug from the squad's pitcher.

"Then don't compare my cooking with the General's guy," Cimon complained.

"I didn't. It was you who compared your cooking to the stew," Drustanus protested.

"No. You said my cooking was not as good as the staff's cook," Cimon declared.

The rest of the squad shook their heads as if they'd heard the conversation many times before. Alerio reached out and grabbed the vino pitcher. After refilling his mug, he leaned over and refilled Cimon's.

"Do you think it's going to snow?" Alerio asked in an attempt to change the subject.

Drustanus shielded his eyes with his hand, turned to look over their tent, and away from the fire.

"The clouds are fat and it's cold enough," he said while looking up at the dark sky. "And it smells like snow."

"I already told you it was going to snow," offered Cimon.

"You said. Why are we out here when it's going to snow?" Drustanus added. "If you're done in, then turn in."

"I wasn't talking about sleeping. I meant why is the Legion out here in the early spring?" Cimon asked.

"A friend of mine with the wagon drivers said General Gurges thought the Legion could take Volsinii in a day. Then spend a day sacking the town, shackling slaves, and putting rebel leaders up on the wood," explained Drustanus. "The wagons were ordered not to unpack all the gear. The plan was for us to break camp and march south on day five. Didn't work out for us, did it?"

"Five days would have been good for me. After this, I'm headed for my father's farm before reporting back to the Southern Legion," Alerio stated. "But why march in the early spring? Why not wait for summer?"

"The General's term is up in a week," Cimon said bending towards the fire and dropping his voice. "He couldn't lead a Legion when his term as Consul is up. No Generalship, no Legion, and no glory. So, here we are waiting for it to snow with a busted Legion."

"And Insubri warriors lounging on our doorstep," added Drustanus.

A sharp cry of pain came from down the road. The anguished scream carried from the medic's tent. It traveled along the clear path between the neat rows of Legionary tents before reaching Seventh Squad's camp.

"That's a hand," proclaimed Cimon. "If the medics had taken anything bigger, the scream would have been longer. Anybody disagree?"

"Not me. Besides, I'm too tired to walk down and ask the medic," another member of the Seventh declared. "Keep your coin."

"Lads, if you don't bet you can't make extra coin," Cimon advised. "Probably a right hand. Some cūlus of a mounted Insubri rode by, swung his long sword, and chopped into a Legionary's wrist. That's a medical discharge with no pension."

"Mounted barbarians are frightening," the squad member commented as he poked at the campfire.

"Unless you have a squad leader with a long swinging mentula," Drustanus declared while glaring across the campfire at Alerio.

"Animals are afraid of flames. One time on my father's farm a field caught fire. Every animal nearby ran just from the smell of the smoke," Alerio said in his defense. "I figured the ponies were half wild so they would bolt from the smoke and sight of the flames."

"And if they hadn't?" inquired Drustanus.

Another yell came from the medic's tent. This one, a high pitched and prolonged scream.

"If the ponies hadn't panicked, there wouldn't be enough left of me for the medics to saw on," admitted Alerio.

"That's a leg," Cimon announced. He held up his mug of watered vino and used it to point down the road in the direction of the medic's tent. "For sure, a leg. Anyone disagree?"

***

Alerio was curled up in a blanket with his armor, gladius, and most of his personal gear at his head. Surprisingly, the goatskin of the ten-man tent kept the cold air out. Unfortunately, the ground where the eight Legionaries slept held the cold. Anything soft they owned was spread out under a second blanket to provide a little insulation.

"Lance Corporal. Sisera. Wake up," Cimon whispered as he shook Alerio's foot.

"What? Is it my watch?" Alerio asked as he shielded his eyes from the lantern's light.

"No. Meleager wants to see you," Cimon explained. "He said to leave your armor but get dressed. Oh, and I suggest you take your cloak. It's starting to snow and it's cold."

"On the way," Alerio promised as he slipped out from under the blanket.

Thankfully, his tunic and wool trousers were warm from his body's heat. After getting dressed, strapping on his gladius, and securing the long knife with the black and yellow hilt to the small of his back, Alerio wrapped the cloak around his shoulders and tossed back the tent flap.

"Good morning, Lance Corporal," Meleager greeted him.

"Just a moment Sergeant. Cimon, how many turns?" Alerio asked his Left Pivot while glancing down at the squad's hourglass.

"Four turns, and the sand is about to run out," Cimon announced. "Drustanus is on perimeter duty. I'll collect him once I wake our camp guard. Run along with the Sergeant and tend your NCO business. We have this under control."

"What can I do for you, Sergeant?" Alerio asked as he turned to face Meleager.

"Walk with me, Sisera," the Century's Sergeant ordered.

***

They left Seventh Squad's area and Meleager guided them towards the center of the Legion camp. As they strolled along the road, the Sergeant glanced around at the squad tents lining the road. If any neglected to have a guard by their campfire, he would roust the entire squad and have them all stand guard until sunrise. Theft was rare but he'd seen squads fight each other over missing gear more than once. Satisfied the squad areas were secure, he turned and studied the crescent shaped scar on Alerio's head.

Lance Corporal Sisera had arrived as Centurion Seneca gathered a Century from Central Legion to fill out Gurges Legion. A senior Tribune's recommendation spoke highly of the weapon's instructor, so they'd given Alerio Sisera Seventh Squad. From watching the young NCO and based on reports, he had done a good job.

"While I was touring the perimeter, I had a chance to speak with Private Drustanus. Were you a Raider with the Eastern Legion," Meleager inquired but continued without a pause. "He also told me about the smoke and fire pony trick. He promised not to try it. You?"

"I don't believe I'd do it again," Alerio assured him.

"No. Were you with the Raiders?" Meleager corrected.

As an experienced Sergeant of a Century, Meleager often tested his Legionaries to see if they were paying attention. Plus, it was interesting to hear which question they chose to answer. Sisera addressed the inquiry concerning his squad. It was what the Sergeant wanted to hear. If he hadn't been on loan from the Southern Legion, he would promote Sisera to Corporal.

"I was with the Raiders," Alerio confirmed. "Why the early morning stroll? Is something wrong? Can I help?"

The Sergeant looked between the snowflakes and peered at the Lance Corporal. Is he waiting to see which question I answer? Deciding he wasn't being tested, Meleager exhaled creating a cloud with his breath.

"We're surrounded by barbarians and half the Legion is wounded or dead. Coronel Pholus is dead, and General Gurges awaits the arrival of Morta," Meleager stated grimly. "So, in reply to your question, a lot is wrong. Can you help? That's up to Tribune Peregrinus and Centurion Seneca."

***

As they progressed down the road, Alerio saw a large tent on the same camp square as the staff and command tents and the General's quarters. Two men stood outside with their heads tilted up letting snow hit and melt on their faces. A large fire burned behind a covered wagon and four braziers cast light on the entrance to the tent.

A medic pushed aside the tent flap with his shoulder. He emerged sideways and as he straightened, Alerio could see a large pan clutched in his hands.

"Barrel and wagon," the medic ordered.

One of the snow gazers walked over to a barrel and lifted the lid. While a dark liquid from the pan was emptied into the container, the man carrying the lid went to the wagon and tossed back the goatskin cover.

After pouring out the liquid, the medic walked to the wagon and swung the pan as a farmer would while spreading seed. An object flew out of the pan and sailed into the bed of the wagon. Before the man could pull the cover back into place, Alerio and Sergeant Meleager came close enough to see details.

All three men wore blood-stained leather aprons. Alerio hadn't seen so much blood since he gutted a deer after a successful hunt. In the wagon were arms, legs, hands, and the bodies of dead Legionaries. The medics had been busy amputating limbs left hanging by bad sword strokes or pony hooves. In the coming days, the medics would remove other limbs as wounds festered. In a way, taking off a hand, a leg or an arm was better for a Legionary's health. Although maimed, the hot iron sealed the sawcut and prevented the rot.

"The command tent is over there," Meleager instructed. "They'll use the blood in the barrel to consecrate the burial sites."

Alerio turned away from the medical tent and shuddered. Hacking off a limb with a gladius may be harsh, but it was done in the heat of battle. Medics achieved the same result, but they did it in a slow deliberate manner. There was one commonality, both actions were accompanied by screaming and bleeding.

Chapter 10 – Command and Control

Generals lived far differently than the average Legionary squad. Alerio felt the warmth as soon as he and the Sergeant stepped into the command tent. A bowl on a side table held grapes, pomegranates, and apples. The fruit left sitting there so anyone on the staff could choose one and eat it. On another side table, cheese and olive bowls were separated by little pieces of toasted bread. Alerio's mouth watered, and his stomach growled. Cimon had called it. The General's cook did have the better pantry.

Centurion Seneca, three other Centurions, and a heavily bandaged Tribune stood around a map. The map covered the surface of a large table occupying the space between the end tables with the ornate rations.

"Meleager, you have a shadow?" Seneca asked looking up from the map. All the officers' eyes lifted. The Centurions nodded at the Sergeant and Alerio while the Tribune scowled.

"Lance Corporal Sisera was a Raider with the Eastern Legion," the Sergeant stated. "I thought he might have a suggestion or two about our situation."

"A Legionary?" growled the Tribune. "Sergeant if you please, remove him. We are the command staff and do not consult with common soldiers. What's next? We ask the Centuries to vote on the Legion's attack plan?"

Alerio's mind drifted as he prepared to turn around. Maybe the Legion wouldn't be in this situation if the Centuries, or at least the Centurions, had been asked to vote on the ill-fated assault plan. One thing disappointed him about being dismissed so abruptly. He hadn't had an opportunity to liberate an apple, or two. Or maybe five, so each member of Seventh Squad could have a half an apple.

"I'd best go check on the guard rotation," Alerio said to Meleager. Then he saluted Seneca. "Sir, by your leave?"

The old Centurion had a sour look on his face as if he'd eaten some bad pig.

"Dismissed, Lance Corporal," Seneca replied.

Alerio pushed aside the flap of the command tent and stepped into the cold night air. Wrapping the cloak tighter to keep out the blowing snow, he shivered and headed for the squad area.

***

Shortly after Alerio left, Tribune Peregrinus, a doctor, and an older man pushed through an inside flap. As they stepped from the General's sleeping quarters, all the officers and the Sergeant looked over.

"The Goddess Morta has severed the threads of life freeing the Commander of Gurges Legion from his pain," announced the doctor. "Quintus Fabius Gurges, Co-Consul of Rome, Senator, General, loving father, and faithful husband is dead."

Sergeant Meleager and the Centurions, men experienced with death, did not react. The older man did.

"What are we going to do?" he cried out. "This was supposed to be a short expedition. Now, we're surrounded by barbarians and the General is dead. Tribune Griffinus, you'll assume command and we'll march back to the Capital. The sooner the better."

The wounded Tribune gulped and looked over at the younger Tribune.

"Lieutenant General Silenus Eduardus, you are now general of the Legion," Peregrinus pointed out. "I'm elected to control the camp, but you are now our commander."

"Armenius Peregrinus. You are too young to be in charge of anything. I've apprentice lads older than you," observed Silenus Eduardus. "Gentlemen, I'm a simple wine merchant. I extended a loan to Gurges to pay for this army and he suggested I take a commission. In no way am I qualified to be a general. My expertise is in business not in military matters."

Silenus Eduardus bobbed his head up and down as if he'd delivered a profound statement. Then he strolled to a chair, sat down heavily, and poured a mug of vino. Waving a hand in a dismissive manner, he announced.

"Tribune Griffinus, define the problem. Discuss possible solutions with your staff. When you're done, bring me the best ideas. The process has served me well in business and I can't image it wouldn't for military problems."

The staff officer who had tossed out the Legionary and lectured the Centurions on speaking with common soldiers stood stiff and unmoving. As most young men from noble families, Tribune Griffinus was trained to know what shouldn't happen to maintain the status quo. However, he had no concept of what should happen to gain control of a complicated situation.

Sergeant Meleager felt sorry for the young man, and he began to speak. Then he noticed the faces of the Centurions. In the Legion men often had to perform distasteful tasks. Universally, the men showed their opinion about the orders by putting on a blank face and keeping their mouths shut. Meleager caught on and clamped his lips closed and relaxed the muscles of his face. No help would be offered to Tribune Griffinus.

***

"Maybe we should plan on defensive patrols in the morning," offered Peregrinus.

Coming awake at the one suggestion, Griffinus stated, "No. We will not. In the morning, we'll march for the Capital. Centurions, prepare the Legion to march."

The three Centurions dropped their chins and stared at the map. Only senior Centurion Seneca responded to the Tribune Griffinus' order. He cocked his head to the side as if listening to a faint and distant noise.

"I said we will march out in the morning. Prepare the Legion," shouted Griffinus. When none of the military professionals in the tent responded, the Tribune turned to Silenus Eduardus. "Lieutenant General, I've issued a command. I order you to instruct these men to follow them."

"Tribune Griffinus. Did you discuss the idea with your staff? That's the first step in the process," the merchant instructed. He took a sip of vino, looked down into the mug and back at Griffinus. "Come to think of it, your family owes me for a shipment of excellent wine that I delivered last spring."

Griffinus clinched his fist and tightened his jaw. Before he could unleash the building anger, Peregrinus pointed to the young nobles' leg.

"Griffinus. You are bleeding all over the command tent's rug," Peregrinus stated.

"I'll bleed wherever I choose," the Tribune yelled. "My family can buy a new rug. My family can buy...Get off me, cūlus."

And Tribune Griffinus collapsed into the arms of Sergeant Meleager. The NCO had recognized the signs of physical distress, raced across the room, and grabbed the nobleman.

"Doctor, please escort the Sergeant to the medical tent," instructed Centurion Seneca. "I believe Tribune Griffinus' wound wraps have become unraveled."

"Well, that was interesting," commented Silenus Eduardus. "Who is in charge now?"

Centurion Seneca hammered his fist in a crossed chest salute and bellowed, "Tribune Peregrinus. Orders, sir?"

"Now I see. The Centurions do have a choice in leadership," the wine merchant said as he took a sip of vino and stood. "My experience with teamsters and shipping managers is to get out of their way when there's a dispute. Please informed me of your decision."

Silenus Eduardus bowed to Peregrinus and strolled to a side tent flap. Once he was gone, Peregrinus lifted both arms in a sign of helplessness.

"I wouldn't know where to start," he admitted.

"You start with the security of the Legion camp and work your way outward," suggest Seneca. "Once we have the camp under control, we'll talk about defensive patrols in the morning."

"That sounds familiar," teased Peregrinus.

"Yes, sir. A good commander allows his men to express their ideas," replied Centurion Seneca. "Even if it's the Commanders to start with."

"I suppose there's no chance of breaking camp and marching south?" ventured Peregrinus.

Another Centurion cleared his throat and spoke up.

"No sir. We've too many wounded to transport. And a large force of barbarians to fight," he described. "However, we have enough Centuries to push them back."

"What good would that do?" asked Peregrinus.

"We'll keep the path to the river open for fresh water," the Centurion stated. "Plus, it'll let the Centuries get a little revenge. Defeat is a bad thing to sleep on. Better we draw some blood and improve the Legion's morale."

"It really is about the men," Peregrinus explained a new-found insight. "No matter how often you beat them to maintain discipline. Or how hard you march and train them, it comes back to the care of the common Legionary,"

"Tribune. There are no common Legionaries. Every one of them has passed a series of difficult tests. At the end, they won the honor of standing and dying in a shield wall against the enemies of the Republic," explained the Centurion. "I'd put our heavy infantrymen against any army in the world. Spartan, Athenian phalanxes, or Qart Hadasht mercenaries, the Legion will beat them all because of the individual Legionary."

"Let's not take on the world just yet," declared Peregrinus. "I'm more concerned with the Insubri right outside our gates."

"As you should be Tribune," admitted Seneca. "And getting a message out before the snow gets much deeper."

"What does the depth of the snow have to do with getting a messenger to the Capital?" asked Peregrinus.

"Our Legionaries from this region tell me a spring snow will only stay on the ground for a week," Seneca explained. "We could wait a week to send the message, or we send it out tonight before the snow finishes falling."

"I'm confused. What does the depth of the snow have to do with the message?" demanded the young Tribune.

"The Insubri riders can spot and track a messenger's footprints in the snow," Seneca clarified. "He wouldn't get a quarter of a mile before they chased him down."

As they talked, Sergeant Meleager pushed into the command tent letting in a cold wind and a flurry of snowflakes.

"Sergeant. Please retrieve Lance Corporal Sisera," instructed Seneca.

"Right away, Centurion," Meleager replied.

***

"What do you mean, he's not here?" demanded Meleager.

"Cimon said he went with you, Sergeant," the camp guard for Seventh Squad's area pleaded. "I haven't seen Lance Corporal Sisera since dinner."

The Sergeant stomped off. Where would he go if he was a young Lance Corporal again? Volsinii? When Meleager was a young Legionary, he slipped into an enemy town for a little vino and company. But the siege had been just outside the walls and half the town supported the Republic. No, Sisera wouldn't have gone to Volsinii.

Heading for the stockade walls, he planned to have the men on guard duty pass the word. It was quicker than him walking the Legion camp. Plus, it would test the Legionaries stationed around the perimeter to assure that they were evenly spaced and awake.

The street he was on ran directly to the eastern wall. It was as good a place to start as any.

***

Sergeant Meleager strolled confidently towards the embankment where the sentry would be walking his post. He left the last squad tents and campfires behind and began to cross the dark transport road. At five paces across, a figure reared up from the dark and tackled him.

Before he could bellow his outrage, a hand clamped over his mouth.

"Sergeant. Be quiet," whispered a Legionary as he removed his hand.

"What's going on?" the Sergeant demanded.

"I heard digging sounds outside the wall," explained the sentry. "Lance Corporal Sisera woke two squads and they're collecting barbarians."

"Collecting what?" inquired Meleager.

Before the sentry could reply, a Legionary came out of the dark with a body over his shoulder.

"Give him to Thirty-First Century, First Squad," the sentry instructed, "One road over, third tent on the left."

The Legionary walked away with his load and Meleager pushed to his feet. It was dark near the stockade wall as it should be to preserve the sentry's night vision. A noise sounding as if a melon had been thumped with a shovel reached him. Shortly after, a Legionary passed by carrying a load over his shoulder.

Meleager eased forward and as he came closer, his eyes adjusted to the dark. A half circle of Legionaries crouched facing the logs. Silently, a figure appeared from under the stockade wall. A Legionary put out a hand as if to help the person clear the trench. Once the two joined hands at the writs, the Legionary jerked the barbarian up onto the hill. Another Legionary clotted the barbarian over the head with his gladius. In one swift movement, the barbarian was hoisted onto the Legionary's shoulder and totted away.

The Sergeant had organized a lot of military operations over the years but never one where enemy warriors simply walked, or in this case crawled, into captivity.

"I think that's all of them. Collect some stakes and seal the hole," Lance Corporal Sisera whispered. "Nice work lads."

"We'll put extra watchers on this post," offered a squad leader.

"I'll find Sergeant Meleager and check the rest of the posts," Sisera said as he walked towards the transport road.

"Would you mind telling me what that was?" asked Meleager as he fell in beside the Lance Corporal.

"After leaving the command tent, I was wide awake. So, I went to check the guard posts," Alerio explained. "One heard digging. After waking up two nearby squads, I sent a Legionary looking for you and another to warn the other posts."

"How many Insubri made it into camp?" asked the Sergeant.

"Twenty. It got a little busy for a while," admitted Alerio. "but we managed to get them all."

"Why didn't you sound the alarm?" demanded Meleager.

"I figured if we woke everyone, the noise would drive off the raiding party," Alerio said. "After what they did to us, I wanted to take as many as possible."

From down the road, they heard the unmistakable stomp of Legion units on the run. Shortly after, four fully armed squads turned a corner and jogged towards the Sergeant and Lance Corporal. Out front and running ahead of the squads were Centurion Seneca and Tribune Peregrinus.

"Report, Sergeant Meleager," Seneca requested as he and Peregrinus came to a stop.

"Lance Corporal Sisera and two squads have captured a raiding party of twenty," Meleager replied.

"Where are they?" asked Peregrinus while peering around at the campfires and the empty road.

A scream rose from two streets over.

"They're in the custody of scattered squads," Meleager informed him. "I think we should collect them soon if we want to have any left to question."

"Sergeant. Gather the Insubri and put them in a stock pen," instructed Seneca. Then turning to Peregrinus asked, "If that's alright with you, Tribune."

"That will suffice, Centurion," Peregrinus replied.

From back in the quick reaction force, a Legionary called out, "Tribune. What if one is too ugly to live?"

Peregrinus whipped around and looked over the four squads for a long while. Long enough for Centurion Seneca to worry if the power of command was going to the young nobleman's head. Long enough for snow to settle on the Legionaries. Finally, Peregrinus slowly shook his head in an exaggerated manner.

"I've given it a lot of thought," the Tribune announced. "In my opinion, they are all too ugly to live. However, they need to be questioned by command staff. Afterwards, I'll need a wood lined lane right outside the gate. Can you do that for me?"

"We'll put them up on the wood in straight lines for you, sir," another Legionary called back. "Just give us the word."

"Thank you," Peregrinus replied. "Lance Corporal Sisera. Accompany Centurion Seneca and I to the command tent."

"Yes, sir," Alerio said as he fell in behind the Tribune and the Centurion.

"If you have an Insubri, bring him to me," yelled out Sergeant Meleager.

A street over, someone shouted back, "But he bleeds so pretty. Can't we keep him."

"I know you lost a lot of friends yesterday. Don't be selfish. We'll all enjoy it when we crucify them tomorrow," Meleager replied. "Now! Bring me my prisoners."

Chapter 11 – Cold, Exhausted and Wet

"The solution is to get a messenger on the way south before dawn," Centurion Seneca explained. "The problem is how to get him passed the Insubri on the riverbank and those patrolling the hills."

Alerio leaned over the map, reached out with an extended finger, and traced the course of the Tiber river.

"Take the river down passed the foothills," he suggested. "But, once the messenger comes ashore, there will be prints in the snow. Unless the barbarians are drawn away, they'll find the footprints quickly."

"Wouldn't they be expecting something from the raiding party?" asked Peregrinus.

"They only sent twenty warriors," Seneca stated. "Not enough for a major attack. More than likely, they had specific targets. I'd guess the Legion command area and the main gate."

"If they are staged and waiting for the gates to open, why not open them?" Alerio offered.

"You want to open the gates?" Silenus Eduardus asked in horror.

He'd wandered in and stood beside the Centurion. The wine merchant hadn't said anything until the possibility of opening the gates was mentioned.

"I believe what the Lance Corporal is suggesting is we open the gates and greet them with several Centuries," Seneca explained. "Isn't that right, Sisera?"

"Yes, Centurion. They are gathered to the west so why not give them a fight," Alerio said. "It'll serve three purposes."

"There are reasons to open the gates?" inquired Silenus Eduardus. "Other than blood lust."

"Yes, sir. A quick fight will put the Insubri on notice that we are not beaten. And it'll be good for the Legionaries to get some revenge," Alerio listed. "In addition, a fight at the gate will draw the southern warriors away from their posts."

"Giving the messenger a head start," blurted out Peregrinus. "When the Insubri break off from the gate engagement, he can be on shore and jogging south."

"Lads, I know I'm not a military man, but scheduling, using my resources to gain an advantage, and attention to details have made me a rich man," Silenus Eduardus announced. "There are issues with sending a messenger. How does he get to the river? How does he survive the cold water? And, who does he deliver the messages to for the quickest response?"

Everyone stared at the map as if an answer would emerge in glowing letters. But no revelation appeared on the map. Long moments later, Tribune Peregrinus straightened up.

"I need to deliver the message," he announced. "We need someone who can get an audience with Consul Vitulus and the Senate. A Legion courier will simply deliver the messages to the first Centurion he finds. To speed up the response, you need a nobleman to deliver the message."

"That was unexpected," Silenus Eduardus admitted while bowing his head to the youth. "But, like an amphora of fine vino, transporting the merchandise undamaged to the customer is just as important as making the wine. How do you, Tribune Peregrinus, get to the Capital undamaged?"

"Sisera, you were with the Raiders. How does the Tribune get to the Capital?" Seneca asked. "Undamaged as Lieutenant General Eduardus put it."

A strange expression crossed the wine merchant's face. In all his years of crawling to the pinnacle of business, he never thought he'd one day be acknowledged as Lieutenant General Silenus Eduardus. While the honor wouldn't last beyond the Legion camp, for this moment in time, he relished it. So, lost was he in his own thoughts, he almost missed it when the Lance Corporal began speaking.

"Four barrels lashed together," Sisera described. "Oiled goatskins for our gear and our legs to protect from the dampness and the cold."

"Excuse me. I missed the first part," insisted Silenus Eduardus. "Who needs barrels?"

"Lance Corporal Sisera has offered to guide me," Tribune Peregrinus stated. "Apparently, we are rafting down the Tiber."

"We'll use the skirmish at the gates to cover your exit," advised Centurion Seneca. "It makes sense for unengaged units to sweep around the camp. You can use them as cover to reach the Tiber. Lieutenant General Eduardus, did we miss anything."

"Tribune Armenius Peregrinus and Lance Corporal Sisera. May the God Kratos give you power for the endeavor. And his sister, the Goddess Bia, grant your bodies the strength to survive," Silenus Eduardus pronounced. "I'll have my slaves empty four wine casks. Centurion Seneca, ready the Legion."

"Yes, sir," Seneca replied as he strutted out of the tent.

"What else do you need Lance Corporal?" Peregrinus asked.

"I need to retrieve some items from my squad area," Alerio responded. "Also, would it be out of line to ask for five apples?"

"Whatever for?" inquired Silenus Eduardus.

"For his squad, Lieutenant General," Peregrinus answered. "Taking care of your Legionaries is a priority for Legion leaders."

"I see. In that case, take ten apples," advised Silenus Eduardus.

"Thank you, sirs," Alerio said as he scooped apples from the bowl. "By your leave?"

"Dismissed, Lance Corporal," Eduardus ordered before turning to Peregrinus. "I could get accustomed to this military life, if it wasn't so dangerous."

***

"Private Drustanus. You're acting squad leader," Alerio announced as he passed out apples to the nine Legionaries. "I've been ordered to assist in getting our message to the Capital. If I don't make it back, ship my helmet, armor, and gladius to Master Tomas Kellerian at the Historia Fae in the Capital."

"This is good, thanks Sisera," Cimon said as he bit into the apple. Ignoring the negative idea of his squad leader getting killed, he asked, "Won't you need the gladius?"

Alerio set his half-eaten apple down and reached into his personal pack. Slowly, he drew out a dual sword rig of tooled leather with two gladii.

"I'm taking my private gear," he advised the squad. After slipping on the rig, he retrieved his apple and clasps wrists with each member of Seventh Squad. "Make me proud in the morning."

"Deliver the message," Drustanus encouraged him.

From down the road, Sergeant Meleager shouted.

"Forty-five, Forty-six, Forty-seven, gear up and get on the road," he called. "I'm waiting people. The snow's not getting any lighter and there's Insubri who need killing."

As squad leaders from twenty-four squads hustled their ten-man tents into action, three Corporals roamed the road in front of their Centuries' tents. They repeated the Sergeant's words and counted Legionaries as they emerged. Soon, three Centuries of heavy infantry were formed up and awaiting orders.

***

There were three stacks of unsorted helmets, armor, and gladii. Not surprising, there were fewer shields on the piles. It was tough to run with a shield and the last Legionaries to make it back to camp had been running for their lives.

Alerio didn't need gladii or shields. He found two cloaks in relatively good shape and tugged them out of a pile. Then, he walked around the medical tent heading for the command tent.

As Alerio approached, a Corporal stepped forward blocking his path.

"And where do you think you are going?" the veteran NCO asked. "Name and unit?"

"Lance Corporal Alerio Sisera, Seventh Squad, Forty-Seventh Century," Alerio told him. "I have an appointment with Tribune Peregrinus."

"The Forty-Seventh has been called up. Where's your armor?" the Corporal inquired. Then to one of the squad members behind him. "Private, check with the duty Centurion. See if Tribune Peregrinus is entertaining visitors."

"Right away, First Corporal," a hard-looking Legionary replied.

Alerio didn't relax. The title of First Corporal referred to the NCO of the Legion's First Century. All the Legionnaires were assigned to the third maniple, and all were men who had earned their place through war and skill. They also had a reputation for bullying other Centuries.

"I asked you a question," the Corporal reminded Alerio. "And what's that on your back and over your arm?"

The hilts from the gladii protruded above his shoulders. It wasn't regulation and the idea of carrying two gladii was foreign to the Legion.

"My personal gear," Alerio replied. "Like I said, I have an appointment with Tribune Peregrinus."

"You know what I think? I think either you are a coward, here to beg the Tribune to relieve you of duty," the Corporal said with a sneer. "Or you're touched and want to kill the Tribune. Which is it?"

"Neither. But since you're being a mentula, I'll tell you one thing," Alerio said as he leaned in towards the NCO. "If I'm still here at daylight, I'm going to take you to the training area and teach you a few things with these gladii."

"Are you threatening me?" demanded the NCO.

"No, Corporal, that's a promise," Alerio stated.

Before the tension between the two Legionaries escalated to physical violence, a voice shouted from the command tent.

"Lance Corporal Sisera. Get your cūlus in here," Centurion Seneca bellowed.

"You got lucky, Sisera," growled the NCO.

"Let's just say your lesson has been delayed," Alerio replied as he took a step to the side and strolled to the command tent.

***

The map on the table had been replaced by layers of oiled goatskin.

"How does this work?" inquired Peregrinus.

"The cloaks are for our trip to the river," Alerio stated while offering the Tribune one of the soiled cloaks.

"This is nasty," Peregrinus observed. He held the cloth between two fingers and away from his body.

"The cloak is just covering until we reach the Tiber," explained Alerio. "We'll drop them on the riverbank."

"And what do we wear for our swim?" inquired Peregrinus still holding the cloak as far from his body as his arm would allow.

"Nothing. Wet wool is heavy. Even holding onto the barrels, the wet cloth will drag you under," Alerio answered. "Our gear and clothing will be wrapped in goatskin to keep it dry. Believe me, you'll be grateful for the dry clothing once we've passed the foothills."

"I'd be happy for clean clothing before we go for the swim," Peregrinus stated.

The First Corporal stuck his head into the command tent.

"They're opening the gate, Centurion," he announced before ducking out.

***

"Lance Corporal Sisera, attend me," Seneca ordered while walking to a corner of the command tent.

Alerio followed the old Legion officer to the spot.

"What do you need, Centurion?" he asked.

"Take care of the Tribune's pack. The Legion dispatches are in it," Seneca instructed. "And do your best to keep Tribune Peregrinus alive."

It wasn't lost on Alerio, the Centurion had emphasized the dispatches before the Tribune.

"I'll get the dispatches and the Tribune to the Capital," Alerio assured him.

"Yes, of course you will," Seneca stated. Then, he pulled a folded piece of parchment from his belt. "After you deliver them, take this to Senator Spurius Carvilius Maximus."

"Yes, sir. Shouldn't it be with the Legion dispatches?" inquired Alerio.

"Lance Corporal Sisera, if was a Legion dispatch, I would have added it to Peregrinus' pack," the Centurion advised. "The letter is for the Senator. Eight years ago, I was the first Centurion for Maximus Legion. The General lead us to victory against the Samnites and marched us through the

Capital in a victory parade. It was a glorious day. Think of the letter as a personal note from an old Centurion to his General."

"I will deliver it, sir," Alerio promised.

A commotion at a side entrance drew their attention. Silenus Eduardus appeared from his quarters followed by two slaves. Each of the eastern tribesmen carried two wine casks bonded together with hemp line.

"They look a little small," observed Peregrinus.

"We use them as floats to keep out hearts and lungs out of the cold water," explained Alerio. "Kicking will keep us warm and low in the water. We don't want to attract the attention of an Insubri patrol if they're watching the river. Now Tribune Peregrinus, strip and wrap your pack, clothing, and weapons in goatskin. Then wrap your body up in the cloak and grab a pair of barrels, sir."

Chapter 12 – A Dip in the Tiber

Torches and campfires behind the entrance lay cold and damp. When the gates parted, a roar from hundreds of Insubri warriors shattered the quiet of the night. Their view of the opening gates revealed dark rows of neatly spaced tents partially covered in snow. Realizing their raiders succeeded in launching a surprise attack, they rushed forward.

Long swords flashed and fur covered bodies charged. So many attempted to be the first between the gate posts, it became a log jam. Expecting to enter a sleeping Legion camp, the first to break free sprinted forward. In praise of their victory, they screamed war cries. Then the view of neatly organized tents vanished behind moving shields. By the time the Legion shields tapped their edges together, the war cries became cries of agony.

Those seeing the shields changed direction and charged to the sides. But they ran into more overlapping shields. After the first flourish, the Legionaries remained motionless. Except for a gladius stabbing out to injure a warrior who got shoved near a shield, the Centuries stood silent. With eyes limited to a space three fingers over the top of the shields, the infantrymen appeared to be clay figurines with helmets and slits for eyes. The three-sided shield wall bristled with gladii at waist level and javelin tips at shoulder height.

Yet the warriors outside in the dark saw none of this. They continued to shove forward seeking fame and glory. Not wanting to be left out of the plunder and killing, they shoved harder and pushed those in front. Those trapped at the front of the horde died against the unmoving shields.

Finally, the Insubri stopped. Realizing they were stuck in a motionless mass, the warriors fell silent. Then a deep voice called out shattering the silence.

"Legion, stand by," he sang out and two hundred forty right feet lifted and stomped the snow-covered ground.

"Standing by," the Legionaries thundered a reply.

"Front rank," he crooned. "Advance, advance, advance."

And the first row of Legionaries propelled their shields forward. As the shields drew back, they were replaced by gladii stabs. With each advance, the heavy infantry repeated the synchronized motions. And with each advance, Insubri warriors fell to the ground. Those just injured lay wounded until the line of Legionaries passed over them. None survived the Legion stomp.

As the two rows moved forward, the Legionaries on the sides fell in behind. By the time they shoved and killed their way to the gate posts, the legionaries were stacked in rows twenty deep. Once beyond the gates, the legion line spread out.

***

The Legion's First Corporal waited for the stretcher bearers to haul away wounded Legionaries. When the space was cleared, he turned to face the four squads behind him.

"Tribune Peregrinus. On your order, sir," he announced.

Armenius Peregrinus and Alerio Sisera stood on one foot while massaging blood flow back into the other. Barefoot and naked under their cloaks, they both shivered.

"Yes, Corporal, please," Peregrinus responded. "Anything to get us moving."

"First Century, stand by," the NCO called out.

Forty feet lifted and stomped the ground.

"Standing by, Corporal," the squads answered.

"First Century, by rows of four, forward march," the First Corporal ordered.

Hearing just four squads referred to as a Century spoke of a brutal reality. Gurges Legion's First Century had lost their Centurion, their Sergeant and half their Legionaries in the assault on Volsinii. Alerio picked up his wine casks and shuffled forward on the slush created by the Legionaries marching in front of him.

***

The back rows of the attacking Centuries moved laterally right and left as they drove back the Insubri warriors. Blowing snow hid the Legionaries on the flanks but the overlapping shields created contact from one end of the battle line to the other.

Behind the extended lines of advancing Legionaries, First Century marched out of the gate, performed a right flanked, and headed for the corner of the Legion camp.

Another right turn and the squads marched on fresh snow along the outside of the stockade wall. His feet numbing from the icy snow, Peregrinus began to hobble.

"Co-Co-Cold," commented the young nobleman.

"It'll gets worse before it gets better," Alerio replied.

"No talking in the ranks," the First Corporal hissed.

As the half Century neared the back corner of the Legion camp, the Corporal tapped two of his Legionaries. They jogged forward and disappeared in the blowing snow.

Thumps of bodies and long swords colliding with infantry shields drifted to Alerio. Out of habit, he reached for his hip gladius. It wasn't there. But the infantryman on his left shifted his shield to covered Alerio. Glancing towards Peregrinus, he saw the Legionary on that side of the formation also shift his to cover the Tribune.

The squads moved forward. Out of the heavy flakes, the two infantrymen materialized. Sprawled on the ground in front of them were three Insubri warriors. One of the Legionaries turned his head.

"Clear," he announced, and the formation moved beyond the pair.

***

The soil under Alerio's feet changed to gravel as the ground sloped. They marched onto the riverbank and the gurgling of water overrode the crunch of hobnailed boots on gravel. The pebbles leading to the river pressed on the soles of his feet and snow clung to his ankles. Alerio wished he could pull on his boots. Promising to be more miserable than the rocks and snow, the icy water sent a shock up his spine.

Out of the corner of his eye, Alerio caught Peregrinus stepping backwards.

"It's too, too cold, cold," the Tribune stammered.

He retreated three steps until stopped when his back hit a heavy infantry shield.

"This is the hardest part," urged Alerio while gripping Peregrinus' upper arm. "When it's over, you'll have bragging rights around your family's dinner table."

"My father will never believe it," Peregrinus explained.

"He will when you show him the missing toes from the frostbite," Alerio suggested.

"Missing toes?" Peregrinus inquired.

The First Corporal stepped forward and explained, "If you stand here long enough your feet will rot from the cold. Medics remove the blackened toes to save the foot."

"How long until I catch the rot?" asked Peregrinus.

"No problem, Tribune," the First Corporal assured him. "You won't be standing here long enough."

"How do you figure?" begged Peregrinus.

"Because, sir, you are…," and the Legion's First Corporal grabbed the back of the cloak and shoved Peregrinus into the river. Holding up the cloak, the NCO glanced at Alerio. "Good luck with that one, Lance Corporal Sisera. And may Volturnus grant you safe passage."

"If it's the will of the water God," Alerio replied handing his cloak to the Corporal.

***

Alerio's cōleī tightened down to the size of raisins and his mind screamed for him to get out of the chilly river. Despite the goosebumps that rose like Mount Vesuvius, he plowed into the Tiber. Partially because it was his duty but mostly because the panicking Tribune and he had a mission to complete. And if he didn't settle down Peregrinus, the kicking and thrashing would draw the attention of any nearby Insubri warriors.

The worst case would be to suffer and survive the Tiber, only to be slaughtered by a band of barbarians, when they crawled out of the water.

Peregrinus' wine casks were drifting downstream. The first thing Alerio did was stroke to the small barrels. Once in hand, he towed them to the floundering Tribune.

"Put a hand on each end of the casks and pull your chest out of the water," urged Alerio as he took one of Peregrinus' hands and placed it. "Kick with your legs."

"I can't, can't feel my legs, legs," Peregrinus pleaded between chattering teeth.

"In Legion training they taught us to fake a motion when your too tired or numb to feel," Alerio explained. "Fake it until your body begins to respond. Now kick Tribune because your life depends on it."

"I am kicking. I think," Peregrinus blurted out along with a mouthful of river water.

"Keep going and say nothing," Alerio ordered. "And don't let your feet break the plain of the surface."

"More from Legionary training?" inquired Peregrinus through clenched teeth.

"Splashing in enemy waters is an invitation for poets to sing your tragic tale," Alerio informed the Tribune.

"The only song I want is of a roaring hearth and strong wine," Peregrinus stated.

"Embrace that thought," Alerio suggested. "And kick silently, we're moving beyond the Legion camp."

***

Torchbearers guided units of Legionaries around the stockade walls. All Alerio and Peregrinus could see from the river were the lights bouncing as the holders walked. One torch's flame headed south almost keeping pace with the floating wine casks.

Another torch flared to life followed by three more. Coming online, the flames identified a row of Legionaries moving steadily south.

"How far are we going?" an infantryman asked.

"Far enough for the Insubri on the riverbank to be more concerned with us than anything floating on the river," the First Corporal replied. Then he shouted so the words carried, "Keep your lines straight!"

***

Alerio kicked and watched the high ground as the flames were left behind. The torch lights dimmed until they winked out. In the darkness, the snow fell unseen. Only when several flakes stuck to his eyebrows did he know it was still coming down. Kicking with dead legs, he and the Tribune continued down the Tiber. His belly tightened trying to generate heat. But the warmth was swept away by the cold water before it spread to his numb limbs. Alerio's eyebrows caked over, and his nose tingled. He wanted to scratch the bridge of his nose and wipe the snow from his eyebrows, but his fingers refused to release the edge of the wine cask.

Temptation urged him to swim for shore and leave the icy water. The dark riverbank beckoned as no movement appeared and no campfires blazed. If he could see the foothills south of Volsinii, or an Insubri camp, or any sign of their location, Alerio would kick for shore and escape the Hades of the river.

***

When Alerio was a lad, he watched an old goat lay down gently in the snow. As if to take a nap on a cold winter's day, the animal seemed to be sleeping peacefully. When he nudged the goat, Alerio discovered the body was stiff and lifeless.

A shiver rippled through Alerio shaking him out of the memory. Looking over, he noticed Peregrinus had ceased kicking. Between his misery and the lack of movement from the Tribune, Alerio decided it was time to leave the Tiber.

"Tribune Peregrinus. We're heading for shore," slurred Alerio.

"Why? I'm not cold any longer," whimpered Peregrinus.

From the Legion's march up and the map, Alerio knew the Tiber widened at the foothills. Although he couldn't tell where they were in relationship to the landmark, he felt the current slow as the river broadened. Alerio had enough of the cold, and he feared for the Tribune's health. Grabbing the rope around the Tribune's wine casks, Alerio forced his legs to move quicker. Slowly, the pair angled towards the far-off riverbank.

Chapter 13 – Death in the Foothills

Sometime before dawn, in a windy gust that blew falling snow almost sideways, Alerio staggered out of the water. One hand lagged, dragging an unresponsive Peregrinus.

"Come on Tribune, wake up," Alerio begged as he rubbed the legs, arms, and hands of the unconscious nobleman.

Alerio's own arms and legs tingled to the point of pain. But he ignored his discomfort to focus on reviving the Tribune. Getting Peregrinus up and moving was the immediate concern. Exposed on the riverbank made the officer and Legionary easy prey for any roving patrols of Insubri warriors.

"So cold," mumbled the Tribune.

"Ten steps from here is a tree line," Alerio informed him. "Can you walk ten steps?"

"Yes, ten steps," Peregrinus replied.

Alerio half pushed and half lifted the young man. Once on his feet, they leaned on each other, crossed to the riverbank, and staggered up the rise. Where the ground leveled, the snow deepened.

"Ten steps?" asked Peregrinus.

"Ten more and we'll be in the trees," Alerio lied.

Fifty paces from the riverbank, Alerio shoved aside a branch laden with snow. The shove caused an avalanche from the higher branches that almost buried them. Shaking free of the pile, Alerio supported Peregrinus as they stooped under the thick branches of a fir tree.

"Fire," suggested Peregrinus before sinking to the layers of dry pine needles around the trunk of the tree.

"Sorry Tribune, no fire. The Insubri would see the smoke," Alerio explained. He fumbled with the bindings before finally undoing his pack. After retrieving the knife with the yellow and black hilt, he cut the ties on the oiled skin around Peregrinus' pack. "All I can offer you are dry clothes, a warm cloak, and a solid pair of hobnailed boots."

***

The sun rose bright and strong, and the clouds blew away. It was a morning that promised warmth after the late spring snowstorm. Alerio, on his knees, watched the river and the land between, from under a branch.

"How are you feeling, Tribune Peregrinus?" he asked while keeping his eyes on the melting snow.

When Peregrinus didn't reply, Alerio turned his head. The Tribune was curled up in his cloak with his eyes wide open.

"Sir, how are you feeling?" Alerio insisted.

"Cold. So cold," Peregrinus mumbled.

"We'll be leaving soon," Alerio informed him. "You'll warm up on the run."

"My feet hurt. Do you think I have the rot?" asked Peregrinus. "I don't want to lose my toes."

"You're fine, Tribune," Alerio assured him. "When I put on your boots, I felt your toes. They were warm."

"So, the medics won't cut on me?" Peregrinus inquired brightening up a little.

"Not that I can tell," Alerio said turning back to peer out from under the branch. "But those three Insubri riders may have a different idea. Are you able to fight?"

"I'm stiff and my arms and legs feel like they're covered in clay," Peregrinus replied. "I don't know."

From the northern direction, three warriors wrapped tightly in furs let their ponies pick the way forward. Unfortunately for the Legionary and the Tribune, the ponies choose a path along the tree line.

"Not hunters, they don't have their bows strung," reported Alerio. "And they aren't in a hurry. Probably a routine patrol."

"You said there are three of them?" Peregrinus whimpered. "I survived freezing to death in the river only to get perfututum by three barbarians before I can even get warm. It just doesn't seem right."

"Swing your arms around and rub your legs," Alerio instructed. "When I leave, wait for the Insubri to pass by then follow. Do what you can. Oh, and sing along with me."

"Sing?" asked Peregrinus. "Why are we singing?"

"Softly for now," advised Alerio ignoring the questions. "When we attack them, sing louder."

"We're going to attack them?" questioned Peregrinus.

Under his breath, Alerio began to sing.

Inspection, Inspection, I'm Ready for inspection

I hone the edge, polish the blade, clean the guard, and oil the hilt
My gladius for inspection

I stitch the hide, tighten the grab, repair the frame, and oil the face
My shield for inspection

I pound the dents, buff out the rents, adjust the guards, and oil the   joints
My helmet for inspection

I check the clasps, replace the grabs, straighten the plates, and oil the straps
My armor for inspection

By dawn, I'm ready for review
On savages with no regard, I use them hard
Wrecks my repairs and restorations
Grinding himself on my gear, before dying with cheer
He ruins my good intentions

Inspection, Inspection
I'm Ready for Inspection
I hone the edge, polish the blade, clean the guard, and oil the hilt
My gladius for inspection

I stitch the hide, tighten the grab, repair the frame, and oil the face
My shield for inspection

I pound the dents, buff out the rents, adjust the guards, and oil the joints
My helmet for inspection

I check the clasps, replace the grabs, straighten the plates and oil the straps
My armor for inspection

By eve, I'm ready for relaxing
Savages who should stay away, I've been killing all day
Dulls my grinds and alterations
Blocking and stabbing fools, as they die upon my tools
Ruins my good intentions

"Inspection, Inspection," Alerio sang as he crawled to Peregrinus. "Sing with me, Tribune. *I'm ready for inspection.*"

Alerio jerked his cloak up to cover the two hilts sticking above his shoulders. Then, he pulled the long knife, looked at the Tribune and winked.

"*I hone the edge, polish the blade, clean the guard, and oil the hilt. My gladius for inspection*," he sang softly while ducking low and slipping out the backside of their shelter.

As afraid as Peregrinus was, the awful tone-deaf singing by the Legionary made him chuckle. He had never actually sung the song. But late in the evenings, Legionaries sang it while servicing their equipment, so the Tribune knew the words.

"I stitch the hide, tighten the grab, repair the frame, and oil the face. My shield for inspection," Peregrinus sang while stretching, briskly rubbing his legs, and rotating his shoulders. As he moved to the same exit used by Alerio, he stopped.

***

The three Insubri warriors and their ponies clomped casually along the tree line. They were scouting for Republic forces coming up from the south. Warned not to engage, their orders were to race back to the picket line at the first sign of Legionaries.

While the orders from their Chief were specific, the warriors didn't think it included the man standing in a clearing deeper in the woods. Although seemingly relaxed, the man stared straight at the warriors. His cloak bunched up around his neck as if cold, the Legionary pointed a knife at them in a challenge. A challenge the warriors couldn't ignore.

They pulled long swords from sheathes and easily dropped off their ponies. Without taking their eyes off the Legionary, they tied the reins to a tree's branches, tossed their fur robes over the backs of the ponies, and stalked into the woods.

***

Big lads, Alerio observed as the Insubri warriors brushed aside tree limbs. They came for him two abreast. As soon as they reached the clearing, the northern warriors separated and swung their swords around to loosen up their shoulders. Big swords, Alerio thought.

"Do me a favor," he called across the clearing.

"What's that?" one inquired in broken Latin.

"Drop dead and save me the trouble of spilling your blood," Alerio suggested.

"Little soldier, little knife, you face the Insubri," replied the warrior while twirling his sword so it made a whirling sound. "It is your blood that will nourish the forest this day."

"You insult my knife?" Alerio responded.

Reaching back, he tucked away the long knife. As his hand rose, it caught the edge of his cloak, and he tossed it off to the side of the clearing.

"How about you insult these," he said while reaching up over his shoulders. As his hands wrapped around the hilts of his two gladii, Alerio asked, "Can you guess their name?"

Alerio pulled both gladii from their sheaths and pointed the blades at the warriors.

"What do you call the fat blades?" inquired the warrior.

"It doesn't matter what I call them," Alerio announced. "For you, they mean death."

From the tree line, one of the ponies whinnied. The three warriors turned just as Tribune Peregrinus vaulted onto a mare's back. He kneed it into a fast trot.

Alerio used the distraction to step forward. With the distance closed, he bent his knees to appear the same height. Turning back around, one of the Insubri cocked his head to the side and squinted his eyes at Alerio.

"You sacrificed yourself to allow another to steal a pony?" inquired the warrior.

"That wasn't the plan," Alerio assured him. "But if he gets away, so be it."

"Does the coward know we have a war party to the south?" the Insubri asked.

The Legionary's reply wasn't what the warriors expected.

***

"Inspection, Inspection. I'm Ready for Inspection," Alerio sang as he began to twirl his gladii. *"I hone the edge, polish the blade, clean the guard, and oil the hilt. My gladius for inspection"*

His blades spun, so fast they created more noise than the warrior's long blade. The show seemed to entertain them until Alerio surged forward. Before the Insubri could react, the Legionary was between two of them. Too tight for their long swords but perfect for the short gladii.

Spinning so his blades circled, he cut two of the warriors. One collapsed with a deep gash in his side. The other danced away with only a slash to his arm.

"I stitch the hide, tighten the grab, repair the frame, and oil the face," Alerio sang as he jumped over the fatally wounded warrior. Using him as an obstacle, the Legionary beckoned the two Insubri forward. *"My shield for inspection."*

"You sing like rancid boar meat," an Insubri observed.

"Then aged boar meat must be delicious," Alerio responded. "Are you going to fight, herd animal, or stand around chewing your cud?"

The two warriors charged forward. Their long swords swiping inward at an angle.

"I pound the dents, buff out the rents, adjust the guards," Alerio belted out as he dove under the blades and off to the side. *"and oil the joints. My helmet for inspection."*

His left gladius lashed out as he rolled slicing across a warrior's thigh muscle. Alerio hit on the back of his shoulders and continued to roll. When he regained his footing and twisted around, he saw the result of his pass. The wounded warrior lay across the body of his dead companion.

The last warrior began to run for his pony.

"Coward!" shouted Alerio. "My father has milk cows with more honor and courage than the Insubri."

The warrior stopped and turned. He looked at the dead tribesman and at the one attempting to stem the flow of blood from the deep cut. Then, his eyes drifted up to the Legionary.

Alerio held a gladius at his own neck while pointing at the wounded man. He was mimicking cutting the injured man's throat.

"I check the clasps, replace the grabs, straighten the plates, and oil the straps," Alerio continued singing. *"My armor for inspection."*

The warrior bashed a tree branch creating a shower of snow. As if a legendary hero coming through a sparkling portal from another world, the big man stalked forward.

"By eve, I'm ready for relaxing. Savages who should stay away, I've been killing all day," Alerio sang the last words with a smile. *"Dulls my grinds and alterations."*

Approaching slowly, the Insubri held his blade up and to one side. From there he could chop downward, stab, or slice laterally.

"Blocking and stabbing fools," Alerio chanted as he moved within range of the long sword.

The warrior dipped the tip forward and with all the strength of his powerful shoulders drew the blade down and across. His aim was to cleave deeply into the Legionary's chest, if not all the way through his torso.

Alerio bent his left knee while raising the left gladius. The Legionary couldn't stop the long sword's momentum. The edges met and the Insubri's blade skated along the gladius being redirected upward. It passed just over the Legionary's head.

Extending his right leg, Alerio thrust his right gladius deeply into the warrior's groin. He twisted the blade before yanking it free. The Insubri dropped his sword and grabbed his crotch as he fell to his knees.

"As they die upon my tools. Ruins my good intentions," Alerio finished the verse as he stood up. Walking to the bleeding warrior, he leaned down and wiped the blood from his blades on the warrior's pants.

He picked up the long sword, measured its weight in his hand, and looked down at the dying barbarian.

"You should have attacked as soon as you entered the clearing," Alerio instructed as he rested the long blade on his shoulder.

***

After retrieving his cloak, Alerio ducked under the fir tree and strapped on his pack. Pushing his way out from under the fir, he approached the ponies. They stood calmly munching grass they located after nuzzling aside the thinning layer of snow.

One pony was red and distinct. Alerio yanked the fur robe off its back, untied him and pulled the reins off. With a swat to its hunches, he sent the pony towards the river. After a quick trip into the woods to hide the robe and reins, Alerio came back and inspected the other pony.

She was plain grey with no distinguishing marks, and she was calm. Not the sort of mount a tribal leader or an outstanding Insubri would ride. In short, an unidentifiable ride for a lackluster warrior. Hopefully, nobody would recognize the pony or her rider at a distance.

Chapter 14 - War Party Games

Alerio nudged the pony away from the tree line. They strolled along the flat ground until they approached a steep grade. Angling to a point where the land fell away on two sides, he drew the pony to a stop.

Far below, a campfire burned and five Insubri warriors sat facing in one direction. Two more stood with bows in hand also facing in the same direction. All their focus was on a tree. Tied to the tree was Tribune Peregrinus.

His legs were wide apart and bent back in what had to be an uncomfortable sprawl. With them tied that far apart, all his weight rested on partially bent knees. His arms were no help. They were strapped to either side of the tree trunk. It was a ridiculous attempt at imitating a crucifixion.

"Lazy barbarians. Won't take time to put a man up on the wood properly," Alerio mumbled. Then one of the bowmen notched an arrow and shot it into the tree. The arrow quivered a couple of fingers width from the Tribunes left elbow. "But not bad for target practice."

The other bowman caught sight of the rider and pony on the hill. He acknowledged Alerio with a wave of his bow.

What the bowman saw was a robed figure sitting on a drab pony. Alerio pulled the long sword and waved it in the air returning the greeting. Then, he kneed the pony into motion and guided her back the way they had come.

He hadn't seen any red spots on the Tribune's body. That spoke well of the Insubri archery and presented him with a problem. Now, instead of sneaking into their camp and recovering the dispatches, he had to rescue the coward of a Tribune.

Once out of sight of the war party, Alerio turned the pony. He pondered the tasks as he rode towards the trees closest to the drop-off. It would be easy to slit Peregrinus' throat while getting the Legion's messages. Then he remembered the trapped and wounded Legionaries. Without the Tribune's political connections, reinforcements would be delayed.

Alerio tossed back the fur robe letting it bunch up on the pony's haunches. After a search, he located a trail and urged the animal into the forest.

***

The trail snaked through the trees in a southwestern direction. Where the land to the east fell, the track climbed higher into the foothills. For animals passing through the forest, the trail provided easy passage. But not so for a rider. Soon the trees closed in and Alerio had to dismount. He pondered leading the pony further but, a glance at the steep grade ahead convinced him to set her free.

He slipped the robe back on, not to wear it for comfort but, for the ease of carrying the bulky fur garment. As the pony picked her way back down the path, Alerio climbed the trail to the top of the foothill. At the center of a flat area, he turned left and began to descend. If he figured correctly, below him at the edge of the thick trees was open grassland and the Insubri war party's camp.

***

Alerio, wrapped in the black fur robe, peered between branches. Down on the grassland, three of the warriors squatted beside the campfire. The other four, either on patrol or lost behind branches, were not visible. Peregrinus also was out of his field of vision. He couldn't tell if the Tribune lived or had the good manners to die making Alerio's task simpler.

The sun's rays filtered straight down through the trees letting him know it was midday. Digging in his pack produced a wheat cake and a strip of dried meat. Once the food was consumed, Alerio leaned back on the slope and closed his eyes.

A cool breeze across his exposed hands alerted him to the setting of the sun behind the foothills. Snugged inside the warm robe, Alerio had to fight the urge to remain motionless and go back to sleep. But, he had come too far, not in distance but in suffering, to ignore his duty. Plus, if the Tribune lived, he'd need awhile to figure out a way to extract the gutless nobleman.

As the sky turned grey, Alerio rolled onto his hands and knees and began carefully picking his way down the slope. With the black fur robe blending into the deepening shadows, he made it to the bottom of the hill unseen. There he crept forward as daylight faded. Two trees back from the grassland, he squatted and studied the Insubri camp.

***

Off to the left of the camp, ponies whinnied. They were tied to a picket line not far from the campfire. Only two warriors tended the fire. Close to them, a Legion leather pack rested unopened next to several sacks of Insubri supplies. Ten paces to the right lay the big tree where Peregrinus was tied.

The pack with the Legion dispatches held the highest priority. The Tribune, if he lived, was secondary. However, if Alerio tripped up, alerted the Insubri, and had to run, freeing Peregrinus became a non-issue. Legionaries ran a lot and fast. But not if slowed down by a weak Tribune who left a companion to face three big barbarians alone.

One of the warriors pulled a stick from the fire and walked towards the big tree. Alerio followed the burning ember as the barbarian approached Peregrinus' location. He squatted and held out the stick.

Alerio expected to hear cries of pain as Peregrinus' face was horribly burned. When no screams carried across from the big tree, Alerio squinted his eyes in an attempt to better see the shadowy figure.

"Eat," ordered the barbarian.

Alerio didn't know if he was relieved or disappointed. The Insubri wanted the Tribune healthy, so they were feeding him. Unreliable coward or not, he had to be freed. Once Alerio settled on the idea, he mostly released his resentment.

Alerio eased back into the forest, faced left, and headed towards the ponies.

***

Between the smell of the Insubri robe and the slow approach, the ponies paid him no heed. They continued to munch on grass as Alerio came up behind the two. From this vantage point, he could see the pair of warriors at the campfire.

Should he attack them, grab the Legion communications, free…

His chain of thought broke when another two riders trotted into camp. They said a few words before leaping to the ground and walking their ponies to where the Legionary hid.

Alerio back away and squatted down. In the dark, the black fur robe blended in with the grassland. Once tied to the picket line, the new ponies snorted greetings at the others. Using the noise as cover, Alerio crept in among the mounts and rubbed one muzzle as he studied the camp, now with four Insubri guarding it.

A sliver of moon rose in the night sky promising a dark night. At least he wouldn't have to deal with moonlit shadows. High in the hills, a wolf howled for its mate and Alerio had his plan.

***

Soon the reins on the four ponies hung un-looped and draped over their necks secured only by slipknots. After loosening one end of the picket line, Alerio laid it on the ground. Back in the forest, he leaned against a tree, watched the camp, and waited.

The wolf howled again and, although no closer, the ponies snorted their displeasure at the presence of a predator. Alerio feared one of the ponies would bolt and reveal the undone ropes. But the mounts settled and the night quieted.

Eventually, the small talk ended, the warriors stretched out and the campfire died down. Still Alerio waited. He wanted them deep asleep and dreaming of hearth and home. If barbarians even dreamed of civilized things like those. Also, he needed another wolf call and three fist sized rocks.

A little toe nudging and he located the rocks. With them in hand, he continued the vigil.

***

The gash of a moon passed its zenith in the starry night and a wolf howled. Alerio reared back and launched the first rock. A pony whinnied and stomped the ground. The other three snorted loudly. One of the Insubri rolled out of his furs and the Legionary hurled the second. This time all four ponies pawed the soil until one pulled back. As if still tied to a picket line, the four rose and spun. Alerio pitched the third rock and the ponies fled in panic.

The warrior stood and shouted. The other three leaped to their feet. Following the ponies, they ran from the campfire disappearing into the night. Alerio jogged along the tree line until he was even with the camp. Then he pivoted left and broke into a sprint. With no change in his stride, he snagged the Tribune's pack, swung right, and vanished into the night.

***

Peregrinus' world had gone from bone chilling cold to hot fear and scalding panic to aching joints and bone chilling cold. His misery knew no bounds. His mind had long since abandoned rationality or his ability to sort out the screaming of his senses. When a voice whispered, he couldn't place the person, or understand the meaning of the words.

"Tribune, keep quiet," insisted the voice.

"Ugh, ah…" and a hand, smelling like pony sweat and dirty fur, clamped over his mouth.

"Peregrinus. For Angerona's sake, shut up," urged Alerio as he cut the Tribune's binding with one hand while holding the other over Peregrinus' mouth.

"Lance Corporal Sisera? I thought you were dead," he mumbled under the smelly palm.

"Later. For now, keep your questions to yourself," ordered Alerio.

"As if a priest of the Goddess of silence," Peregrinus promised.

The bindings on both legs hung sliced but the Tribune's legs didn't move. A bad sign thought Alerio as he cut away the binding on the right wrist. Peregrinus swung away from the tree trunk like a broken window shutter - unanchored except for the suspended left wrist. Once that rope parted, Peregrinus tumbled to the ground, his legs unable to support his weight.

An arm snaked under the Tribune's arm and across the small of his back. Suddenly, he was airborne and slung over the Legionary's shoulder. In ten jarring steps, his ribs hurt from bouncing off the Legionary's shoulder bones, and his head ached from slamming into Alerio's pack. He didn't complain out loud but, in his mind, he prayed to Angerona to keep his words of agony in his mind and off his lips.

Peregrinus expected the pain to increase as he was carried across the grassland. Instead, his head hung away from the Legionary's pack and the pace slowed. He felt the shift and realized they were heading up hill.

***

Alerio's lungs inflated and deflated. With each cycle, he struggled to find enough air. As his thighs began to burn, he concentrated on lifting and placing one foot at a time. It wasn't so much the extra weight of the Tribune. In Legion Training, Recruits ran with sandbags on their shoulders. If a trainee fell and didn't get up, two bags were added to the load. For those slow to reach the top, only a single sandbag was added when they ran the hill a second time. No, it wasn't the weight. It was the steepness of the hill and the rush to put as much distance between them and the Insubri camp as possible. Breathing like a bull and digging deep into his guts for reserve energy, Alerio continued the climb.

***

Peregrinus flew through the air and landed on his back. He heard another body fall beside him. That body breathed hard and groaned.

"You came for me," blurted out the Tribune.

A leather pouch slammed into Peregrinus' stomach driving the air from his lungs.

"I came for the dispatches," gasped Alerio. "You, sir, were a secondary priority."

Chapter 15 – Dash Down Hill

"Can you stand, Tribune Peregrinus?" Alerio inquired as he struggled to his feet.

"I believe so," replied the nobleman.

"That's good, sir. We should get moving," Alerio stated formally.

Peregrinus pushed back until he was on his knees. After testing to see if his legs would support his weight, he managed to stand. Reaching down and picking up his pack, he reported his success to Alerio.

"Ready to march, Lance Corporal," he announced.

"Yes, sir, follow me and take care with your footing," the Legionary warned.

Turning left, they hiked over the crest of the hill and began to slip and slide their way down the far side. From tree to tree, they crept downward each getting a share of scratches from low hanging branches.

***

"We should wait for daylight," Peregrinus suggested.

Alerio stood within the tree line staring across the dark grasslands.

"Is that an order, Tribune?" he asked.

"Well no. I was simply voicing my opinion," Peregrinus explained.

"In that case, sir, we should move," Alerio stated and began walking away from the forest.

Caught by surprise, the nobleman rushed to catch up with the Legionary.

They walked for a long time before Alerio asked, "Can you run, sir?"

"My knees are sore but yes, I believe so," Peregrinus replied.

Alerio stepped off and broke into the Legion jog. The Tribune, again caught off guard, raced to catch up with the Legionary.

In the quiet and dark of the early morning, the two men moved rapidly across the gentle hills and dales of the rolling land. The only sound, their hobnailed boots pounding the short grasses and the occasional stretch of bare earth.

***

Alerio fell into the rhythm of the run, and they covered a lot of ground. He could hear Peregrinus breathing hard and noticed a few times when the young nobleman stumbled. Then, the Tribune wasn't beside him. Turning, Alerio saw his shape sprawled in the grass.

"Do you need to rest, sir?" Alerio asked as he knelt.

"Knees hurt," reported Peregrinus. "Head hurts."

Thinking the Tribune had injured his head in the fall, Alerio probed his scalp before placing a palm against Peregrinus' forehead. The nobleman burned with fever. Moving to the young man's knees, Alerio felt the joints and found both swollen.

"We'll take a rest period," stated Alerio as he slipped Peregrinus' arms out of the pack's straps.

From their packs, he pulled out wheat cakes and meat strips. While they ate the horizon lightened. This was good as they could see further and judge the direction to the Tiber. Somewhere further south, the Northern Legion had a fort on the riverbank, a dock, and patrol boats. On the other hand, the rising sun was bad as they were visible to any Insubri patrolling in the area. Alerio wasn't sure which he preferred. Then, he wished it was still night.

"Tribune, can you stand?" Alerio asked as he stood.

"What? I just sat down," mumbled Peregrinus. "A moment to dine in peace would be appreciated."

Reaching down, Alerio grabbed his arm and jerked Peregrinus to his feet. The Tribune's head wobbled, and his knees began to fold. If it weren't for Alerio's grip on his elbow, he would have fallen.

"Brace up, Tribune. I need you to stand tall and look in this direction," Alerio instructed as he turned Peregrinus to face east. "Stay right there. If you can, wave with your arms."

"I don't understand," pleaded Peregrinus. His eyes were unfocused, and he had a blank look on his young face.

"I'll explain later," promised Alerio as he turned and jogged away.

***

The lone Insubri warrior saw the two strangers. As he urged his pony closer, he recognized the hobnailed boots and the short hair worn by soldiers of the Republic. Hatred set his heart aflame, and he kneed the pony into a charge while drawing his long sword. To cut them down and bask in their pain while they died by his hand, fired his mind.

One stood as helpless as a bait goat staked in place for a cougar hunt. He would die first. The other ran towards him holding a short sword. That one, he would spare for now. After slaughtering the goat, he would return and slay the armed man.

***

Alerio had spotted the mounted Insubri in the distance. With Peregrinus standing, he hoped seeing two Legionaries would send the rider to get help. That at least would give him and Peregrinus a chance to move out of the area. Unfortunately, the warrior decided to attack.

Drawing one gladius, the Legionary ran to engage the Insubri. But the rider nudged his pony to the side, and they began to veer around Alerio. Unaware of the danger, Peregrinus stood dazed and unable to defend himself.

With the rider attempting to bypass him, Alerio drew his other gladius. Not having a javelin or a distance weapon, the Legionary changed course and sprinted in a direction to cut across the pony's path. But it was too far. The rider would be by him and on Peregrinus before he could intercept the warrior. In frustration and with a prayer to Diana, Alerio hoisted both gladii and flung them at the fast-moving warrior.

End over end, the short blades spun sailing in a flat arc across the distance. From Alerio's hands the gladii traveled to a spot just in front of the mounted Insubri. The Goddess of the hunt must have heard Alerio's plea as the warrior rode into the path of the tumbling blades. One slapped into his shoulder. Its edge leaving a thin cut on the skin. The other gladius rotated a little faster allowing the pummel to slam into the warrior's temple. He toppled from the pony.

The pony, surprised by the sudden loss of weight from its back, slowed to a trot. A tasty spot of green drew the mare's attention. She walked over and began grazing.

Alerio reached to his back and drew his knife as he ran. Before the Insubri regained awareness, his heart pumped the last of his blood onto the soil. Alerio wiped the blade clean on the dead warrior's leather pants before collecting his gladii and the pony.

Act 3

Chapter 16 - Legion Post Umbria

The on-duty Legionary leaned against the gate post. After yesterdays' cold and snow, the spring sun warmed without the oppressive heat of summer. He'd been at his post since daybreak and was looking forward to some vino while he fished off the pier after his shift.

He alternated between watching the light traffic of merchants on the road running south and the empty northern route. A Legion had marched through just days before and since then, no merchants had come from that direction. It took him by surprise when far up the northern road, a pony, ridden by a fur covered barbarian, and led by a man wearing Legion boots, came trotting and jogging towards the Legion Post.

"Sergeant of the Guard," he yelled through the open gates. "You've got to see this."

Moments later, the on-duty NCO walked out and looked at the strange makeup of the travelers.

"Not Legion couriers," observed the Sergeant. "What do you suppose?"

"Deserters. The one on the pony seems like he's hiding and the one on the ground has two sword hilts sticking over his shoulders," the Legionary replied. "Nothing about them is regulation except the boots. Think they'll try to get passed us."

"Corporal of the Guard. Get me a unit on the main road," the Sergeant shouted. Then to the guard commented, "And I thought this was going to be a boring watch."

"I was hoping it would be," the Legionary confessed.

***

After the grassland, Alerio was tempted to climb the next hill and approach the Legion Post from the west. But Peregrinus' fever and chills forced him to choose the Republic road. While running and leading the pony, he constantly watched to be sure the Tribune didn't lose his seat and the road behind them was empty. Even with Legion Post Umbria in view, they could be run down by mounted Insubri warriors.

Relief ran through him when ten Legionaries poured out of the Post and took up positions across the road. A Sergeant stood in front of the shields holding up his hand.

"Halt. State your unit and purpose," he shouted as Alerio, and the pony slowed.

"Lance Corporal Alerio Sisera. Seventh Squad, Forty Seventh Century," Alerio reported. Then as he began to point upward, Peregrinus collapsed and tumbled from the pony. Alerio managed to catch him as he fell. After lowering the nobleman to the road, he continued, "This is Tribune Armenius Peregrinus of General Quintus Fabius Gurges' staff. And the Tribune needs immediate medical attention."

"Purpose," demanded the Sergeant.

"We have dispatches for the Senate," reported Alerio. "The Legion is sheltered in place and surrounded by tribal units of Insubri and Etruscan warriors."

"Alright, carry the Tribune to medical," ordered the Sergeant. "We'll let the Centurion sort this out."

"Sergeant. I'll need someone to bring those packs tied over the pony's neck," explained Alerio as he lifted the Tribune.

When no one moved and the Sergeant didn't assign a Legionary, Alerio hoisted Peregrinus and draped him over the back of the pony. Then, he tugged on the reins and guided the animal into the Legion Post.

"Dispatches for the Senate?" asked the Sergeant of the squad leader. "What do you think?"

"Merda. One is sick, I could see that. The other is delusional," replied the Lance Corporal.

"Follow them and take those gladii off the Lance Corporal's back," the Sergeant ordered. "He may be too afraid to fight barbarians, but it could be a problem if he snaps."

"We're on it, Sergeant," the squad Leader said. "Squad. Right face. Forward march."

***

Alerio pulled the packs off the pony, slung them over his shoulders, pulled Peregrinus down and into his arms. He struggled through the door to Medical.

"The Tribune needs helps," he announced.

A medic sitting in the corner looked up from a scroll.

"What seems to be the lad's problem," he asked without moving.

"I don't know, medic," Alerio said between clinched teeth. "It could be drowning in cold water. Being use for target practice by a war party. Running on injured knees. Or maybe he's just exhausted from organizing a Legion under siege. But I'm a Legionary not a medic. What do you think?"

Two Legionaries stepped into the room and separated to either side of the door. A Lance Corporal entered and walked up to Alerio.

"I'll take the rig and the gladii," he stated. "Take them off or we'll take them off for you."

Alerio turned his head and glared at the two Legionaries by the door. Here he stood, with packs hanging over his shoulder and a feverous Tribune in his arms and they wanted him to disarm.

"No problem, Lance Corporal. Just have the medic tell me where to lay the Tribune,"
 Alerio replied. "But I can tell you, I've had a really bad day. If I don't get a hot meal and a nap soon, you just might have to try and take them from me."

"You are up on charges for refusing an order," the Lance Corporal said. Then to the two Legionaries at the door. "Remove the Lance Corporal's gladii."

Alerio kicked the squad leader in the thigh sending him reeling back into one Legionary. Using the Tribune's legs, he swept the other off to the side where the man tripped over a chair. Then Alerio walked to the medic and dropped Peregrinus into the man's lap.

"Take care of him," Alerio ordered as he reached over his shoulders and drew the gladii. Spinning back to the three Legionaries, he warned, "You want these? Come and take them."

"Squad," shouted the Lance Corporal.

Eight Legionaries filed through the doorway with their javelins leveled at Alerio. He smiled at them and twirled his blades.

"This is going to be interesting," he exclaimed.

Without armor and in a confined space, the javelins out matched the gladii. Everyone knew it and that's why the squad leader hesitated.

***

"Where is the Tribune?" a voice outside demanded.

The doorway darkened as a huge Centurion blocked out the sunlight. When he entered, he shoved the Legionaries aside and scowled at the man holding two gladii.

"Who are you and what are those?" he growled.

"Lance Corporal Alerio Sisera, sir," he answered while smoothly jerking the blades up, over his shoulders and into their sheaths. "Weapon's instructor and Legion scout for Tribune Peregrinus. We're carrying messages for the Senate."

The officer looked at the medic holding the Tribune in his lap.

"Strange treatment for a staff officer, Doc," he pointed out. "Is suckling now a Legion approved treatment?"

"No, Centurion. It's just I was taken by surprise when they came in," stammered the medic.

"And ended up holding him like a babe in arms?" the Centurion stated. "Someone help the medic move the Tribune to a surgery table. The rest of you, clear this room."

"But Centurion, the Sergeant said to disarm…" the squad leader began when the Centurion chopped the air with his hand.

"What part of clear this room did you not understand?" he inquired.

"Squad, dismissed," their leader ordered.

He followed eight of them out while the last two helped move Peregrinus to a table. Then they scrambled to escape the glare of their Century's Centurion. Once the room was cleared, the officer looked closely at Alerio.

"You resemble your father," he said. "How is Sergeant Sisera?"

"I wouldn't know, sir," Alerio replied. "I've been stationed with the Southern Legion. They sent me north with Gurges Legion so I could take leave and visit my family after the engagement."

"So why are you here?" he inquired.

"General Gurges and Colonel Pholus were killed, and half the Legion is dead or wounded," Alerio reported. "Lieutenant General Silenus Eduardus sent Tribune

Peregrinus out with dispatches. I'm his guide and bodyguard."

"And how is that working out?" the Centurion asked indicating the Tribune.

"It's been a busy night," reported Alerio.

The Centurion took Peregrinus' pack and walked over to the medic's table. After pulling out the Legion dispatches, he sat and read through the stack of reports.

"Doc, how's the Tribune?" the officer inquired as he rewrapped then stuffed the reports back into the pack.

"From my initial examination, I'd say exhaustion," the medic replied. "But his knees are swollen, and he has deep rope marks on his wrists and ankles. He needs rest."

"I'm sending over hot food," the officer informed the medic. "Whatever they need, get it. They leave at first light for the Capital. Sisera, take care of the Tribune."

"Yes sir. Will we see you again?" asked Alerio. "I think Tribune Peregrinus would like to thank you."

"No time, Lance Corporal," the Centurion announced as he reached the doorway. "I'm marching my Century north to block the road. If the barbarians decide to come south, I'll have a surprise for them."

***

Before sunrise, four Legionaries carried Tribune Peregrinus to the docks. Alerio walked behind with the torchbearers at the rear of the procession. They filed through the rear gates, down a narrow wood walkway and onto a pier.

"We'll have you at the Capital in two and a half days, sir," the Corporal of the patrol boat informed Peregrinus.

His answer was a half raised right hand that dropped almost as quickly as it had lifted from under the blanket. With a wave from the Corporal, the bearers carried the Tribune onto the boat. She was a thirty-oar, single banked Legion river patrol boat. They placed the Tribune in the center of the boat and Alerio to the rear.

"You can store your packs under the bench," the Corporal offered.

"These packs stay by my side," Alerio informed him. "Although, I'd like a turn on an oar tomorrow."

"You know rowing?" the NCO asked.

"Southern Legion training," Alerio responded. "I need to stay in shape."

"I don't think anyone will have a problem with a break," the Corporal replied. Then he announced to the oarsmen, "Blades up."

Fifteen oars on either side of the boat were raised straight in the air. A Legionary on the dock shoved the boat and it drifted until the current caught her.

"Ready all. Oars in," the NCO ordered. "Pull through. Stroke, stroke, stroke."

The patrol boat surged forward as thirty oars, in perfect unison, rowed them down the Tiber river.

Chapter 17 - Capital City Docks

The NCO was true to his word. The patrol boat approached the Capital docks two and a half days later. The half was a guess as pouring rain and heavy clouds blocked the sun. Alerio watched as the Corporal leaped to the dock while the boat was still being secured to the pier.

He approached a man holding a slate tablet and dressed in an oiled goatskin coat. Two slaves stood in the rain a respectful distance behind the man. After a few words, the Corporal returned to the patrol boat. The man with the slate tablet sent one of his slaves racing off towards the city.

"The Harbor Master is securing a carriage for you, Tribune Peregrinus," reported the NCO.

When Peregrinus didn't respond, Alerio spoke for the Tribune, "Thank you, Corporal. Your crew did a good job. If the Tribune were able, I'm sure he would express the sentiment himself. If you're staying for the night, I'd like to buy you a mug of vino and a meal."

"Both sound good but, we have orders to report back as soon as possible," the Corporal replied. Then he shouted to the boat's three Lance Corporals, "Give me four bodies to carry the Tribune to the carriage."

A small, enclosed coach, pulled by two ponies, rolled onto the pier. The Harbor Master spoke to the driver before walking away followed by his two slaves.

Peregrinus groaned as he was lifted from the boat. When his cloak shifted, he shivered violently. Alerio reached out and adjusted the covering. He also pulled his own cloak up to keep the rain off his head.

Once the Legionaries placed the Tribune in the carriage, Alerio climbed up and placed the warm fur robe over the Tribune's cloak. He dropped their packs on the floorboards and climbed down.

"To Villa Peregrinus. Do you know it?" he asked the coachman.

With his cloak over his head, only Alerio's face showed. He and Peregrinus appeared to be two young men from wealthy families. Most likely, based on their mode of transportation, returning home from playing Tribune with the Legion.

"I know the Capital, lad," the coachman replied. "Don't you think I know the city?"

"Fine. But take it slow and don't jar the Tribune," he warned.

"Are you telling me my business?" demanded the driver. "If you don't think I know what I'm doing, let's have the city guard and a Magistrate decide."

Alerio was shocked. He didn't know what he had done to the anger coachman.

"Sir. I'm just trying to get the Tribune to his father's villa," Alerio pleaded.

Suddenly, the Harbor Master appeared through the rain. The two slaves were now standing right beside him. Up close, the slaves were thick with corded muscles and both their faces displayed scars from prior fights.

"What seems to be the problem?" the Harbor Master asked. "You can't block the pier with this coach. Move along!"

"I'm not going anywhere until the city guard gets here," the coachman declared. "I'm a freeman and a Citizen. I will not be insulted."

The Harbor Master lifted a hand to his chin as if in deep thought about the situation. Finally, he dropped the hand and looked at Alerio.

"See here, young sir. Why don't you offer a tip to the coachman?" he explained. "You know, just to clear this up, so you can be on your way."

Then to the coachman, the Harbor Master asked, "Would a gold coin sooth your feelings?"

"Two golds and I will forget the whole thing," announced the coachman. "And I'll happily drive the young gentlemen to their grand villas."

Being worried about the Tribune's health and wanting to get him home as soon as possible, Alerio started to reach for his coin pouch. But the coachman's words echoed in his head. The hand stopped in midair.

"I'm a farm lad. My father's small villa is over a hundred miles from here," Alerio stated as he slung back his cloak. "And I'm a Lance Corporal, not a gentleman."

When the cloak slipped from the lad's head, the wealthy youth facing the Harbor Master vanished and a scarred

Legionary took his place. Although young, the Legionary was obviously a veteran.

While pointing at the two slaves, Alerio glared at the Harbor Master and suggested, "Let's call the city guard. Unless you think these two can take my coin pouch. However, before you decide, understand this. The Tribune is a courier for Gurges Legion bearing dispatches for the Senate. So please, call the city guard and explain why you and the coachman delayed the Senate's messages. Oh, and I'm his bodyguard. What will it be Harbor Master?"

"To Villa Peregrinus, off you go," urged the harbor master.

"Right away, master," the coachman said as he cracked his whip over the ponies' heads.

The carriage rolled away and Alerio placed a hand on the rear to keep pace. They moved off the docks and were soon heading towards the Temple of Portunus.

Chapter 18 - Villa Peregrinus

The Villa Peregrinus occupied a wide strip two blocks north of the Capitol building. While not as large or ornate as those villas clad in clay bricks to the second floor, it did have a half bricked first floor with carved wood for the second floor on the main villa. The rounded clay tiles of four large outbuildings were observable over a substantial wall.

The coachman guided the ponies onto the paved drive, passed the carriage gate, and halted the team at the main entrance. Alerio took the three steps up to the door and rapped hard on the carved oak. When no one answered, he pounded harder.

Standing with rainwater pouring off his head, Alerio looked back at the coachman and shrugged. The driver purposely turned his head away ignoring the plight of the wet Legionary.

Another series of hard fist-to-wood strikes brought a pair of eyes to the barred peep hole.

"Deliveries at the merchandise gate," a man advised through the head high opening. "Around the corner on the east side."

"Is this Villa Peregrinus?" inquired Alerio.

"Yes! And delivers are made at the east entrance," the man insisted.

"In the coach is Armenius Peregrinus," Alerio informed him. "I don't think the master of the villa would require his son to be delivered at the merchandise gate."

"Wait, wait," the man shouted. Then away from the door, he yelled, "House guards. To the main entrance."

The door opened and Alerio saw a bald, older man.

"Where is he?" the man demanded.

"In the coach. But, he's ill," Alerio replied. "Are you his grandfather?"

"No. I'm Photius, the villa's administrator," the man corrected. He walked on old stiff legs to the carriage and struggled until he managed to climb up. "Young master Peregrinus?" he asked. "Are you well?"

Two large, armed men came through the doorway. Photius waved at them. "Come here. Be gentle. Take Master Peregrinus his room."

After the Tribune was handed down from the coach and carried away, Alerio reached in and pulled out the packs. Then, he took out a coin pouch, extracted five silver coins and handed them to the coachman. The man sneered at him, cracked the whip and the carriage rolled away.

Alerio watched the coach until it left the drive and made a U-turn on the street. Hoisting the packs, he shook the water off his head and turned towards the doorway. The intricately carved oak door was closed.

After mounting the steps, he pounded on the door. On his third attempt, one of the house guards peered out.

"You've made your delivery," the guard sneered. "If you expect a reward, you've come begging at the wrong villa. Be gone."

Alerio started to explain but realized he would be arguing with a house guard. Not Armenius' father or even Photius, the villa's administrator, both with the power to admit him, he was presenting his case to the person with the least authority. Shaking his head at the ill-mannered treatment, he adjusted the packs and pulled the cloak over his head. At the end of the drive, he turned left and headed for the Capitol building.

***

Two blocks later and across the manicured grounds, Alerio stepped under an overhang at the Capitol building.

"No loitering, Legionary," a city guardsman states as he marched up.

"I'm looking for directions," Alerio said then he paused because he wasn't sure where to take the Legion dispatches. A moment later, he asked, "Where is Villa Maximus? I have a letter to deliver to Senator Spurius Carvilius Maximus."

The guardsman pointed to the northeast.

"Cross the boulevard, walk three blocks and turn north," he instructed. "Look for the villa with the marble statue of Bia. You can't miss the Goddess. She's life size."

The guard chuckled at the comment. When he motioned for Alerio to move on, the Legionary ducked his head and marched back into the rain.

He followed a gravel path and stopped at the boulevard. After looking up and down the usually busy road, he jogged across. Following the directions, he turned left after three blocks, walked another two blocks, and stopped.

The statue of Bia, Goddess of Might, Force and Bodily Strength, stood higher than the villa wall behind her. As one of Jupiter's winged enforcers, her wings spanned more than two arm's lengths to either side of the Goddess. Alerio now understood the guardsman's reaction to the life size description. Life size only counted if you were referring to giants.

Alerio bowed to the Goddess and thanked her for giving him the strength to escape the Insubri. Then he marched across the pavers to the main door and knocked.

"Your business?" demanded a man through the peep square.

"I've a letter for the Senator," Alerio stated. "From Centurion Seneca."

"Wait right there," blurted out the man before Alerio could tell him about the Legion dispatches. Moments later, the man's face appeared in the cutout, and he mumbled, "Good, good, you're still there."

The door swung opened and the man waved Alerio through the doorway.

Chapter 19 - Villa Maximus

Alerio was directed to a space next to a floor trough. The channel would carry any dripping rainwater away from a mosaic of a hunting scene. On either side of the fine tiles, couches rested against short dividing walls. Glass figurines of Gods and Goddesses, gold plates and porcelain vases lined the tops of the walls.

"Letter. Hand me the letter," urged the man who had opened the door. "Quickly. The Senator is busy."

Alerio dug into his pack, produced Centurion Seneca's letter, and handed it to the man.

"There are also…" Alerio began but the man cut him off.

"Wait here," the man ordered before he rushed down a hall and disappeared into a room.

While he waited for the man to come back, Alerio gathered his cloak and squeezed out as much water as he could. The water ran down the trough. As it traveled, shiny inlays shimmered in the bed of the channel. He wondered if the objects would twinkle if the trough was blocked off and flooded.

The man reappeared at the end of the hallway and beckoned Alerio to come. Dropping the end of the soaked cloak, he marched towards him. At the end of the hallway, the man indicated for the Legionary to enter a room.

***

"What in Discordia's name is this?" growled a large man sitting behind a desk. He waved a recently unfolded piece of parchment in the air and glared at Alerio.

Although older and a little thick around the middle, the man maintained enough muscle to present a formidable figure. His hair was gray and cut short as a Legionary would wear it. Alerio had no idea who the man was or what was in the letter. The gray-haired man calling on the Goddess of Strife and Discord gave no clue. So Alerio did what every enlisted soldier does when confronted by a person of importance, he saluted.

"Lance Corporal Alerio Sisera. 47th Century, Seventh Squad, Gurges Legion," he announced with a cross chest slam of his fist. "And sir, I have no idea what's in the Centurion's letter."

The man glanced down, read a section, and peered at the Legionary over the top edge of the parchment.

"Lance Corporal Sisera, I am Senator Spurius Carvilius Maximus," the man stated. "You can call me General Maximus. Seneca was my First Centurion when we beat the Samnites. See that shield?"

The General pointed to a wall behind Alerio. Turning to look, the Legionary saw a Legion heavy infantry shield that had been cleaved half its height by a sword. Mounted on the walls to either side of the doorway were damaged weapons. A broken javelin, a chipped gladius, as well as tribal implements of war. All showing use during a battle.

"General that shield is in need of repair," Alerio observed.

"Eight years ago, that shield saved my life, Lance Corporal," related Senator Spurius Carvilius Maximus. "We had the Samnites leaders trapped in their last fort. My third maniple had the honor of the final surge. Then, I did something stupid. Yes, Generals do stupid things. I rode parallel to my lines. I stopped behind the second maniple, ahead of my personal guard, to get a look at the barbarian's defenses. A unit of Samnites cavalry smashed through and surrounded me. My horse went down, and I leaped to the ground drawing my gladius. All I could see was ponies, hairy savages, and long swords. I deflected several but something rolled into my legs, and I fell. One brute jumped from his mount and ran at me, his sword held high for a killing blow."

The Senator reached out and took a gulp from a silver chalice. After wiping his mouth with the back of his hand, he continued.

"Four thousand heavy infantrymen under my command and I lay like a lamb on an altar," Maximus described. "The barbarian rushed at me yelling a victory cry. I feebly pointed my blade at him as if he would be kind enough to run himself through and die for me. Three steps from me, he began the kill strike. My world shrank to his thick, hairy forearms and the long, wide sword. It was falling towards my face and there was nothing I could do to stop it."

The Senator stood up and walked around his desk. He marched across the room and stood by the damaged shield. Placing a hand on the oiled surface, he spanned the split with his fingers.

"Suddenly my view of the savage and the sword was blocked by a Legionary's body and an infantry shield. This shield," Maximus explained while running his fingers up and down the edges of the cut. "The sword's blade sliced the infantry shield almost in half. Deep enough that the Legionary holding it began to bleed heavily from a cut on his left forearm. Most normal men would have retreated to care for the wound. Or, at least, use the shield for self-protection. Not him. The shield was at first in front of me, then behind me. Next it appeared on my side to stop strikes before shifting to the other side where it defended me against more attacks from the savages. All the while, the Legionary bled. Yet the shield never failed to protect me from Samnites' blades."

Standing taller and seeming more like the General he'd requested Alerio call him, Maximus crossed in front of the doorway and lifted a long, tribal sword off three wall pegs.

"This blade should have ended my life," he explained holding the blade in two hands. "When my personal guard finally fought their way to me and drove off the Samnites, the Legionary and his shield were in front of me defending against any last attempts. By then, he was on his knees. The shield holding him up instead of him holding the shield. Covered in his own blood from helmet to knees, he turned his blood-streaked face to me and said – General, the line belongs to the Legionaries of the heavy infantry. Generals belong with the command staff. Then, he toppled over. I thought him dead."

General Maximus reverently placed the Samnite sword back on the wall pegs. He strolled across the room and resumed his seat behind the desk.

"I was informed that Centurion Seneca had seen my brash ride," Maximus related. "He grabbed the shield from a wounded Legionary and sprinted a quarter of the length of our line to defend me. While he was recovering, I foolishly asked him what reward he would claim. He asked for two things. One was to give a share of the Samnite's spoils to the Legion. That one cost me a fortune. Second, he asked if I ever received a letter from him, I would drop everything and read the note. No gold or public awards for him, only that I pay personal attention to his communiqué."

Alerio watched as a smile broke the creases on the Senator's face.

"In this case, the letter is worth more than the spoils I shared with the Legion," declared Maximus. "Where is Tribune Peregrinus?"

"At his father's villa," Alerio replied. Maximus' smile faded and he shook his head in understanding. "But I have the Legion dispatches in his pack."

General Maximus' eyes popped wide open, and the smile returned.

"I'll take the dispatches," he instructed while clearing scrolls and parchment from his workspace.

Alerio dug into the pack and pulled out a packet of oiled goatskin wrapped letters. He peeled back the waterproof skin and handed the sealed parchments to Maximus.

The Senator read the names on the outside and separated them into four stacks. He selected one and opened it. Then, he stopped, studied Alerio and opened his mouth.

"I want to know what happened. But hold it until I get Marcus here," the Senator tilted his head back and yelled, "Belen!"

The man who had opened the door for Alerio strutted into the room.

"Yes, General?" Belen asked.

"Send word to Villa Flaccus. It's important that I see Marcus Fulvius this afternoon," directed Maximus.

"Senator Fulvius is holding a reception for his selectors," Belen reminded Maximus. "He is likely to beg off your invitation."

"How do I phrase this?" Maximus asked sarcastically. "Inform him that if he wants my block of voters to elect him Consul tomorrow, he'll get his cūlus over here, now! Of course, phrase it more diplomatically."

"Of course, General," Belen assured the Senator.

"Lance Corporal Sisera. My secretary will show you to the cook shed. Have something to eat while I read the dispatches," instructed Maximus. "When Senator Flaccus arrives, I'll need you to tell us about Volsinii. So, go light on the vino."

"Yes, sir," Alerio assured him as he followed Belen out of the room.

Behind him he heard General / Senator Spurius Carvilius Maximus swear as he opened another letter.

Chapter 20 - Consul Elect, Senator Marcus Fulvius Flaccus

"Spurius, this had better be worth it," a tall, thin man warned as he walked into the General's study.

"Senator Flaccus. May I introduce Lance Corporal Alerio Sisera," Maximus exclaimed while directing the man's eyes to a Legionary standing off to the side of the room. "He was with the late Quintus Fabius Gurges at Volsinii."

"You summoned me here to see a Legionary…," Flaccus stopped, and stared at the old General. "You said the late Gurges. As in, Quintus Fabius Gurges is dead?"

"Yes, killed in action at Volsinii," confirmed Maximus. "Per Legionary Sisera."

"How can you take the word of a single Legionary?" questioned Flaccus.

"I have the Legion's dispatches," explained Maximus while holding out both hands as if presenting a work of art. "Armenius Peregrinus was the courier. But his family locked out our Legionary, and the dispatches, once Armenius was carried into the villa."

"If Peregrinus had gotten his hands on the dispatches, he would have used them for political ransom," Flaccus stated. "Can you imagine the mess Codex would have made if he got his hands on them?"

"But he didn't. Thanks to an eight-year-old pledge, they were delivered to me," Maximus gloated. "Here is your chance to bask in glory and the adoration of the public."

"What do you have in mind?" asked Flaccus.

"Tomorrow, as soon as you're confirmed as Consul, you ask for a warrant to raise a Legion," explained Maximus. "Lance Corporal Sisera, in brief, tell us the state of Gurges Legion."

Alerio cleared his throat. He hadn't expected the death of a Senator to be brushed aside without a least the appearance of grief. These powerful men were playing a political game far beyond a farm lad's comprehension. Gathering his thoughts, he addressed the two Senators.

"Sirs. The Legion is secure behind their defenses," Alerio reported. "There are too many wounded to retreat and not enough Centuries to continue the assault on Volsinii."

"In your opinion, what was the cause of the Legion's failure to capture the city?" asked Maximus.

"Hold on, what makes you think a Lance Corporal would know about military tactics?" asked Senator Flaccus.

"Let me see," Maximus said as he picked up Seneca's letter. "Lance Corporal, where were you during the initial assault?"

"With the reserve Centuries at the Legion camp, General," replied Alerio.

"And after the Legion was routed?"

"I commanded the squads guarding the gate."

"And how many barbarians did you and your squads engage while holding the gate?"

"I'm not sure, General. We were kind of busy."

"According to your Centurion, you fought off over five hundred warriors," explained Maximus. "While letting wounded and retreating Legionaries through to the safety of the camp. So, I ask you again, what was the cause of the Legion's failure to capture the city?"

"Cavalry, General. We committed ours too soon and the Insubri's mounted warriors hit the lines from the rear," Alerio stated. "Too many of them. Not enough of ours. The maniples had the Etruscī from the city stopped and moving back. It was their cavalry that broke our lines."

"Gurges' tight purse strings were his end," Flaccus commented. "It's also our problem in the morning."

"Granted, the Flaccus Legion will take all the reserve budget," Maximus admitted. "But let me handle that. You give a rousing speech to energize the Senate and the public and I'll work a few deals to free up the gold."

"Didn't you say Armenius Peregrinus was the courier," Flaccus pointed out. "He could be a problem. His father will use him as a first-hand witness in every public square in the Capital."

The General again referred to Centurion Seneca's letter.

"It seems young Peregrinus has a genius for organization," Maximus ventured. "I believe he will make an excellent assistant to our governor in Crotone province. I'll make the motion for his appointment along with an award for valor for the young man."

"And what of Lance Corporal Sisera?" inquired Flaccus.

"Our Legionary doesn't need anything, yet," Maximus explained. "However, in a few years, he'll need a sponsor to appoint him to Centurion. Plus, he'll need coin to outfit his Century. That's if the Lance Corporal can keep his lips sealed about what was said in this room."

Alerio's mind had drifted back to a comment someone made about needing a sponsor and a heavy coin pouch to be a Centurion. He missed the last part of Maximus' statement.

"Well, Lance Corporal, can you keep this discussion to yourself?" demanded Flaccus.

Coming back to the present, he stammered, "Yes Senator. Yes, General and thank you."

"I want you cleaned up and at the Senate at sunrise," instructed Maximus. "You won't be called upon to talk. But, if I point to you during the proceedings, simply snap to attention and salute me. Understand?"

"Yes, sir."

"Belen will show you out. Senator Flaccus and I have a speech to write," Maximus ordered. "Dismissed."

Alerio picked up his pack, slammed a salute to his chest and marched out of the Senator's study.

Chapter 21 - Chronicles Humanum Inn

It was a long way from the Senator's villa to the Legion Transfer building near the port. But Alerio didn't realize it. His mind was full of the possibilities of becoming a Legion officer in the future. Once he reached the boulevard, he settled into the rhythm of the Legion jog and the distance vanished under his pounding boots.

"Lance Corporal Alerio Sisera, Seventh Squad, Forty-Seventh Century, Gurges Legion," he reported to the duty Corporal in the building.

"Noted, Sisera. First time in the Capital?" asked the NCO.

"No Corporal, I've been here before," Alerio informed him. "Is the city guard still a problem?"

"The city guard is always hunting Legionaries. Just don't give them a reason to lock you up."

"They'll get no trouble from me," Alerio assured him as he left the Transfer building.

***

Heading east, Alerio decided to walk. Although the clouds threatened, the rain had stopped, and he enjoyed the familiar stroll. Once over the boulevard, he took the last few turns and stopped at the cloth sellers.

"Master Zacchaeus. I am in need of your services," Alerio called out as he pushed through the door.

From the back room, the old tailor shoved aside the curtain and stopped.

"Legionary Alerio Sisera. What can we do for you today?" inquired Zacchaeus.

"Interesting turn of a phrase," Alerio replied. "As it is, I need a military tunic for a sunrise visit to the Capitol building. Tomorrow morning."

"For anyone else this late in the day, it would require a purse of gold," Zacchaeus informed him. "But for you, step into my fitting room."

The tailor ushered him into the back room.

As the old man climbed onto a stool, he asked, "Weapon's instructor, raider flag from the eastern Legion, Lance Corporal designation, any new awards or units since the last time?"

"You can add a combat rowing insignia," Alerio said as he stripped off his wool shirt.

"Seeing as you keep adding to your display, I would recommend a shoulder scarf," suggested Zacchaeus. "It will hasten the process of dressing you for the morning. We can work on the tunic and the scarf separately."

"Excellent idea," agreed Alerio.

Once Zacchaeus had fitted a rough tunic to the Legionary, the old tailor climbed off the stool.

"Go have a bath and a bite to eat," Zacchaeus instructed. "Come back at sundown for a final fitting."

Alerio paid the tailor, shouldered his pack, and left the cloth seller's establishment.

***

Across the street and a little further down the road, Alerio stopped to admire the tiered stories of the Chronicles Humanum Inn. He mounted the steps up to the porch and pushed into the great room.

Junior officers and senior NCOs sat at tables eating and drinking from mugs of vino. Alerio wove his way between the tables until he reached the long granite countertop.

"Innkeeper. Can a Legionary get a vino in this place?" he called across the counter. His voice carried down the center hallway.

"Hold your mentula," Thomasious Harricus called from the storage room.

He appeared moments later with a basket and a stack of clay mugs. His eyes were on the stack.

"Service sure is slow in this place," Alerio teased.

"If it's not to your liking, you can take your business elsewhere," Thomasious shot back.

"And miss out on your pleasant personality?" Alerio replied.

Thomasious carefully set the mugs on a shelf and spun to face the mouthy customer. Seeing Alerio, he smiled, snatched up a mug and drew vino from a cask.

"There's nothing worse than a smelly Legionary who doesn't respect his elders," Thomasious said while placing the mug on the counter. "Just off the road, are you?"

"Do I smell that bad?" Alerio asked as he took a sip.

"A bath, I can help you with. But a room is harder," Thomasious explained. "After firebreak district burned, the Senate decided not to let anyone rebuild it. The plan is to extend the Capital outside the defensive walls. They have hundreds of slaves building roads and installing utilities around the hills and out into the fields. And with slaves comes Legionaries."

"I take it you're booked up?" guessed Alerio. Then something the Senators discussed came to him and he asked, "Are the roads and utilities expensive?"

"Expensive? My little clay ears tell me all the Senators are worried about financing the expansion," Thomasious replied. "Just fielding Gurges Legion required them to borrow from this year's budget."

"So, any new costs will add to the debt?" inquired Alerio.

"And put the budget into a deficit. Empty coffers are not a good way to start the year," Thomasious added. "When did you become interested in finances?"

"I'm not," lied Alerio. "I just thought if I talked to you long enough, you would think of a place for me to sleep."

"I guess, I can give you a storage room. At least it'll be a roof over your head."

***

Long before sunrise, Alerio slipped on his new blue tunic and slung the yellow scarf over his shoulder. As expected, he found the innkeeper sitting alone eating his breakfast in the great room.

"Sorry to intrude on your morning meditations," Alerio said as he crossed the room. "Care for some company?"

"Lance Corporal Sisera. Please take a seat," Thomasious Harricus invited him with a wave of his hand at an empty chair. Then, he slid a platter of cured ham and assorted cheeses across the table. "Eat, I took more than I could handle. Your questions about finances got me thinking and thinking always makes we hungry. Unfortunately, the conclusions I reached swept away the hunger."

"Is the Republic in trouble?" Alerio inquired as he picked up a slice of ham and laid a piece of cheese on top.

"Not in the short term," Thomasious explained. "Once the harvest is in and the stockyards are full, the coin will flow. At least enough for the Senate to pay on demand bills.

But the long-term solution will require huge influxes of capital to maintain the city's growth."

"Where will the coin come from?" Alerio asked as he chewed on the ham and cheese. "Trade and shipping? Better crop production?"

"There is the cause of my heartburn," stated Thomasious. "We're becoming a player in city / state politics. I fear war is the only way to fill our coffers. And with war comes the possibility of losing. The Republic has any number of potential enemies. Take your pick, Athens, Sparta, Syracuse, Egypt and, the big bear in the woods, the Qart Hadasht Empire."

"But we have the Legion. None of them would dare invade the Republic," Alerio assured him. "The heavy infantry would drive them back into the sea."

"Spoken like a true Legionary," Thomasious said with a chuckle. "On our shores, yes. But what about a Legion in a distant land? How would they perform away from the Republic and the support of our citizens?"

"A Legion has never fought across a sea," reported Alerio.

"Not yet, my young friend," confirmed Thomasious. Then in an exaggerated manner, he inspected the Legionary's uniform. "Something is missing from your toga and brightly decorated scarf."

Alerio looked down and ran his eyes over the new uniform and the scarf with the crests and badges. Seeing nothing wrong, he glanced up at the innkeeper.

"Is it too much?" he asked. "They said to present myself at the Senate. I thought I should look my best."

"I didn't say anything was wrong," Thomasious assured him. "Only that something was missing."

The innkeeper pushed back his chair and walked away. Moments later, he came back through the double doors and laid a long cloth covered item on the table. Alerio peeled back the cloth and gasped.

"I couldn't wear my dual gladius rig with a uniform," announced Alerio. "But this is way beyond my personal hip gladius."

"It's on loan to you for the day," Thomasious explained. "Tomas Kellerian built it for a Centurion. Unfortunately, he was wounded and is recovering. Until he arrives and pays for it, it's just sitting in one of my stockrooms. Might as well put it to use."

Alerio stood and wrapped the tooled leather belt around his waist. Then, he wrapped his hand around the gold threaded hilt. The blade came free from the brushed leather sheath, and he admired the gold inlays on the handguard.

"Don't let the decorations fool you," Thomasious assured him. "It's an Historia Fae forged blade. Kellerian said it'll cut from dawn to dust and still have edge enough to behead a barbarian chief."

"I'm just going to observe the Senate," Alerio assured him. "The blade could be wrought iron and soft as cheese for all the use it'll get."

"It completes the uniform," Thomasious boasted. "You look like the perfect Legionary NCO."

"Do you still do your gossip scrolls in the afternoon?" inquired Alerio.

"Yes. Once the Clay Ear hears from his little spies," Thomasious replied.

"You'll have to wait until much later in the day to record this. But the Republic will be sending another Legion to Volsinii," stated Alerio. "Senator Gurges was killed during the assault and his Legion is trapped."

"That's why you were interested in the Republic's finances?" Thomasious asked.

"No sir. I'm a simple Legionary and that would be above my pay grade," Alerio assured the innkeeper. "Thank you for the loan of the gladius. Now, I'm going to play Legionary statue at the Senate."

"Let me know who does the nomination first," instructed Thomasious.

"I don't know what you're asking," pleaded Alerio.

"Pay attention and let me know," Thomasious repeated as he selected a piece of ham and placed a fat piece of cheese on it. He took a bite and declared, "Delicious. Run along now, you don't want to be late for the Senate of the Republic."

Act 4

Chapter 22 – The Senators and Guests Arrive

Vendor carts occupied areas on the streets bordering the grounds of the Capitol building. Some offered cooked meats, their aromas competing with baked good carts a few yards away. Alerio joined a crowd moving in the predawn threading their way between the lanterns of a beverage seller and a lamb cart.

As they neared the Capitol building, the dark gave way to lights flooding the granite steps, porch, and the doors leading to the Senate's auditorium. The throng slowed as it joined other citizens. Some people were visible at the edge of the light but, most were back in the dark. Alerio pushed his way forward and approached a Sergeant standing under a torch at the edge of the light.

"Sergeant. I'm Lance Corporal Alerio Sisera. I am under the orders of Senator Spurius Carvilius Maximus to make myself available to the Senate," he explained.

"See the Centurion at the bottom of the stairs," the NCO advised while pointing across the lighted but mostly empty grassy expanse.

Alerio marched to a set of blazing braziers where a Centurion stood scanning the illuminated front ranks of the crowd.

"Centurion. I'm Lance Corporal Alerio Sisera," Alerio stated with a salute. "I am under the orders of Senator Spurius Carvilius Maximus to make myself available to the Senate."

The officer glanced at the Legionary's uniform, nodded approvingly, and ordered, "See the Tribune at the top of the stairs."

As Alerio climbed the steps, he glanced back to see other NCOs spread out along the length of the lighted area. Citizens spoke with the Sergeants, and some were allowed forward to speak with the officers at the bottom of the steps. In turn, a few were sent up to speak with the staff officers.

Most of those allowed on the porch by the Tribunes clustered around in small groups talking. Men, who seemed to know what they were doing, quick walked between the groups. They selected individuals or pairs of citizens, and these were escorted through the doors.

At the top of the stairs, Alerio saluted a staff officer.

"Tribune. I'm Lance Corporal Alerio Sisera," Alerio repeated the speech. "I am under the orders of Senator Spurius Carvilius Maximus to make myself available to the Senate."

The Tribune inspected the Legionary before turning his face and calling out, "Belen! I've got one of yours."

"Be there shortly," Maximus' secretary replied from behind a crowd.

He pulled three people away from a group and held the door so they could enter the Capitol building. Then Belen pointed at Alerio and motioned him to a space between two doors.

"Wait there until I collect you," the Senator's secretary ordered. He spun away and rushed to greet a pair of men climbing the steps. Both wore togas with gold trim. Belen bowed and motioned them to proceed directly into the building.

Out on the Capitol grounds, several lantern-lit processions snaked through the dark. As their lights converged with the steps' torches, a tall thin man emerged from the building. He stepped out on the speaker platform that divided the staircase.

"Senators of the Republic are arriving," he announced.

From the dark, Alerio heard cheers, although a few boos could be heard in the crowd's response. The processions materialized out of the dark revealing about a hundred older and middle-aged men. As the Senators climbed the steps, their secretaries jockeyed for positions so they would be in the proper place to greet their masters.

Alerio observed Belen chatter into Senator Maximus' ear as they crossed the porch. The Senator scowled and his lips moved rapidly before he vanished through the doorway. Belen fast walked to a Tribune, and they exchanged words. The Tribune descended the steps and spoke to a Centurion who crossed the grass to speak with a Sergeant. After a quick exchange, the Centurion and the Sergeant raced off into the dark.

***

The number of people seeking to climb the steps increased once the Senators had arrived. Many made it to a Tribune but only a few were allowed into the Capitol building. The rest were dismissed by a Senator's secretary despite the gold rings, ornate sandals, quality togas, and other trappings of wealthy men. The criteria for who entered and who was rejected was beyond Alerio's frame of reference. However, he had sense enough to recognize someone using exclusion and limited access to a Senator as a lever of power.

The porch cleared and all the secretaries vanished. Even the Tribunes relaxed and gathered to chat. Only the Centurions, Sergeants and Alerio stood in their posted positions.

Another procession of lanterns crossed the grounds from the north. As before, the crowd parted, the lights bounced and headed towards the Capitol building. When it neared, a middle-aged man, sneering and muttering, surged ahead and jogged up the steps to the gathering of Tribunes.

"What is the meaning of this?" he yelled. "My son is ill. He should be allowed to rest. Instead, he's ordered from his sick bed and summoned by the Senate."

"Please wait here, Master Peregrinus," a Tribune suggested before marching to a door and entering the Capitol building. Moments later, the Tribune reappeared followed by Belen.

"Belen! I knew Spurius Maximus was behind this," he accused. "Only a miserable old man would drag a sick lad from his mother's arms."

Belen ignored the raging father and peered down at the procession. A sedan chair carried by four slaves appeared at the bottom of the stairs. Beside the enclosed coach stood Photius, the bald old man from Villa Peregrinus. The same administrator who had locked Alerio out. A squad of City Guardsmen, the Sergeant and the Centurion surrounded the coach.

"Bring the sedan chair up to the porch," Belen shouted with a wave of his arms. "Hurry up. The Senator wants him in place before the voting begins."

The slaves carefully carried the sedan chair up the steps and gently set it down on the porch. Tribune Armenius Peregrinus climbed out with the help of the old administrator. He was dressed in a white tunic with bronze trim and, although standing on his own, seemed unsteady.

"Right this way," Belen informed him and the three headed for a center doorway. Seeing the elder Peregrinus following, Belen stopped the group. He pointed further down the porch and directed, "Master Peregrinus, kindly take the end door. Senator Maximus has granted you access to the public gallery."

With a huff and more mumbling, Armenius' father shuffled towards the door. Inside, no doubt, he would be guided to a place where invited citizens could stand and watch the Senate.

Chapter 23 - The Senate in Session

No more solicitors arrived at the stairs or on the porch. Alerio decided, he either had been forgotten or his presence deemed unnecessary but, no one decided to tell him. In both cases, it meant the same thing. He stood watching as weak, defused light from the rising sun revealed the masses of citizens. Lounging around in clusters, people filled the Capitol grounds waiting for announcements from the Senate.

A door opened and very young man marched towards him.

"Lance Corporal Sisera, follow me," he directed.

They entered a center door, crossed the corridor outside the senate chamber, and stepped into a huge room filled with loud voices speaking to be overheard by other loud voices. The Senate of the Republic was in full volume debating issues that would affect all the citizens.

On the flooring by the doors and across the chamber, people stood. Some left and ran to a Senator who beckoned them. Alerio spied Belen on the far side of the chamber.

Alerio expected to be taken to the public gallery behind the sitting Senators. Instead, the lad guided him down the curved walkway in the opposite direction. Legionaries stood guard on this end of the chamber. The lad nodded at the guard and walked Alerio by him.

He ended up in a small gallery, high up but behind the speaker's podium. Alerio had a view of the tiered rows of extra wide seats that wrapped part way around the chamber. Unlike those in the public gallery, he could see the faces of the Senators. Also, in the private gallery were a cavalry officer in full armor standing off to the side, several older and obviously important men, Armenius Peregrinus, and the Peregrinus' household administrator Photius.

Alerio marched to Armenius and whispered, "How are you feeling, Tribune?"

"They administered a drug, and I can't remember the last three days," admitted Armenius.

"You will not speak to young Master Peregrinus," ordered Photius.

"The Tribune and I fought our way through patrols of murderous barbarians," Alerio growled.

"We did?" inquired Armenius.

"Yes sir, we did. You were captured and tortured. After I freed you, you ran on painful legs like a veteran," Alerio stated while glaring at the household administrator. "Despite all the obstacles, we completed our mission."

"We did?" asked Armenius.

"Yes sir, we did. And because we shivered, bled, and sweated together," Alerio spoke to the old man. "No one can prevent me from speaking to my Tribune."

"You had a mission?" demanded Photius. "What mission?"

Before Alerio could explain, a tall man at the podium pounded a gavel and shouted for silence.

***

"The next order of business before the Senate of the Republic is the elections of Consuls," the man announced. "Who will nominate first?"

All the Senators looked in the direction of one Senator. Spurius Maximus sat relaxed and appeared bored. With a dismissive gesture of a hand, the chamber erupted. The man at the podium searched for another Senator willing to propose a candidate for Consul.

One jumped to his feet and shouted, "I nominate Senator Appease Clodus Codex for Consul of the Republic!" The Senator sat and another stood and raised his arms.

Senators around Maximus appeared confused while those around the Senator with his arms in the air pounded their armrests and yelled in delight.

"I accept the heavy responsibility of the office bestowed on me by the Senate of the Republic," Consul Codex boomed. "My duty to expand our Capital will continue until we are the envy of the world."

He was interrupted by outbursts from Senators on his side of the chamber. Only a few on Maximus' side joined in the jubilation. When the Senators settled, Codex continued.

"We have budgeted for community services and public utilities for the new growth," he boasted. "When we sell the available lots, our coffers will fill, and our hearts will swell with pride."

Another round of cheering broke out. Again, those around Codex were the loudest. Across the chamber, only a few joined in. Codex smiled and glanced around at his supporters.

"From my own funds, I declare a city-wide holiday in two days to show my pleasure at being elevated to the office of Consul of the Republic," he announced.

His supporters, vocal as before, shouted out their pleasure. Even those in the public gallery raised their arms and shouted their delight at the proposed festival. This time more of the Senators around Maximus added their cheers.

With bows to both side of the Senate, Consul Appease Clodus Codex sat down.

***

The man at the podium tilted his head in question and looked in Spurius Maximus' direction. After a dramatic pause to allow everyone to cease their celebration, the Senator rose from his seat.

"I nominate Senator Marcus Fulvius Flaccus for Consul of the Republic!" Maximus stated with authority. Then he sat and Marcus Flaccus stood.

"I accept the heavy responsibility of the office bestowed upon me by the Senate of the Republic," Consul Flaccus exclaimed. "While I appreciate my Co-Consuls ambition to improve our Capital, there are more pressing issues."

Instead of the cheering that greeted Appease Codex's speech, Flaccus' elicited murmurs of confusion. With no need to wait, Consul Marcus Flaccus resumed.

"Late yesterday evening, dispatches from our Legion at Volsinii reached me," Flaccus explained. "With a heavy heart, I tell you that General Quintus Fabius Gurges was wounded in the attack and has died."

Now, the entire Senate erupted in calls for avenging their fellow Senator. Especially loud were the Senators around Consul Codex.

"Our response will be swift, terrible and total," Flaccus promised.

The Senate chamber filled with angry voices. Their emotions running wild and their hearts pleading for revenge. Flaccus' words hit the right cord and he had the backing of the entire Senate.

"While I gather the heavy infantry for Flaccus Legion, I took the liberty of calling up units to support our Legion trapped at Volsinii," Consul Marcus Flaccus exclaimed. "Is it the will of the Senate?"

Every senator shouted his agreement with the plan.

"Tribune of the Horse!" called out Flaccus. "Are you and your Legionaries prepared?"

The armored cavalry officer, who stood off to the side of the private gallery, marched forward.

"We are ready to obey the orders of General Marcus Fulvius Flaccus," the cavalryman replied.

"You and your five hundred mounted Legionaries will ride north to support our Legion at Volsinii," directed Flaccus. "These are your orders from your General."

The Tribune slammed his fist into his chest armor. It rang around the Senate chamber.

"Yes, General Flaccus!" replied the Tribune.

Then he marched out of the private gallery. However, he didn't exit at the first door. As if on parade, he extended his march passed each door so everyone could hear the slap and click of his hobnailed boots. At the last door, he left the chamber, but the echo of his boots lingered.

"Senators and citizens of the Republic, I regret that these events preclude me from attending my Co-Consul's holiday and festival," Marcus Flaccus explained. "I will be heading north to enforce our laws and to protect the integrity of our Republic."

Over one hundred voices, and as many pounding on the wood of their armrests, sent an almost physical force swirling around the chamber. In the noise and chaos, Consul Flaccus bowed to his supporters and sat down.

The man at the podium pounded for quiet and cried out for silence. After long sessions of pounding and pleading, the volume in the Senate chamber fell to a manageable level.

"Let it be known throughout the Republic," the man announced. "The Senate has declared this the year of Consul Appease Clodus Codex and Consul Marcus Fulvius Flaccus. May the Gods watch over and assist them in their endeavors."

***

Senator Maximus stood and held out his arms for attention.

"The Consuls will sacrifice to Jupiter this afternoon on the Capitol grounds. All citizens are welcome," he announced. "We have committee business for the rest of the day. However, before we break up, there is someone I'd like to recognize."

He pointed at the private gallery. Lance Corporal Alerio Sisera proudly slammed his fist into his chest. Regrettably, he wore only cloth, so his salute lacked the thunder of the cavalryman's salute.

"Three days ago, Tribune Armenius Peregrinus and this single Legionary slipped out of our besieged Legion camp in Volsinii. They swam the freezing waters of the Tiber and evaded barbarian patrols. Although ill with fever, Tribune Armenius Peregrinus delivered the news of the stricken Legion to the Capital," Maximus stated. "Before venturing forth on this dangerous mission, Tribune Peregrinus organized the Legion camp when the command staff was decimated in the fighting. To honor Armenius Peregrinus, I propose he receive an accommodation for bravery, fifty gold coins, and an appointment as Assistant Governor to our eastern province at Crotone. Can I get a yes vote on this resolution?"

The full Senate shouted their agreement. How could they not for a hero of the Republic?

Chapter 24 - Reassignment

Alerio stood and watched as the Senators clustered around secretaries obviously discussing elements of state business. The public gallery emptied, and the visitors gathered around the exit doors. With no escape available, he stared at the Senate chamber and marveled at the political maneuvering he'd just witnessed. While the rewards were beyond his experience, he was smart enough to recognize a well-played game and the winners.

One of the winners, who had not been a player, was Armenius Peregrinus. The old administrator took the young man by the elbow and guided him towards the edge of the private gallery. Before they reached the Legionary stations at the entrance, Armenius' father came stomping down the walkway.

"You had the dispatches?" he screamed. "Do you know what political favors I could have earned? What business arrangements I could have done with those dispatches? And all the while, my idiot son had them."

Armenius shook his head as if to clear his vision. Then he threw off the hand gripping his elbow and straightened up.

"When I was covered in blood from carrying wounded Legionaries and ten more were begging for my guidance, I wondered what my father would think," Armenius explained. "When I sank beneath the cold water ready to give up, I thought, what would my father think. When the savages tied me to a tree and used me for target practice, I wondered what my father would think."

The young Tribune turned to Alerio.

"Lance Corporal Sisera. We did complete the mission and relief is on the way to our men at Volsinii, am I correct?" he asked.

"Yes, Tribune. At great personal risk to you and despite your injuries and illness," Alerio assured the young man. "We completed the mission, sir."

Armenius stepped up and stood nose to nose with his father.

"I am a Tribune of the Legion. A decorated hero of the Republic. And, I am the Assistant Governor for the eastern province," explained the younger Peregrinus. "Do you know what I am not worried about?"

"What?" questioned his father.

"I am going home to say goodbye to my mother and organize transportation to Crotone," announced Armenius Peregrinus. "The thing I am not worried about, is what my father thinks."

With those words, Armenius Peregrinus brushed by his father and slung people out of his way as he reached and exited through the doorway.

***

The elder Peregrinus and the old administrator were shocked. They looked confused until Peregrinus raised his eyes and locked them on the young Lance Corporal.

"You. You had the dispatches," he mumbled. "You've made an enemy. And I am not a man to be trifled with."

"You, sir, are a father who raised a brave son," Alerio replied.

"Don't patronize me," shot back Armenius' father. "I am going to…"

"Going to do what, Master Peregrinus?" Belen inquired.

The Senator's secretary stood with an older Legionary. A man who appeared to be far beyond retirement age. Tribune Velius, head of Intelligence for the Southern Legion, tilted his head in greeting.

"Master Peregrinus, understand this, Lance Corporal Sisera is a patron of Senator Spurius Maximus," explained Belen. "Any threats directed towards him will be considered as threats to the Senator. Now, I believe you have a son who will soon leave the Capital. I suggest you go and make peace with him."

Peregrinus and his administrator gave Belen and Velius a wide berth as they hurried for the exit.

"Thank you, Master Belen," Alerio said.

"No need, Lance Corporal," the secretary replied. "The Senator thought something like that would happen. Now, I must get back to Senate business."

Belen rushed away and Alerio caught Velius shaking his head and grinning at him.

"Tribune Velius. Is something funny?" asked Alerio.

"No, not really," the head spymaster for the Southern Legion admitted. "It's just if you don't come back alive, I'll have to answer to Senior Centurion Patroclus and First Sergeant Gerontius. Plus, explain why to one of the Republic's most powerful Senators."

"I thought I'd go north with Flaccus Legion. Afterwards, I'll go and visit with my family," Alerio ventured. Then he paused, thought about the Tribune's statement, and inquired, "Come back from where?"

"Sicilia, Lance Corporal Sisera," Tribune Velius explained. "I need you in Syracuse."

Chapter 25 - Historia Fae, Armorer to the Gods

Alerio rapped on the exterior door of Historia Fae. When no one answered, he knocked again but harder. An iron plate slid open, and an eye stared out from the small square.

"What?" a deep voice demanded.

"Master Kellerian, I am in need of your assistance," Alerio stated.

"You're too pretty to need weapons or armor," Tomas Kellerian challenged. "In that uniform, you should be at a nobleman's villa sipping quality vino and chasing kitchen wenches."

"As handsome as I am, I should be," replied Alerio lifting a scarred arm and rubbing the crescent shaped scar on the crown of his head. "Yet here I am speaking to a cyclops and asking for admittance to his den of iniquity."

"I've been called worse, and the description of my work depends on if you're standing behind or in front of the pointy end," Tomas Kellerian, the Armorer to the God, shot back. "Hold on."

Iron bars grating on iron hooks reached Alerio's ears. He waited on the street until the locking braces stopped screeching and the door opened. Quickly, he crossed the first threshold and four steps later the second doorway.

"I don't know why you refuse to oil those rods," ventured Alerio as Thomas noisily shoved the iron bars back into place.

"Rust is the enemy of smoothly operating armor and the edge of a steel gladius," replied the Armorer as he closed the interior door. "However, rust makes the iron squeal. It reminds anyone entering my establishment that the door is barred. Just in case they think about coming back later, uninvited."

"So, rust is a tool of your security?" inquired Alerio.

"It is. Now what can I help you with?" Thomas asked.

"I'm going to Syracuse and carrying Legion gladii isn't the best way to blend in with the citizens," Alerio explained as he pulled his dual gladius rig out of his pack. "I need another pair of swords."

Tomas Kellerian reached out and took the harness and gladii from the Legionary. He examined the leather rig and full sheaths by gripping them in one hand and then in the other.

"Too bulky to hide and too heavy to conceal, you're right," proclaimed the Armorer. "Come with me."

They walked through the showroom. Along the way, they passed rows of stands displaying gold plated and gold trimmed sets of ceremonial armor.

"That set is for General Quintus Gurges when he returns from Volsinii," Tomas said as they walked by a beautiful set of armor.

"Unfortunately, General Gurges will not be coming to claim his armor," Alerio stated. "He died in the battle along with a lot of good Legionaries."

Tomas Kellerian stopped short and Alerio almost collided with the Armorers broad back. Looking first at the armor, then at Alerio, he exclaimed, "That is disheartening news."

"Did you lose a large commission?" inquired Alerio as he turned to look at the intricate gold work on the polished armor.

"No. My heart goes out to the dead and wounded Legionaries," Tomas explained. "I collected half the commission in advance from Gurges before I started the project. Some other nobleman, after playing General, will buy it. Enough talk. Follow me."

***

They crossed through the large workroom where two craftsmen sat shaping armor sections. And by areas where less gaudy armor and gladii were stored. At the backdoor door, the Armorer pushed through and led them into the rear lot.

Several outbuildings, a stable, a smoking forge, and a gazebo with leather hanging from the rafters occupied part of the walled compound. One corner had a sand pit with grinders. Two mounted whet stone wheels, one rough sandstone and the other smooth granite, sat beside a worktable. They had square holes in the center of the stones, and both were plugged with wooden blocks. Running through the blocks were iron bars holding the whet stones on frames. Handles attached to the bars allowed for manual turning of the stones. However, attached to the handles were rods connecting to pedals for steady foot powered motion.

All the stations were manned by workers with massive scars or missing body parts.

"Here we go," announced Tomas as he reached into a shed and pulled a covering from a pile of rusty items.

"Rust?" noted Alerio as the Armor moved a few items.

"Surface rust," Tomas explained as he selected four blades from the pile.

Without another word, he carried them to the grinding area.

***

The Armorer ran his fingers along the flat of the first blade. After holding it up, eyeing the length for straightness, and taking a couple of practice swings, he set the blade on the workbench. The next blade he tossed to the side with no more inspection than the finger test. When he glanced down the length of the third blade, he shook his head and tossed it to the side. The fourth blade caused him pause but, eventually, he placed it with the first.

Alerio could see the blades were old gladii. The guard, grip and pommel had been removed and the blades ground down. Whether from years of maintenance by Legionary metalworkers, or from hard grinding to remove gouges and chips from the blades, they were barely recognizable as Legion gladius blades.

"Those look rough," Alerio commented.

"I bought them from a supply Sergeant," the Armorer explained. "Some of them I can grind down into knives or short swords. Others are useless because the temper is gone, or they have cracks. In both cases, the blade will snap under stress."

"And those two?" Alerio asked pointing towards the workbench.

"Solid steel, mostly straight and thin enough to pass as reworked gladii to an expert," Thomas assured him. "There are enough old blades around that they won't mark you as a Legionary. But, your haircut will."

"My haircut?" asked Alerio as he ran a hand over his short-cropped hair.

"Most freemen in Hellenistic countries don't have Legion haircuts," Tomas observed as he picked up a handful of sand and began buffing the rust scales off the first blade.

"I'm leaving on a mail boat tomorrow afternoon," explained Alerio. "I don't think my hair will grow much between now and then."

"Corporal. Can you leave the felting and get our customer a hat?" Tomas shouted to a man stirring a kettle with a paddle.

"It's at a critical heat. Can you get me someone to keep it moving?" the man inquired while still stirring whatever was cooking in the pot. "Do you want a phrygian or a petasos?"

"Lance Corporal Sisera go relieve Corporal Gilibertus at the pot," Tomas ordered. Then to Gilibertus instructed, "Bring one of each. We'll see which hat frames his baby face best."

As Alerio took the paddle, he glanced into the kettle. A mass of wet wool swirled around in murky water stinking of stale meat and urine. He wrinkled his nose, breathed through his mouth, and continued to stir the mixture.

He noticed the missing foot as Corporal Gilibertus walked stiffly away. On the end of the stump and wrapped around his ankle was a piece of fabric. Below the cloth, a block of wood held in place by strips of leather added enough height, so the legs were the same length. Despite the appendage, the man's stride was stinted. He vanished into the main building and Alerio concentrated on twirling the ball of wool.

***

Tomas called the Corporal over when he came back with two hats. After a few instructions, the Armorer took the hats and turned over the blades to Gilibertus.

"What's in this?" asked Alerio as Tomas crossed to the kettle. "And why are you not separating the wool? Bundled up like this, it'll never untangle for the spinner."

"Tallow and lye. And we don't want the sheep hairs to separate," explained Tomas. "Beef fat and lye water thickens the wool and once it's knotted up properly, Corporal Gilibertus will spread it on a bronze form. Another bronze piece will be placed over the mixture. Once the pieces are clamped together, the Corporal will mount it over a fire and keep the bronze rotating for a full day."

"To what end?" asked Alerio.

"The phrygian, like this hat," exclaimed Tomas holding up a cone shaped hat. "It's made from a flat piece of felt. Rolled and trimmed with the top bent forward at a jaunty angle, it's very popular with ship's crews."

"The hairs in the cloth remind me of a beaver dam. Logs and sticks crisscrossing so tightly, they hold themselves in place," observed Alerio.

"That is the beauty of felt. Soft and durable and not labor intensive," suggested Tomas. "And speaking of beavers. This is a petasos and it's not wool felt, it's felt made with beaver hair."

The hat was shaped with a wide brim around a low, rounded crown. The Armorer reached out and placed the phrygian on Alerio's head. He stepped back and shook his head while studying the Legionary.

"No, definitely not the phrygian," Tomas said as he snatched the hat off and replaced it with the petasos. Then he reached out and cocked the hat to one side. Nodding his satisfaction, he announced, "Better."

A workman strolled across the lot. Tomas pulled him over and pointed with pride at the brimmed felt hat.

"I was with the Eastern Legion and some of the rich folks from Greece wore those," the workman said. "It looks good on him, Centurion."

Alerio knew Tomas Kellerian had retired from the Legion after twenty years of service before becoming an armorer. Looking around at Tomas' staff, he realized all of them were scarred and wounded.

"Your craftsmen are Legion veterans?" asked Alerio.

"You think I'd buy slaves and teach them how to make swords and armor?" replied Thomas. "I spent half a life defending the Republic. I'll not teach our enemies how to defeat us."

They were interrupted by a call from Corporal Gilibertus at a grinding wheel.

"Swing the kettle away from the fire so it can cool," he instructed. "Come here, I have an idea."

Alerio used the paddle to pivot the pot from over the fire. He and Tomas strolled back to the grinding area.

"That petasos looks good on you, Lance Corporal," Gilibertus said as he lifted his good foot from the peddle. Without the pumping of the foot peddle, the limestone grinding wheel slowed. "It's one of my best. Took me a full day to pound out the bronze plates to get that shape. And I left the clamps in place to keep the felt under pressure for two days."

"You are a felt craftsman, I agree," mumbled Tomas. "Now, what idea did you have?"

"These gladii have the most wear at their tips and in the center of the blades," the former Legion Corporal explained. "I saw several Qart Hadasht swords a few years ago. Sharpened point, edge on one side and a blade that tapers to a thin belly. These blades have enough heft that I can grind out that shape."

"That shape will work," Tomas observed. "Make sure they're matched and balanced. Our young Lance Corporal likes to use two swords at the same time."

Gilibertus shot Alerio a quizzical look before he reached out and spun the grinding wheel. Once it reached speed, he began pumping the peddle to maintain the grinding velocity.

"What about handles?" Alerio inquired while pointing to the bare hilts.

"We'll keep them simple. No big pommels as I don't think you'll be fighting in a shield wall," Tomas informed him. "If you do end up in a blood bath, grip them tighter. Because you won't have a ball on the end to keep your hands from slipping."

"Will they fit my rig?" Alerio asked.

"You're supposed to be sneaking and peeking. Wear a sword fighter's harness and you'll have eyes on you everywhere you go," Tomas explained. "I have a better idea. Now, get out of my shop so we can get some work done. Come back at first light."

"Thank you, Master Kellerian," Alerio said as he headed for the door of the shop.

Chapter 26 - The Clay Ear

"That's a pretty cap you have there," Thomasious Harricus said as Alerio opened the front door and stepped into the Chronicles Humanum Inn.

"They call it a petasos," Alerio stated while crossing the great room to reach the granite counter.

"Do they now?" teased the Innkeeper. "What did you learn at the Senate?"

"Senator Codex was nominated first," reported Alerio.

"How did Maximus allow that to happen?" Harricus asked more to himself than to Alerio. "When is Codex holding the big party to woo the citizens?"

"In two days. But, I believe Senator Flaccus stole his thunder when he announced the formation of a Legion to march north," Alerio added. "Senator Maximus staged the nomination, the announcement of Flaccus Legion, and the promotion of my Tribune to a post with the eastern province's governor. He played a masterful game."

"That sounds more like the old war dog," the Innkeeper stated. "I bet Consul Codex is chewing clay bricks at having his chance for fame taken by the other Consul getting a Generalship."

"Is fame important to him?" inquired Alerio.

"Consul Codex is a man who believes he has a destiny," Thomasious Harricus responded. "Building out the city should have been his benchmark project and his legacy. The Consul who almost doubled the size of the Capital. It does have a nice ring to it. I imagine you'll be marching north with Flaccus Legion?"

"No, I've been recalled to the Southern Legion," Alerio told him. "But I don't leave until afternoon tomorrow. So, I have time for a mug of vino."

Chapter 27 - Qart Hadasht Swords

In the morning, Alerio ate with the Innkeeper before shouldering his pack and marching to the Historia Fae. Although the sun lightened the eastern sky, there were shadows at street level. He rapped loudly. Surprisingly, the Armorer unbolted the security bars immediately and opened the door.

"Can't sleep?" Alerio asked as he stepped over the threshold.

"Excited for you to try the Qart Hadasht swords," Tomas Kellerian explained. "They're on the workbench in the back."

After the Armorer finished latching the door, they walked to the assembly room.

***

The workbench held several pieces of steel for armor, leather straps to mount the pieces, squares of felt to protect the buyer's skin from the straps of the armor and a bedroll.

It was a nicely done bedroll with a leather tie buckled around one end, a leather cap sealing the other end and a shoulder strap for carrying it. But in all the searching, Alerio couldn't locate a pair of swords.

"I don't see them," Alerio confessed.

"You don't?" inquired Thomas. He snatched the bedroll off the bench and headed for the backdoor. "Let's go check outside."

**

The sunlight had yet to reach the armorer's compound, but it wasn't necessary. Around an open space between the workstations, braziers burned. Their light illuminating a circle and four straw-figures. Thomas' crew of former Legionaries sat on barrels beyond the light. They were eating from clay bowls and watching Alerio closely as he emerged from the building.

"The Centurion said you are a weapon's instructor," Corporal Gilibertus called out. "Time for a class, Lance Corporal Sisera."

Some of the other craftsmen mumbled agreement between mouthfuls of Legion mush. A porridge made from whatever grain was most plentiful and whatever flavoring was handy.

"I can demonstrate with my bare hands," Alerio replied as he slipped the pack off his shoulder and the petasos from his head. He sat the hat on the pack and continued, "But the best I'll do to your straw barbarians is dent them."

Alerio indicated the four, full sized straw men standing in the circle of barrels.

"Here, try this," Thomas suggested as he tossed the bedroll to Alerio.

Catching it in one hand, he almost dropped it. Where he expected only the weight of a wool blanket and an oiled waterproof wrap in the bedroll, it was far heavier. Alerio turned the bedroll and noticed two leather flaps on the uncapped end. He pulled the flaps and saw two bone knuckles nestled in the folds.

"I seemed to have missed these at first glance," Alerio stated as he pulled on the bone pommels. Two swords emerged from the end of the bedroll.

The blades were shorter than a gladius, but the leather braided bone hilts were longer. Overall, the extra length of the handles gave them a longer reach than the Legion gladius. The top of the blade ran straight to a point while the underside tapered from a wide top into a narrow belly. Unlike the gladius, only one side had a cutting edge, and the point was sharpened.

"These are beautiful," exclaimed Alerio as he rested the bedroll beside the pack.

Swinging the swords so the blades crossed, he whipped them back and out as far as his arms could reach. Standing with the swords parallel to the ground at shoulder height, he looked from one craftsman to the other and nodded.

"Corporal Gilibertus, what's in the morning mush?" Alerio asked still standing as if he were crucified.

"Boiled oats and honey," boasted the former Legion NCO.

"Honey from the Golden Valley?" inquired Alerio. He began to make small circles with the tips of the swords.

"As a matter of fact, yes. We just opened the amphora, and the honey is fresh," Gilibertus replied.

"Fill a mug with honey," Alerio instructed. "And we'll see if the weapon's class is worthy."

Suddenly, bowls of mush were set down and coin purses appeared. Gilibertus tossed a coin on a pile and reached back. Turning around, he held up a small amphora of honey and a clay mug.

"To small?" Gilibertus asked with a smile. "I can find a bigger mug."

Alerio stared at the mug as if he were contemplating the offer. The small circling of the sword tips became larger, and he looked at Thomas.

"Armorer. Please put a mark on the mug," Alerio instructed as he swung the swords in bigger circles that engaged his shoulders. "About halfway from the top."

More coins hit the piles as the Armorer pulled a knife and etched a deep scratch in the fired hardened clay. Holding up the mug, he showed the craftsmen the line. Then, he pulled out a coin and dropped it on one of the piles. All the bets were in the two piles and the craftsmen sat back to watch.

"Corporal Gilibertus. Fill the mug with honey," Alerio explained. "On your count."

Gilibertus tilted the amphora of honey over the empty mug and said, "Three. Two. One. Vade."

At the word vade, honey dribbled from the mouth of the amphora and Alerio leaped.

Still swinging the swords, he landed between the first two straw figures. Then he hopped across the circle, leaned out, and chopped another one in the midsection. Without pausing, he twirled around backwards and split the fourth strawman's head in two.

Spinning back, he hacked with both swords and split the fourth straw figure in half. As the upper half toppled, he ran to the third and completed chopping through its middle. Before the top could fall, he swung and severed the straw head.

Instead of turning around, Alerio dropped to his back, somersaulted across the circle, and twisted as he rose to his feet. One sword snaked out and cleaved through one straw middle while the other angled downward to completely sever the last strawman's torso. Both tops fell to the ground.

Alerio held up the swords and bowed.

"Time," shouted Tomas.

Gilibertus jerked the amphora upright and away from the mug stopping the flow of honey.

"He left the heads on two of them," one of the craftsmen challenged.

Alerio glance behind him and back at the man.

"Sorry," he said as he walked to the straw torsos. With a flick of his swords' tips, he cut the last two straw pieces holding the heads in place. Both straw heads rolled away from the now headless torsos. "Better?" he asked.

Thomas strolled over and took the mug from Gilibertus.

The former Corporal had been so busy watching the lighting quick attacks by Alerio, he'd neglected to watch the mug. When a couple of craftsmen shot him questioning looks, he held up his hands to show he had no knowledge of how much honey was in the mug.

"Besides the mug, was the weapon's class informative?" asked Alerio.

"Finest I've ever seen, weapon's instructor," admitted Gilibertus. "And with swords strange to your hands."

"The long handles remind me of the sickles we use to harvest grain on my father's farm," explained Alerio. "And, they are well balanced. Thank you for that."

The Armorer pulled his knife and placed the blade against the mug. First above the marked line, then below it. He seemed to be having an issue deciding where to mark the honey fill. Finally, he smiled and ran the blade along the original line.

"The honey is exactly at the marked line," Tomas announced while handing the mug to a craftsman to pass around for inspection. A few groans came from the former Legionaries.

***

"Lance Corporal Sisera. Unbuckle it and roll out the bedroll," Thomas ordered. "Let me show you what my team did for your swords."

With the end cap removed and the other end unbuckled, the blanket and a waterproof cover rolled out to reveal two leather sheathes sewn into the blanket.

"With the swords removed, the sheaths make a nice pillow," Gilibertus explained as he walked up and dropped a fist full of coins into Tomas' hand.

The Armorer glanced down at the coins, "I warned you he was a weapon's instructor."

"You said weapon's instructor with a wink," Gilibertus complained. "You didn't say anything about him being a weapon's master."

"I had to find a way to pay for the Golden Valley honey," the Armorer replied while jingling the coins in his hand. "This should about cover the cost."

Alerio inserted the swords in the sheaths and rolled up the blanket and cover. Once the end cap was on and the buckles fastened, he slung the strap over his shoulder. Next came the pack and finally the petasos, which he cocked at a jaunty angle.

"Master Harricus. Thank you for the custom work," Alerio said. "What do I owe you?"

"Let me see. Two rusty gladii, two scrap pieces of leather, two rusty buckles," the Armorer listed. "A good quality wool blanket, a fine goatskin rain cover and an exquisite beaver felt hat. I'm thinking two gold. Got to cover the cost of feeding my lads."

"But, that's not enough," exclaimed Alerio.

"I served with the Eastern Legion," Gilibertus added. "Master Kellerian explained where you got the beauty marks on your head and your forearm. The rest of the craftsmen and I talked it over. Two gold is fair for a man who killed an eastern rebel leader."

"Now, pay up and begone," the Armorer ordered. "This is a business, not a social club. And the rest of you. Don't the rest of you have projects? If you don't, I'll fine something for you to do."

Chapter 28 - Sicilia and Syracuse

Around midday, Tribune Velius stepped from a carriage onto the bricks bordering the dock. The driver handed him a travel bag and the head of Planning and Strategies for the Southern Legion walked around the carriage. As the old Staff officer strolled towards the Tiber river, he had a good view of the busy port.

Three gourd shaped Corbita merchant ships occupied one end of the pier. Two were being unloaded and one was taking on cargo. Five flat barges from upriver unloaded grain, furs, and minerals. Slaves, freemen, sailors, citizens, and foreigners pushed, pulled, or toted the merchandise. While the rounded Corbitas were eight feet in height, the thirty-man, single banked Legion patrol boat, at three and a half feet in height, bobbed on the river below the pier.

Tribune Velius couldn't see the patrol boat at first. It wasn't until he was almost to Lance Corporal Sisera, at the edge of the dock, when he got a look at the Legion boat.

"Where's the crew?" Velius asked while looking around Alerio and down at the sixty-five-foot patrol boat.

"Over by the warehouse, eating," Alerio reported. "I imagine, Tribune, they're waiting for the dispatches and tide at the mouth of the Tiber."

Velius studied the Legionary. He wore a light brown beaver felt petasos and well-used woolen tunic and pants. Over his shoulder were slung a bedroll and a pack. With no weapons in sight, the Lance Corporal had obviously decided to go unarmed.

"I'm surprised you didn't strap on a gladius," the Tribune teased. "You do a dagger stashed somewhere."

"It wouldn't be very spy like to walk around wearing a Legion gladius," Alerio replied. "Why are you sending me to Syracuse?"

"I'm sorry you didn't get to visit your family," Velius offered as a delaying tactic while he gathered his thoughts.

"You gave me the opportunity. It was the Etruscī and Insubri who pulled the lynch pins making the wheels fall of my vacation," Alerio responded. "Sicilia? Syracuse?"

"It has more to do with the Sons of Mars in Messina," the Tribune described. "They've been pirating ships from Syracuse and other city states. That alone would draw the attention of Syracuse. However, they've added overland raids along the east coast of Sicilia. So, they poked the bee's nest and now that the bees threaten to swarm, the Sons of Mars petitioned the Senate for protection."

"Excuse me Tribune, but that seems to be a political issue," ventured Alerio. "Why would the Southern Legion be interested in war between Messina and Syracuse?"

"Normally it wouldn't, unless one of them crossed the Messina Straits and attacked Republic territory," Tribune Velius explained. "But the Sons of Mars have also petitioned the Qart Hadasht Empire for help. If the Empire moves forces into Messina, they'll be an arrow's flight from Rhégion and the Southern Legion."

"That's uncomfortably close," Alerio pointed out. "Why doesn't the Senate send a Legion to Messina. Just the presence of our heavy infantry would prevent Syracuse from attacking and prevent the need for Qart Hadasht to interfere."

"Budget, Lance Corporal Sisera," Velius clarified. "Between the cost of Gurges Legion, Flaccus Legion and the public works for expanding the Capital, the Republic is short of funds."

"On a farm, you plant, grow, and sell your crops," Alerio said. "If you come up short one year, you make a deal with vendors for some coin or credit to tide you over until next year's crop."

"That is an excellent description," complimented Velius. "Now suppose you've borrowed two years in a row plus committed to more expenses. What would you owe?"

"You'd have bet the farm," answered Alerio.

"Exactly. The Senate has bet the Republic," Velius replied. "They don't have the funds to send a Legion to defend the Sons of Mars. Or the will, considering the Sons are pirates and thieves."

"I'm going to Syracuse to evaluate if they are preparing for war?" guessed Alerio.

"There, you've answered your own question," stated the old Tribune.

Act 5

Chapter 29 - Syracuse Harbor

The heavily loaded transport had sailed from Rhégion before dawn. Catching Scendente, the Messenia current when it changed to a southern direction, the crew paddled just enough to keep the vessel in the center of the strait. By sunrise however, they'd reached open water and the boat fought a mild headwind. They rowed to within sight of the coastline and exchanged the headwind for a steady breeze off the starboard side. Their Captain ordered the sail raised, but the crew continued to row. While Mount Etna had been visible since light touched the top of the volcano, the green grass and trees of Sicilia weren't distinguishable until sunlight touched the shore. When the sea level air warmed, the cool air from the mountain flowed down and gave them a favorable wind from the stern. They shipped oars and let the sail carry them south.

Alerio could see why their Captain maintained a distance from the land. Boulders, some above the water line in the shallows, and more below waited to rip open the hull if the transport ventured too near. Further along the coast, the waters deepened but the land rose in jagged cliffs of sharp black rock. Pocked marked with crevasses, caves and ravines, the shore offered no port for a vessel.

It wasn't until the sun was high in the sky that the shoreline receded, and a rocky beach came into view. The crew rolled the sail, grabbed oars, and rowed towards land.

"Hold water," shouted the captain. With the four oars motionless in the waters of the Messina Strait, the transport nudged gently against the beach.

The crew and Alerio hoisted amphorae of olive oil, wine, and bundles of cloth from the belly of the Corbita. Down a narrow ramp and across the gravel of the beach, they carried the containers to where the captain stood with traders from Catania. There, merchandise was exchanged for gold and silver coins. The Captain spent a long time visiting with his customers while the crew and Alerio ate a meal and rested. After the Captain finished, the crew pushed the transport off the rocks and back into the sea.

***

Late in the afternoon, the crew again rolled the sail and manned their oars. But instead of rowing towards the land, they rowed westward out to sea. For a time, the shoreline also rolled west then it rounded and retreated to the east. All the while, the transport continued to distance itself from land. Only when the coastline vanished below the horizon did the Captain track southward. Holding the southern course, the crew rowed in slow, controlled strokes.

"Why are we out so far?" Alerio inquired. "I don't see land anywhere."

He rowed along with the other crewmembers. The man in front of him looked back and smiled.

"The Captain is sweeping around to enter the harbor from the east," he explained. "It's better to avoid crossing tracks with warships and faster transports."

They rowed until the Captain bent the rear facing oar to swing the transport towards starboard. As they rowed on the new track, land appeared. As well as a fast-moving Greek trireme. With one hundred and eighty oars propelling the warship, it cut the low waves leaving a trail of white water in its wake. The battering ram in front and just under the water split the waves and Alerio imagined the horror of the transport being smashed by the rapidly advancing triple banked ship of war.

"Warship," announced Alerio.

"And rowing hard," added another crewmember.

**

The closer to a break in the land they got, the more vessels left the harbor. Most were low in the water transports like the Corbita.

One cargo ship stood out. Rather than the almost flat profile with the wide deep belly, this ship was curved up and out of the water both fore and aft. It was easy to imagine the storage compartments in the bulging ends. Not only was the storage different, the number of oars and the huge sail meant the cargo ship was fast.

"Single banked with twenty oars," Alerio stated in admiration as the sail unrolled. The sail suspended high above the deck with the edges of the cloth extended far beyond the ship's rails. "What is she?"

"Egyptian transport sailing out of Alexandria," replied the rower. "And yes, she is fast. But also, nimble enough to oar clear of us. Unlike the trireme which might sink us just for practice."

"Have they done that before?" Alerio asked in panic.

"I don't know," the rower replied. "Nobody has survived to tell the tale."

The rowers laughed and Alerio concentrated on the wide channel between the end of an island and the toe of a land mass bracketing the entrance to the harbor.

Chapter 30 - The Harbor of Syracuse

"The island of Malta, then on to Oea on the coast of Africa," the Captain offered. "You'll see sights that most people can't even dream about."

"I appreciate the offer, Captain," Alerio replied. "But, I have business in Syracuse. Thank you for the ride, the work, and the pay."

Alerio jingled the silver coins in the palm of his hand. The offer of employment on the transport had caught him by surprise. He had to admit, it was flattering. Hoisting his pack and bedroll, Alerio adjusted the brim of his petasos and marched down the ramp and on to the docks of Syracuse.

On the far side of the harbor, fishing boats were grounded on a narrow beach. On the other side of the sandy beach, tall grasses grew in marshy areas. Closer to where his transport was docked, larger ships lay tied to piers. Spanning from the commercial docks, the city's defensive wall ran over a bridge to the island. Warships floated further along the island with barracks nearby. Behind the troop housing, the walls of Syracuse rose, signaling the border of the city.

"Almost fourteen miles of wall," a street urchin said.

Alerio glanced down at the tow-headed youth.

"I can give you a tour," the lad offered. "All the best eating places, and the best lodging and, and the best shops, and the best…"

"Stop. I'll give you a silver to quit talking and to leave," Alerio said. "If you can tell me where the army drills?"

"Drills?" he asked.

"You know, where soldiers practice with swords and shields," described Alerio.

"Oh, beyond the swamp outside the wall. Take the altar gate for the best view," he replied holding out his hand. "Almost fourteen miles of wall…"

Alerio dropped a silver into the small hand at the same time as a soldier called out.

"You there, don't give them coin," the armed man ordered as he marched up. "You! Get out of my patrol area. And you sailor, are you heading into the city?"

"I am," Alerio responded as he watched the lad scurry away and vanish around a pile of transport crates.

"The gate is the other way, over the bridge," the guard pointed out. "And don't give the street urchins coin. It only makes them brazen."

"Thank you for the directions," Alerio said before noticing the soldier had his hand out.

So, running off the lads was more than securing the docks. They were cutting into his coin. Alerio dug out another silver and gave it to the guard.

"Enjoy your stay," the soldier said as he strutted away.

**

The sun was getting low and Alerio decided he needed a bed for the night. Figuring he'd find an inn closer to where the military drilled, the Legionary set out to cross the city.

Syracuse was old, far older than the Capital of the Republic. And it was built of mud smeared walls and stone more so than wood and clay bricks. A lot of the pitted black rock he's seen during the sea trip had been incorporated into the buildings. For use as a façade material, it was smoothed and carved with figures. Greek symbols and Gods were chiseled into the rock. Although prominent, none of the buildings had been built of the ragged black rock.

Alerio had traversed half the city when the urge to touch the strange black rock overwhelmed him. The street was empty, as most people had gone home to retire for the day. He stopped, set down his pack and the bedroll, and reached out a hand.

**

A shout from an adjacent alleyway echoed down the street. Alerio had turned to face the alley when a man in a military tunic burst onto the street. He stumbled while making the turn and Alerio saw blood on his face. Four men in rough clothing were almost on him. Alerio reached back and drew the long knife with the black and yellow striped hilt.

The military man scrambled to his feet and unsteadily staggered by Alerio. Seven steps beyond the Legionary, the man collapsed. Behind him the four men yelled with joy and raced towards their victim.

Hooking a foot under the heavy bedroll, Alerio launched it into the path of two of them. It spun end-over-end and both men ran into the blanket, cover, and the two steel swords. The weighted bedroll slammed into their shins and their feet got tangled. They toppled to the paved street. The other two, seeing their fellows fall, stopped, and refocused on Alerio.

"Nice petasos," one sneered at Alerio. "I've always fancied a fine lid like that."

"Just take the dēfutūta hat. Do the sailor lad, the soldier, and let's get out of here," the other man urged.

The two on the street were on their knees and brushing off their hands. Both had dropped their knives which had skipped and slid down the street.

The hat fancier held his knife as did the other man. Alerio held his knife beside his leg.

"Excuse me?" begged Alerio. "I'm new in town and I'm looking for an inn. Can you suggest a quality inn for the night?"

He asked so innocently the two street thugs hesitated. Their mistake.

Alerio sliced from beside his leg to the air above the cautious robber's head. Along its path, the blade parted the man's wrist, his chin and lacerated one eye. As the man collapsed in agony, Alerio leaped over him.

Expecting the victim with the beaver felt hat to run away, the last sanding thug stomped towards the downed man in the military tunic. But Alerio wasn't fleeing.

He reached the two kneeling men and rammed a knee into the side of one's skull. The man sprawled into the pavers as only a dead weight could, all loose and fluid. The second man caught the bottom of Alerio's thick sandal in the nose. Blood burst in a spiral shape from under the end and sides of Alerio's foot. The man with the crushed nose flew backward and when the back of his head knocked into the pavers, he no longer knew he was bleeding. He lay unconscious on the street.

Alerio spun and saw the last thug reach out with his knife. As if probing, he attempted to place the tip in the military man's eye. Unfortunately, the man fought off the blade with his hands and forearms. If the two kept up the poking and flesh blocking for much longer, the military man would bleed out before the blade could penetrate his eye and spike his brain.

Flipping the knife with the black and yellow handle, Alerio caught the blade. Drawing back his arm, he threw the knife. It flipped four and a half times before embedding its tip in the outlaw's neck. The man reached over his shoulder. Then he staggered two steps before falling to his knees before sprawling on the street.

Alerio walked over, pull the knife from his neck, bent down, and cleaned the blade on the man's shirt. Then, he went to the military man.

"Can you stand?" he inquired.

The man continued waving his hands in the air as if still fending off the blade.

"Calm down," ordered Alerio. "They're all down and you're safe. Is there somewhere I can take you?"

The man pointed up the street and tried to stand. His wet palm slipped, and he landed back on the street. Alerio looked hard at his hands and forearms. Both were bleeding but none of the cuts pumped or dribbled rivers of blood. Assuming the man wasn't about to bleed to death, he left him. After putting away the knife, Alerio collected his bedroll and pack.

With an arm around the man's back, Alerio helped him stand. Looking around the Legionary didn't see any witnesses or more thugs. He was pleased as he didn't want to call attention to himself. Unseen, he and the wounded military man made their way from the scene of the fight.

However, Alerio was wrong. On a rooftop across the street, an impassionate observer watched as the military man ran onto the street. Her interest still didn't peak when the four-armed men chasing him turned the corner. Even when the stranger tossed the bedroll, she smiled at the move, but remained bored. The knife from behind the stranger's back was rudimentary street fighting and she actually yawned. His hand-to-hand fighting skills were adequate. It was when he flipped the knife. The black and yellow hilt flashed in the fading light of early evening and her spine went cold and her body tensed. Before she could act, the stranger and the wounded man were out of danger and moving up the street.

Chapter 31 - The Somewhat Honorable Macario Hicetus

The soldier staggered and Alerio could smell vino on his breath. Unable to tell if the head wound or the drink caused the man to stumble, Alerio kept a firm grip as they made their way up the street. Eventually, the man lifted an arm and pointed out a pub.

They entered and a man behind the counter looked up and, seeing the blood, indicated a rear doorway.

"Courtyard. I don't want him bleeding on the tile," the proprietor instructed.

"Two mugs of red, a cloth and a pitcher of vinegar," Alerio replied as he guided the soldier towards the doorway.

"This isn't a medical center and I'm not a doctor," the man warned. "If he's going to die, take him back to the street."

"He's not going to die, and I just want to clean him up," Alerio assured the proprietor. "Red, cloth and vinegar."

In the courtyard, Alerio guided them to a rough-hewn bench and table. He eased the soldier down on one end of the bench. After shoving his petasos in the pack and placing his gear behind the bench, he slid in on the other end.

"Let's take a look at those cuts," Alerio offered reaching out and taking the man's arms.

"They tried to rob me," complained the man. He winced as Alerio probed the cuts. "Ouch, that hurts."

The proprietor arrived with a tray. He set two mugs and a pitcher on the table. When Alerio tilted his head back and stared, the man pulled a semi clean cloth from his apron.

"Three silvers and two bronze coins," he stated.

When the soldier didn't reach for a coin purse, Alerio dug into his and paid the man. After he left, Alerio lifted the pitcher and poured a splash over the man's arms.

"Algea bless me, that hurts," the soldier exclaimed loudly.

The pain seemed to have revived the man.

"I'm Alerio Sisera," he introduced himself while washing the blood from the man's head wound. "And you are?"

"Lieutenant Macario Hicetus of King Hiero the Second's mounted Signal Corps," he replied. "And that's why I was banned from the parade."

"Because you are mounted or part of the Signal Corps?" asked Alerio as he moved to gently cleaning the Lieutenant's hands and forearms.

"No. Because I am the son of the Syracusan leader Hicetus," Macario announced.

"Leader, as in the King? You're a Prince?" Alerio inquired.

"No, no. My father was the Tyrant Hicetus. I was born the year he was driven from power and from the city," the Lieutenant explained. "Today's my twenty-third year and I wasn't allowed in the parade."

Alerio's head was spinning from the odd answers from Macario Hicetus, son of a disposed tyrant, mounted signalman, and birthday celebrator. None of which explained why the Lieutenant wasn't allowed in the parade.

"One simple question, Lieutenant Hicetus," probed Alerio. "Why weren't you allowed in the parade?"

"Because King Heiro the Second was reviewing the troops," Macario stated.

"I gathered that, but why?" demanded Alerio.

"I'm not allowed in the presence of the King," Macario finally admitted. "King Heiro's advisers are afraid I might assassinate him and lead an uprising and claim the throne."

"Would you?" inquired Alerio.

"Good Hygieia no, may she prevent the illness of over ambition," Macario pleaded. "I just want to go to war and reclaim my family's honor. A few accommodations, a little blood spilled, and my mother will once again be accepted at Galas held by noblewomen."

Alerio wanted to ask about the Syracusan military plans but suddenly he had to relieve his bladder.

"I'll be right back," he informed Macario. He stood and went through the doorway. The proprietor pointed out the necessary closet.

***

While Alerio used the hole in the floor, he heard loud voices and the vino seller reply to a question. When he emerged, the voices were louder and coming from the courtyard. Moving cautiously, he approached the doorway and peered out.

Five cavalrymen crowded around Macario Hicetus. They were talking over each other about what a grand parade it was and how it was a shame Lieutenant Hicetus had been ordered to stand down. Alerio wanted to join the conversation but one of the troopers grabbed Macario's hands.

"What happened to your arms and your head," the man demanded. "Who did this to you?"

"I don't remember," Macario mumbled. "After you trotted off, I went to have a drink and roll the dice. You know that always cheers me up."

"And makes you coinless and hungover," another cavalryman teased.

"The next thing I know, I'm sitting here cleaning my wounds," he mumbled. Reaching out, Macario picked up the pitcher and sniffed the content. "With vinegar and this rag."

Alerio realized the injured and drunk Macario was confused. While he watched, the proprietor brushed by holding two pitchers and balancing five mugs. Deciding it was time to leave, Alerio followed the man to the courtyard.

"I was here earlier and left my pack," Alerio explained while the men reached out to grab mugs.

He went behind the bench and picked up the bedroll and the pack. Then Macario turned and studied him.

Before Alerio could get to the doorway, Macario blurted out, "Hey, I know you. You were on the street."

"Is this one of the men who attacked you?" asked one of the cavalrymen.

Alerio ran before the obvious answer came. As he reached the front door, he heard Macario shout, "Yes. He was one of them."

By then, the Legionary was out of the pub and racing up the street. The five cavalrymen poured from the establishment and gave chase.

Alerio didn't know the city or, which streets were dead ends. It wasn't in his plan to get into a street fight with five soldiers. Spy on them yes, but not do battle on their home ground. He passed a cross street and several alleyways.

After glancing over his shoulder, he put on a burst of speed. The cavalrymen were gaining on him.

Ahead, a small, hooded figure waved and pointed at an alleyway. Not having any other options, he adjusted and ducked into the dark narrow space. The small figure followed. Ten paces in, Alerio slammed into a stone wall.

The five cavalrymen bunched up at the mouth of the alley. With only a moment of hesitation, they charged into the dark. That's when a stack of barrels along the wall came free and rolled into their legs. The five tripped and ended up sprawled on the pavers.

Alerio swung his bedroll around and began to lift the leather flaps. As his fingers reached into the end of the bedroll, a small hand gripped his arm. It was a small hand, but the fingers squeezed deeply and insistently into the arm muscle.

"This way," came a whisper and Alerio was guided to a rope ladder.

He climbed and before he reached the roof top, he felt the rope sway as his small rescuer scrambled up after him. Once on the tiles of the roof, Alerio fell back and breathed heavily.

 The hooded figure quickly pulled the ladder up. Then the hood turned to Alerio.

"Your name, Ally of the Golden Valley?" a woman's voice asked.

"You're Dulce Pugno," Alerio said. When she didn't reply, he answered, "I know. You don't use that name in the city. I'm Alerio Sisera and I thank you."

"Are you injured?" the assassin from the Sweet Fist inquired.

"I am uninjured thanks to you," Alerio reported.

"Follow the roof line. You'll come to a low building. On the far side, it's a short jump to a set of stairs," the assassin explained. "You will find an inn three blocks from there."

Then she rose to her feet and in four steps was swallowed by the night. Alerio waited for his heart rate to slow and his breathing to return to normal. Then he stood and walked off in the opposite direction.

Chapter 32 - The Altar of Syracuse

Alerio woke when sunlight touched the windowsill. He rolled out of the cot, poured water from a pitcher, and washed his face in the bowl. Once dressed in the workmen's clothing and with the felt petasos set on his head at a rakish angle, he took the stairs down and left the inn.

By keeping the rising sun to his right, he navigated northward through the dense streets of the city. Several blocks from the inn, he allowed his nose to guide him to the west and a market. Vendors offered baked yams and other cooked vegetables. At other tents, he found lamb, beef, and fish on sticks turning over open flames. All the odors made his mouth water and after wandering between vendors, he bought a baked yam and several large slices of lamb. One more stop to secure a wooden mug of cider, and he headed north once again seeking a place to sit and eat.

Ten blocks from the market, he came upon a wall and approached a grassy area. Above the wall, he could see the upper section of a tall structure constructed with granite stones. As if a giant doorway had been removed to reveal a curved but shallow room, columns on each side framed the decorative arched wall to the rear. Alerio sat, leaned his back against the wall and began peeling back the burnt skin of the yam.

***

"There he is!" a voice called out in a breathy flat tone.

Alerio glanced up to see a man standing on the street pointing at him. The man had tiny pieces of cloth stuffed in each nostril of a badly swollen nose. Recognizing one of the street thugs from last night, he took a bite of the yam and tossed it away. Then with a slice of lamb clutched in his teeth, he jumped to his feet and ran along the wall. The mug of cider sat in the grass untouched.

This wasn't turning out to be a quiet information gathering mission. At a gate, he passed under an arched opening and stopped. In front of him was the curved structure. Acting as giant steps, huge granite blocks tiered from the ground to the floor of the curved room. Off to his right, rows of seating wrapped around an amphitheater cascading down to a performance stage. Neither building caused him to stop.

A long flat stone surface spanned the entire distance between the theater and the monument. Knee high walls with access ports cut in at areas along the wall showed steps leading up to the flat stones. Priests in ceremonial robes walked behind the walls sacrificing oxen.

Alerio had seen the death of oxen offered to the Gods before. But, never in such volume. A quick count and he arrived at two hundred oxen laying side by side on the flat rocks. Blood flowed behind the low wall and down the steps. It poured like water into drain channels keeping the blood off any of the assembled crowd who wanted to avoid it. For those seeking a blessing, all it took was to dip a few fingers into sacrificial blood as it flowed by.

The crowd of witnesses was divided into four layers. To the rear were visitors, workmen and slaves. Next were citizens while closer to the massive alter the Syracusan military stood in ranks. The area in front of them held noblemen, senior staff officers, and advisers. One man, in ornate armor, stood on a step. With arms outstretched, he looked towards the sky while an ankle-deep flood of blood washed his lower legs.

When the street urchin mentioned a gate near an altar, he was referring to the Alter of Syracuse. Glancing back through the arched gateway, Alerio saw five men clustered together. Two were speaking and one mimicked touching the brim of a hat.

"That's how he recognized me,' Alerio thought as he stepped away from the opening, pulled off the petasos and stuffed it into his pack.

Walking quickly, he made his way to the end of the workmen and side stepped into that section of the crowd.

***

"Mighty Zeus, we ask you to accept this sacrifice. Grant us your blessing," the man standing in the blood shouted. He reached down and dipped both hands into the flow. With fresh blood streaming off his hands, he turned to the crowd. "And powerful Nike. We beseech you to carry us to Victory!"

The crowd roared back its approval.

"At least there will be plenty of meat," a workman mumbled.

"That's if King Hiero shares it," another craftsman added. "After salting some for the army, and feeding his troops, we'll be lucky if there's any sacrifice left for common folks."

Considering the large sacrifice, the call to the Goddess of Victory, the assembled troops, and the workman's comment about salting the meat, Alerio realized the army was only a few weeks from marching to war. But, marching where?

Two rows in front, a soldier turned and glared at the speakers. Talking while the King was calling to the Gods was frowned upon. Then the soldier shifted his eyes and they locked on Alerio. A nudge and a tilt of his chin caused another soldier to look back. He also zeroed in on the Legionary.

'With the hat on, the street thugs recognize me,' pondered Alerio. 'Without it, the soldiers recognize me. This mission is going bad fast.'

King Hiero the Second called for blessings from other Gods. And why not? His priests had sacrificed enough oxen to cover all the Gods and Goddesses on Mouth Olympus as well as a host of minor deities.

Somewhere during the necessary plea to Poseidon, Syracuse being a deep harbor city and always in need of protection by the God of the Sea, Alerio slipped back into of the crowd.

Chapter 33 - Run, Hide, Escape or Die

Once out of sight of the soldiers and the street thugs, he moved to fringe of the praying crowd. When out of sight from both the street thugs and the soldiers, Alerio ran to the perimeter wall and followed it to the end. Then, he jogged into a wooded area. On the far side, he entered a street and strolled through the upper section of Syracuse. He didn't see anyone following and was happy when he approached the massive city wall.

The street followed the wall and soon he came to a portal. A bored guard stood against the open gate and barely acknowledged Alerio when he walked by and left the city. Beyond the city's defensive wall was a military camp.

Southward and far from the last tent, marsh grass and swampland ran to the sea far in the distance. To the north, cultivated farmland stretched between crops of trees. Alerio had an idea of when the army would march but no clue as to its destination. He turned south and followed the defensive wall along the outer edge of the military camp.

About halfway down the line of tents, he noticed a few soldiers basking in the warm sunlight. One of them raised up and grabbed a wineskin. After a long stream of vino, the soldier lowered his head and looked directly at Alerio.

Lieutenant Macario Hicetus of the mounted Signal Corps did a double take before slamming a fist into another soldier. Alerio didn't wait to see the result of the alert. He ran.

At the next gate, Alerio slowed and walked through with a nod to the guard. As soon as he was out of sight of the gate, he broke into a jog. A few heartbeats later, four mounted cavalrymen charged by the surprised guard. Luckily for Alerio, none stopped to question the soldier on gate duty.

They split up in four directions and trotted down the streets hunting the man who attacked Lieutenant Hicetus.

***

Alerio pushed into the crowd at the market. Glancing around, he felt safe with no cavalry in sight and his head bare. Until he saw the proprietor of the pub where he'd taken Hicetus. Standing with two men by a bronze figurine stall, the tavern owner pointed out Alerio and in exchange he received a full purse. Now, petasos or not, the street thugs knew him.

A man on the side of the market began keeping pace with him. A quick look to the other side and he spotted a second man doing the same. Both were wearing worn and dirty clothing, so he assumed they were street thugs.

It was decision time. Run and try to stay ahead of them until he reached the harbor? Or, find a place to take a stand and fight them. Considering the on-the-take guards at the docks were probably on the thugs' payroll, Alerio pulled his bedroll around. He decided to look for a dead end. A hidden corner of the city where a few bodies wouldn't be noticed.

But first, he needed to get out of the market. It was too easy for an enemy to slip up behind him in the crowd and shove a dagger in his back. Seeing a narrow street between three-story buildings, Alerio walked until he was passed the street. Once the men following him were beyond the street, he stooped down and ducked behind a vendor's tent. A quick run back, a hook around another tent and, while still stooped, he cut across the market. He gained the narrow street, stood upright, and ran.

Chapter 34 - Aphrodite's, The Pub, Not the Temple

The plan was to make the first corner and get out of the line-of-sight from the market and the thugs. His legs churning and his arms pumping, he reached the intersecting street and veered south. Then he pivoted and ran back to the intersection. Down the block and walking his horse was a cavalryman. He was staring into alleyways and side streets as his horse moved. Thankfully, he didn't see Alerio.

Back on the narrow street, Alerio ran for the next intersection.

***

He could see the next street was a wide boulevard. At first, he decided to skip it and move to the next intersection. But as Alerio started to cross the expanse, he noticed the boulevard was empty. Not just lightly traveled, it was deserted. Glancing to the south, he realized why.

A few blocks down, tall temples occupied both sides of the boulevard. With the massive sacrifice in progress, every Priest and disciple for every God or Goddess would be at the massive altar helping to butcher oxen. Changing his mind, the Legionary headed south on the temple street. Staying to the side of the boulevard, he quickly reached the temple structures.

Maybe he could duck into one and hide until dark. But what then? He still needed to discover the target of King Hiero's army. Behind him, he heard yelling and a quick look back showed seven men rushing into the intersection. They pointed at him, and he responded by running.

Alerio swung into the first street he came to and didn't break stride until he heard music. Not an angelic choir or chants one would hear from a temple. This was drunken, boisterous voices accompanied by strings and drums. Following in the direction of the music, he continued down the street.

Aphrodite's Wine and Food occupied a section in the center of a block. Alerio bypassed the street leading to the establishment and ran to the next intersection. Taking the parallel street behind Aphrodite's, Alerio smiled.

Warehouses for temple supplies lined one side of the street. It wasn't the warehouses that caused him to smile. It was the corrals and empty wagon yards between the storage buildings. Figuring the sacrifices would keep the wagon drivers busy until after dark, Alerio stopped and listened to a song.

Oh, the Goddess Aphrodite.
Oh, she of love and beauty.
She of pleasure, and procreation.
Ah procreation!

My wife is like the goddess, let me tell you why.
Showers me with Love, she does. She does!
Ere I come home late, after fellowship and wine.
She blesses me with wash water, or words that ain't refined.
Calling endearments like drunk, rogue, and swine.
It's love like Aphrodite, from that true love of mine.

Oh, the Goddess Aphrodite.
Oh, she of love and beauty.
She of pleasure, and procreation.
Ah procreation!

My wife is like the goddess, let me tell you why.
Shows me her Beauty, she does. She does!
Beyond description I say, is the sight of my own lady.
Sagging in places that shouldn't, all droopy and toothy.
Bowed legs and mention not, the size of her booty.

She's blessed like Aphrodite, my own plumpish cutie.

Oh, the Goddess Aphrodite.
Oh, she of love and beauty.
She of pleasure, and procreation.
Ah procreation!

My wife is like the goddess, let me tell you why.
Soothes me with Pleasure, she does. She does!
Look in the cooking pot, it's a smoldering gastric affair.
Dinner at home is burnt, not always worth the dare.
It's a wonder I don't expire, eating my good wife's fair.
She's special like Aphrodite, for the woman does care.

Oh, the Goddess Aphrodite.
Oh, she of love and beauty.
She of pleasure, and procreation.
Ah procreation!

My wife is like the goddess, let me tell you why.
Sprinkles me with Procreation, she does. She does!
She's as cold as a granite statue, if I desire Procreation.
If I'm feeling amorous, she displays one of our children.
They're always under foot, the fruit of our union.
She's honored Aphrodite, by birthing an even dozen.

Oh, the Goddess Aphrodite.
Oh, she of love and beauty.
She of pleasure, and procreation.
Ah procreation!

Alerio stopped at a wagon yard, unhooked the latch, and pushed the gate open. Then, he walked to the center of the street and waited. While he waited, he sang along with the music drifting from Aphrodite's courtyard.

Oh, the Goddess Aphrodite, Oh she of love and beauty.

The seven men came into the intersection and spotted him.

She of pleasure, and procreation. Ah procreation!

Alerio sang and waved at the seven street thugs when they burst into the intersection. Then, as they ran to him, he strolled through the gate and walked to the center of the wagon yard.

Chapter 35 - Open Field Tactics

Alerio learned the gladius and shield from Legion veterans. Every harvest, a Sergeant and a Centurion came to work on his father's farm. While there, they taught him sword skills as well as tactics. If your mission was to guard or protect a fixed position, you wanted to funnel your enemy and prevent them from surrounding you. If you were attacking, you needed to avoid a funnel which narrowed your line of attack. A third option dealt with a broken Legion line.

If you found yourself separated and fighting multiple barbarians, get to open ground. Any boulder, tree, or wall could be used by them to sneak up on your blind side. Or trap you where the enemy had the advantage of attrition while your back was to a wall. Open field tactics allowed you freedom of movement to fight on many fronts.

The empty wagon yard fit the need and Alerio pulled off his pack and tossed it to the corral fence. Next, he loosened the flaps and rested the bedroll on the ground between his feet.

"My wife is like the goddess, let me tell you why," Alerio sang. *"Showers me with Love, she does. She does!"*

The seven men rushed through the gate, and one stopped to close and latch it.

"Ere I come home late, after fellowship and wine," Alerio smiled while he sang and waited for the men to get closer. *"She blesses me with wash water, or words that ain't refined."*

"You interfered last night, stranger," a big man advised Alerio. He was better dressed than the rest and had a short sword hanging from his hip.

"Calling endearments like drunk, rogue, and swine," Alerio voiced without acknowledging the man. *"It's love like Aphrodite, from that true love of mine."*

"I'm speaking to you, lad," the man said raising his voice.

So Alerio sang louder, *"Oh the Goddess Aphrodite. Oh, she of love and beauty. She of pleasure, and procreation. Ah procreation!"*

"Teach this ignorant Latin to respect his betters," the leader of the street thugs roared.

The six thugs responded to the order. They pulled knives and rushed at Alerio.

"My wife is like the goddess, let me tell you why," Alerio crooned as he dipped both hands into the end of the bedroll. *"Shows me her Beauty, she does. She does!"*

The fastest are not always the smartest or the most skilled. Many times, according to Alerio's teachers, they are just that, fast.

Alerio's hands emerged with the two swords. Both thugs, expecting to strike a standing man were not prepared for the flashes of steel that slit one's belly open and peeled off the side of the other's face.

Suddenly the thugs were down to five and their victim stood with one sword extended and another hanging above his head like a scorpion's tail.

"Beyond description I say, is the sight of my own lady," Alerio sang. *"Sagging in places that shouldn't, all droopy and toothy."*

The thugs, realizing they faced a swordsman, spread out. Even the big one in the nice clothing moved forward. He held his sword's point low.

"Bowed legs and mention not, the size of her booty," Alerio sang as he stood still letting the thugs close the distance. *"She's blessed like Aphrodite, my own plumpish cutie."*

Two moved shoulder to shoulder on Alerio's left. They came in fast before waiting for the other three.

"Oh, the Goddess Aphrodite," Alerio bellowed as he spun to face them while scissoring his blades. *"Oh, she of love and beauty."*

Their rush brought them into range of the swirling sword tips. Both men received lacerations to their chests and thighs. But, none of the cuts prevented them from retreating from the crossing and uncrossing steel blades.

"She of pleasure, and procreation," Alerio sang as he stepped back and twisted his upper body. *"Ah procreation!"*

One thug dove at Alerio's back. After twisting away from the knife, the Legionary hacked down as the body flew by. The fat end of the blade opened the flesh starting at the base of the thug's skull. Alerio's sword sliced the entire length of the man's spine before swinging away to block another's knife thrust.

"My wife is like the goddess, let me tell you why," Alerio bellowed as his second blade swiped down from the opposite direction. *"Soothes me with Pleasure, she does. She does!"*

With a full arc to gain momentum, Alerio's blade severed the hand holding the blocked blade. The knife and the hand fell to the dirt and the man sank to his knees holding the stump. He cried as blood spurted from the neat slice.

"Look in the cooking pot, it's a smoldering gastric affair," Alerio sang. *"Dinner at home is burnt, not always worth the dare."*

The well-dressed man was the last uninjured thug. Looking at his two men with multiple cuts, he shouted, "Get back in the fight."

"It's a wonder I don't expire, eating my good wife's fair," Alerio sang as he circled so he stood between the thugs and the gate. *"She's special like Aphrodite, for the woman does care."*

The two injured men appeared to be confused. They had entered the wagon yard seven strong and full of vengeance. Now, there were three and after witnessing the flying steel of the stranger's blades, they weren't sure they wanted to re-engage with him. Except, their leader had ordered it. And, the stranger with the two swords stood blocking access to the gate and their escape.

"Oh, the Goddess Aphrodite. Oh, she of love and beauty," Alerio warbled. *"She of pleasure, and procreation. Ah procreation!"*

The big thug marched to the two wounded men and put his face close to theirs.

"He's one man. Hades, he's just a lad," their leader explained. "You take him from the sides while he's busy defending from my sword."

"He's pretty fast," one ventured.

"And skilled," the other added.

"I don't care. No one can assault my club and live to tell about it," growled the big man. "Let's finish this."

"My wife is like the goddess, let me tell you why," Alerio sang as he waited for the thugs to come. *"Sprinkles me with Procreation, she does. She does!"*

They split up. Two moving to flank Alerio with their leader coming to face him head on.

"She's as cold as a granite statue, if I desire Procreation," the Legionary sang. *"If I'm feeling amorous, she displays one of our children.*

The leader lifted his sword holding the blade up and to the side. Obviously, he didn't have the training to wield the weapon properly. The other two closed in from the sides.

"They're always under foot, the fruit of our union," Alerio crowed as he leaped at the thug on his right. *"She's honored Aphrodite, by birthing an even dozen."*

Swinging both swords together at the man, he stepped by him, and spun to face the last two.

"Oh, the Goddess Aphrodite," Alerio sang as the man with the deep neck gash and broken ribs lay bleeding to death in front of him. *"Oh, she of love and beauty."*

The last two were forced to shuffle around their dying companion. Alerio held up his right blade as an offering for the thug with the sword. His other sword hovered at waist level towards the man with the knife. The thugs attacked at the same time.

"She of pleasure, and procreation," Alerio sang as he deflected the sword with his right arm. *"Ah procreation!"*

His left blade tapped the knife to the side before sweeping back to slice deeply into the thug's wrist. The man grabbed the injured limb and ran away from the fight, the gate, his leader, and the deadly swordsman.

The leader swung hard at Alerio's sword, and the Legionary allowed his blade to swerve away. Seeing an opening, the thug leveled his blade and charged. Alerio shifted to let the tip of the thug's blade pass him. Then he brought his left blade around. The thin belly of Alerio's sword chopped into the thug's shoulder, through the shirt, the skin and into the bone.

The leader of the street thugs arm went numb, and he dropped his sword. Without pausing, Alerio ran his right blade across the thug's throat.

"My wife is like the goddess, let me tell you why," Alerio sang as he cleaned his blades on the shirt of the well-dressed thug.

Standing, he looked around for the last one. The man's body lay sprawled on the far side of the wagon yard near the corral. Sitting on the fence was a slim woman with her hood thrown back.

"Alerio Sisera," she said in greeting. "The manager of the Golden Valley Trading House would like a few words with you."

Chapter 36 - Syracuse Trading House

There were Golden Valley Trading Houses spread throughout the civilized world, as well as, a number of them in large barbarian settlements. Each house traded in luxury merchandise. One of the staples was honey from the Golden Valley. Another service available at the trading houses, if you possessed the coin, was assassination by the Dulce Pugno. Seeing as all managers from the houses were members of the Sweet Fist, there was no way for Alerio to refuse the invitation.

"Which way?" Alerio asked the woman as he slid the swords into the bedroll.

"Cavalry on the streets and city guards looking for a man with a beaver petasos and a scar on his head," she announced. Then indicating the seven dead street thugs, she added. "No crime syndicates seek that man."

"If not the street, then how do we reach the trading house?" Alerio asked as he picked up and shouldered his pack.

She hopped off the fence rail and looked hard at him. "Why did you block the gate?"

"So none of them escaped," Alerio replied. "As you noted, no crime syndicates are looking for me."

"Truly you are a worthy alley of the Golden Valley," she acknowledged. "This way."

There was a gap between the corral fence and the warehouse. The woman guided them through the gap and around back of the building. At a narrow alleyway, she turned south for two blocks before taking another turn. Soon Alerio was completely lost in the maze of back streets and alleyways of Syracuse.

The city was much older and a lot bigger than the Republic's Capital. Its construction differed as well. Where the Capital used clay bricks, Syracusans preferred large and small stone blocks for their buildings and walls.

After the seemingly endless walk, the woman stopped in an alleyway and opened a door. Alerio entered expecting to find a warehouse attached to the trading house. Rather than organized stacks of quality vino, cheeses, silks, linen, rare fruit, and cured meats and, of course, small amphorae of honey, he walked into an open-air room. Boiling pots of water, stinking of urine and lye occupied most of the open area. The rest was taken up by piles of cloth or clothing hung on lines to dry.

"A laundry?" inquired Alerio.

"The smell keeps most people away," the woman said as she strolled across the compound.

"I can smell why," commented Alerio as he followed her.

One of the men stirring a tub of wash cocked his head at the woman. She raised her hand and waved a pattern. Looking closely Alerio noted the knife scars on the man's arms and one on his cheek. The man was probably a member of the Dulce Pugno which meant he was an assassin. Based on the presence of a Sweet Fist, Alerio figured anyone entering the compound uninvited would not enjoy the hospitality.

The woman walked through an open doorway and the Legionary followed. Inside the building were tables where other workers folded and bundled the clean clothing and fabric. She ushered Alerio into a storage room and bolted the door.

Picking up a steel bar, she shoved it behind a box resting against one wall. With a slight twist, the box rolled away from the wall revealing an opening and the top of a ladder.

"Turn left at the bottom of the ladder," she ordered. "You will be met."

"Thank you. I didn't get your name," Alerio said pleasantly as he squeezed around the box to gain access to the ladder.

"You will be met," she insisted while ignoring his question.

***

There was little head room and by the time Alerio saw the light in the distance, his back hurt, as did his head where he smacked it against the rough ceiling.

"Alerio Sisera?" inquired a man standing at the bottom of the ladder holding a lantern.

"Yes sir," replied the Legionary. Then he asked, "I don't suppose you have a name?"

"You can call me, Milon," the man said indicating for Alerio to climb the ladder.

Alerio emerged in a supply room with shelves stacked with jars, amphorae, and small polished boxes. He had to navigate another box to clear the ladder. Milon came up and used a bar to move the box back against the wall.

"My office is down the hall," he announced as he unbolted the door.

Alerio recognized the layout of the building from past visits to Golden Valley Trading Houses. A long center hallway ran back to the warehouse. To the front, the direction they walked in, the hall passed rooms before doing a dogleg to a foyer and the front door. Milon opened the last door on the right and waved Alerio into an office.

***

"Please, Alerio Sisera, have a seat," Milon said as he stepped around a large desk.

He waited until Alerio began to sit before taking his own chair.

"I understand you wanted to speak with me," Alerio ventured. "Or was it just to get an Ally of the Golden Valley out of harm's way?"

"Both, to be honest," Milon admitted as he pulled a full coin purse from under the desk. He sat the heavy bag down and gently pushed it across the desktop towards Alerio. "Gilibertus sends his regards."

"The Dulce Pugno from Bova Beach," recalled Alerio picking up the pouch and weighing it in his hand. It was by far heavier than the purse he'd given the wounded assassin. "I take it he made it back to the Golden Valley?"

"He did. That is your loan repaid with interest," Milon said. "But it still leaves the scales of trade unbalanced."

"I don't understand," pleaded Alerio. "Unbalanced?"

"In the eons the Dulce Pugno have guarded the Golden Valley, never has one of our Sweet Fist been saved by an

Ally," explained Milon. "We are at a loss as how to repay you."

"I could use some information," stated Alerio. "What is the target of the Syracusan army?"

"Messina. However, the main force will not leave for a month or so," Milon advised. "The King has sent an advance force. They marched this afternoon. But, information, sanctuary, and aid are due an Ally. What additional request would you ask of us? Riches, someone quietly removed, or a lifetime supply of luxury items? What can the Golden Valley do to repay you?"

Alerio let his mind wander. Here was an opportunity with a host of possible benefits. When he spared Gilibertus, he was just doing the honorable thing. Now, the Golden Valley was offering his heart's delight as repayment, and he didn't have a clue.

"Lance Corporal Sisera, there is no need to decide at this moment," Milon assured him.

The use of Lance Corporal jerked Alerio out of his introspection. How did the assassin know? But the use of his rank and the reminder that he was a Legionary gave Alerio the answer.

"I want my banishment lifted," he stated. "I am a soldier of the Republic and if ordered to the Eastern Legion, I would like to sleep peacefully at night."

Milon raised both hands and rested the fingertips together. His arms were muscular and scarred with long healed blade cuts. Even if Alerio didn't know before, the healed knife wounds let him know he was dealing with a Dulce Pugno. The assassin closed his eyes and wrinkled his forehead.

"We've never waved a ban on an Ally," expressed Milon. Then he stopped and opened his eyes. "Gilibertus is my brother. My younger brother to be exact. A promise of life for a life is a good trade. You are welcome to return to the eastern region by the Dulce Pugno of the Golden Valley."

His response explained how he knew Alerio's rank. But there were two other things he needed.

"I have to get out of the city," Alerio said. "Can you get me on a ship to Rhégion and put me up for the night?"

"No ships will row out tomorrow or the day after," Milon advised. "There are storms headed up from the south. Sanctuary is due without asking."

Alerio held out the coin purse before inquiring, "Will you sell me a horse?"

Milon smiled and said, "You plan to ride across Sicilia in a storm, through the lines of an advancing army?"

"How big can an advance unit be?" Alerio asked. "And yes, I plan to ride. If you will sell me a horse."

"We will loan you a horse and give you a letter for one of our customers at Lentini," Milton said. "The city is six miles inland at the foot of Mount Etna. If you ride hard, you can change horses there and get ahead of the advance units. They will follow the coast road."

"I appreciate your help," offered Alerio.

"I will also do the same for a customer in Catania. It's only nine miles further, but you'll be riding across the rolling land along the base of the mountain. The horse and you will both be exhausted," Milon advised. "The ruins of Naxos are twenty-eight more miles and there, I am afraid, I can offer no help. You'll need to rest the horse before the final thirty-one miles to Messina."

"You seem to know the route by heart," Alerio said.

"We are a trading house for the Golden Valley," Milon replied. "It's our business to know. Now, go rest. You have a hard ride ahead of you."

Alerio glanced at the doorway. The assassin from the rooftop and the wagon yard stood looking at him.

"I'll show you to a room," she stated while motioning for him to follow her.

"Thank you Milon," Alerio said. Then asked as he placed the coin purse in his pack. "One last question. Why did Macario Hicetus say I was one of the muggers?"

"Because it wasn't a street robbery," Milon answered. "Lieutenant Hicetus likes to gamble. He also cheats. Yesterday, he lost a large sum of coin despite the cheating. When he fled without paying, the gamblers commissioned a street gang to take one of his eyes."

"But why identify me as one of them?" questioned Alerio.

"To hide the gambling and loss from his fellow mounted signalmen. He owes coin to almost everyone in his unit and most reputable gambling establishments in Syracuse,"

Milton replied. "He claimed it was a robbery. By pointing you out as one of his assailants, he put a face on the criminals. Identifying you deflected attention from his gambling, the real attackers, and the gaming syndicate who hired them."

"In short, I was a scapegoat?" ventured Alerio.

"Yes! Macario Hicetus put all of his sins on you and offered you up as a sacrifice," Milon agreed.

The female assassin at the doorway chuckled.

'I'm glad someone finds this amusing,' Alerio thought as he left Milon's office.

Act 6

Chapter 37 - Leaving Syracuse

Alerio kept to the shadows outside the trading house's front gate. With heavy clouds blocking the moon and stars, the only lights were a few lanterns on the streets. Following Milon's directions, he quickly made his way northward.

The revelers at the altar, those still awake, were chanting. Filling the air with their voices which mixed with the aroma of roasting sacrificial meat. Alerio approached from between the last buildings. Before he reached the priests and worshipers, he turned eastward and re-entered that section of the city.

As promised by Milon, the guard at the defensive wall ignored the man in the beaver felt hat. Far beyond the gate, a horse whinnied and Alerio was greeted from the dark.

"Alerio Sisera. You move like a bull on clay tiles," the female assassin whispered.

"I move like a Legionary," Alerio corrected as he marched towards the voice.

The hooded figure emerged from the dark and the reins of a horse were placed in his hand.

"Can you ride better than you sneak?" she offered.

"All Legionaries can ride," responded Alerio. "We're taught in Legion training. As heavy infantrymen, there's little cause to walk around like a cat stalking a mouse."

"Then stomp your way northward until the ruts in the road deepen. That's where the road splits," she advised. "Wait for enough light to see the three branches. The left heads west, the right follows the coast, and the center is the road for you."

As she spoke, Alerio rubbed a spot between the horse's eyes. When he stopped, the animal moved closer and nudged him in the chest for another round.

"Thank you for your help," Alerio said but the night was empty. The assassin already faded silently into the darkness.

***

The sun didn't rise or so it seemed to Alerio. Instead, a soft light lit the clouds like a candle's flame behind a silk screen. When the three routes became visible, Alerio mounted the horse and trotted off on the road running to the northwest.

Miles later when the horse showed signs of tiring, Alerio dismounted and walked. As a Legionary, he was accustomed to long marches. The road began to climb and after miles of walking and riding, he stopped to let the horse graze while he rested and ate a meal of cheese, bread, and olives. Somewhere on the coastal route, the advance units of the Syracusan army also marched and rested.

Although not steep, the road elevation rose consistently. He continued alternating between walking and riding to keep both of them fresh. The land transformed from trees and natural grass to cultivated fields where the road flattened. By late afternoon, the sunlight hadn't strengthened, in fact, the clouds grew heavier during the day, and it became darker. The storm mentioned by Milon was approaching. Alerio imagined the seas to the south of Syracuse being too rough for ships to leave the harbor. And probably had been since early morning.

Chapter 38 - Through Lentini to Catania

Set in the middle of farmland as far as Alerio could see, Lentini resembled the collective village near his father's farm. Except, Lentini was much bigger. The town had streets of housing, craftsmen compounds, multiple storage buildings for the harvest, and designated wagon yards to hold vehicles for transporting the grain. One prevailing feature of the landscape was the stone walls made by farmers from the rocks they dug up when tilling the soil.

The buildings were constructed of rocks, wood, and rough clay bricks. Alerio marveled at the difference between the uniformed bricks crafted by workers in the Republic and the haphazard clay blocks made for Lentini.

He rode onto the main street ignored by the people. They were too busy rushing around closing shutters and checking rails on corrals to be sure the animals were secure during the approaching storm.

After locating Milon's customer, he traded the horse for a mountain pony and settled down to a meal. Later in a spare room, as he unstrapped the bedroll, thunder cracked, lighting streaked across the sky and rain began to fall.

***

No one was on the street as a lone rider and the mountain pony left Lentini. Rainwater rolled off the bedroll cover, but some moisture found creases and the rider and pony were soon drenched. Between the rain, heavy clouds, and a hidden sunrise, they took the muddy northeast road in the dark. It wouldn't get much lighter as they ascended the mud and rock track towards the coast of Sicilia.

Alerio understood the need for a pony when the trail rose through a section of the black rocks with the holes and crevasses. Footing was difficult even during the times he walked to give the animal relief. As the land fell and the riding became easier, the trip didn't. Chilled from the rain and huddled as best he could under the oiled goatskin cover, Alerio's only comfort was the knowledge the Syracusans were also marching through the downpour.

Nine hard miles and half a day later, the low walls of Catania materialized from the driving rain. Alerio dismounted and walked into the town. He had to bang on several doors before getting directions to Milon's customer. There he received a hot meal and bad news. A unit of Syracusan cavalry had passed through the evening before. Even knowing his route would overtake the mounted patrol, he climbed on the horse. While still damp and chilled, he rode out of Catania.

Chapter 39 - Between Naxos and Hades, the Cavalry

Either the clouds were getting thicker, or the sun was going down. In either case, the light on the muddy road was fading. Crossed wagon wheel ruts, rain filled holes, and high spots became harder to see. After the horse stumbled for a third time, Alerio dismounted.

His world closed down to his feet splashing mud, his legs lifting and lowering, and the limited view provided from under the oiled cover. There were miles to go, rain coming down in buckets and only the breathing of the horse to compete with the drone of the rain. Despite the difficult conditions, Alerio slogged forward.

Training can be useful unless it teaches you to shut down your mind to endure long marches. In the Legion, you traveled in your Century so letting your mind drift as your body performed was not dangerous. Alerio was traveling alone. Allowing his awareness to idle proved costly.

***

The land on either side of the road changed. On one side trees crowded the muddy track, while on the other a grassy field stretched into the gloom of the fading light and the pouring rain. Alerio marched stoically into the rain while the horse walked behind him.

Suddenly, three horses came from the field. Alerio's only warning was the greeting from his horse in response to the whinnies from the cavalry mounts. His mind snapped back to the present, but the Syracusan soldiers were already towering over him. With javelin tips aimed at his head, all he could do was stop and acknowledge them.

"Good evening," he said looking passed the iron points and the long shafts.

"Nice horse, Son of Mars," one said with a wicked smile.

"You sir, have me confused with the Sons of Mars," Alerio tried to explain. "I've never been to Messina. Never met any of those rogues."

"He's Latin," another of the cavalrymen observed. "And you're right. It's a nice horse."

A quick jab from any of the javelins and Alerio would be fatally injured or killed. Rather than waiting to see if they were horse thieves or murders, he dropped the reins and rolled away from the three deadly tips. Using his horse to block the cavalrymen, Alerio sprinted into the trees leaving his horse on the road. Unfortunately, his pack, a change of clothing, personal gear, and his fat coin purse were tied on the horse - as was his bedroll with the swords and blanket.

"Should we hunt him?" asked one of the mounted soldiers.

"Too dark and those trees have low branches," another replied. "We have the horse and his pack. Besides, I don't think he'll be a problem. Did you see how fast he ran?"

"Like a rabbit," the third added. "Let's finish the patrol and get back to camp."

The three rode off. From the tree line, Alerio watched them head south. Once they were out of sight, he sprinted across the road and didn't stop until he was far into the field. There, he turned and continued his march northward. Now however, he was aware and keeping an eye on the road.

***

When it was almost completely dark, three shadowy riders came along the road heading north. Once the cavalrymen passed, Alerio changed course and regained the road.

Legionaries marched and Alerio was a Legionary. Throughout the rainy night, he continued his trek. Stopping only to collect rainwater in his oiled goatskin to slacken his thirst, he reached Naxos before the cloudy sky lightened.

The sight of a campfire protected under a suspended tent-cover made him smile. Mounted soldiers lived good, he thought. To approach the camp, he snaked between toppled granite blocks. They might have once been a temple or a government building. Now they served as cover for the Legionary as he worked his way closer to where the Syracusan cavalry unit slept.

Across the fire but visible at the edge of the light, he spied seven horses and a supply mule. One of the horses was his. Further confirming his count of the enemy force were three two-man tents. Five soldiers were not in sight. Alerio assumed they were sleeping.

One guard sat under the cover staring into the fire. He might have been fantasizing about hot food, warmth, dry clothing, and cold vino. At least that's what Alerio was fantasizing about. But first he had to collect his belongings.

One of the challenges with launching an attack on a superior force was the inability to match the enemy sword for sword. Even with the element of surprise, Alerio was doomed in a stand-up fight against six trained soldiers. Plus, he didn't have a sword to use. He did have a finely crafted knife and that would have to do for now.

Chapter 40 - Natural Selection, Nature Calls

They selected the campsite with an eye towards repelling an attack. Three tents formed a semicircle on one side of the campfire with the tied horses and the mule occupying the opposing space. Toppled but leaning granite blocks formed a defensive structure between the horses and the tents on one side. Across from those blocks, but further back, more of the large blocks were scattered beyond the firelight. The on-duty guard sat on a smaller granite block facing in the direction of the scattered blocks watching the logical approach an enemy would use for an attack.

The cavalry troops had done an excellent job of securing a safe bivouac. If a large, noisy force arrived, the guard would alert his comrades. If, however, one wet, weary, and hungry Legionary crept forward slowly in the pouring rain, it was a different situation.

Alerio moved from block to block, using the granite, not as barrier but, as a way to break up his shape. While still beyond the firelight, he knelt beside a block to wait.

***

Spend time with troops in the field and you'll learn one thing. No matter how good the security, before the sun rose, a soldier would need to relieve his bladder. Alerio had drifted off and didn't see the man emerge from his tent. He did hear grunts exchanged between the sleepy man and the sentry. By the time the soldier walked out of the firelight and into the rain to answer nature's call, Alerio was awake and moving.

The soldier yawned as a stream of his steaming water splashed into the wet earth of the ruins. His blanket over his head and wrapped tightly around his shoulders. He yawned again then attempted to scream when the knife blade sliced into his kidney before traveling to sever one side of his spinal cord. No sounds of agony issued from his lips because of the hand clamped over his mouth.

The soldier was eased to the ground and finished off. His body placed so it sat leaning against a granite block with the sightless eyes reflecting the campfire light.

Alerio moved off to the side and groaned loudly enough for the sentry to hear. Then, he placed his tongue between his lips and made a fart noise. Not a quick one but, a long-drawn-out wet sound. And, he groaned again.

"Gods man," whispered the man on guard duty. "What crawled up your cūlus and died."

Alerio replied with another groan, an even longer episode of passing wind, and topped the performance off with a final groan which he shut off unnaturally.

The sentry walked to the edge of the firelight and peered into the rain. As if it would help, he shielded his eyes with his hand, leaned forward and stared into the black rainy night.

"Trooper, talk to me," the sentry urged as he stepped out from under the cover.

He must have seen the campfire light reflected in the dead man's eyes because he moved directly towards the body. "Are you…"

With his windpipe severed and the weight of his body supported by his head, which was pressed against Alerio's chest, the concerned sentry died without finishing the question. Alerio let the body fall on top of the other dead cavalryman.

When he set out from Syracuse, Alerio's plan was to get to Messina and catch a ship to Rhégion. There he would make his report to Tribune Velius. If the mounted troopers hadn't stolen his horse and his equipment, he would be on the way to Messina. Now, he stood in an unguarded camp of sleeping soldiers and the job wasn't done.

***

An iron pot with tripod legs, ration packs, and bladders of liquid, as well as his pack and his bedroll were stacked beside the campfire. Alerio pulled the swords out of the bedroll and rested them against the granite block beside a pair of javelins. Then he rummaged through the first two food ration packs. Finding a nice stock of supplies, he began to assemble a big breakfast.

He placed the iron legs above the fire and attached the pot. After filling it halfway with water, he ladled in three portions of oats. Laying on more logs, he poked the fire until it blazed up and flames engulfed the base of the pot.

Pulling out three yams, he placed them in the embers below the burning logs between drinks of vino. Mounted troops did live better than the infantry.

In the last ration pack, he touched four wrapped packages. The outsides of the wrappings were gritty and Alerio smelled salted pork when he pulled them out of the pack. He skewered the pork slices on sticks and balanced them on the top of the pot. Soon, the delicious aromas of boiling oats, baking yams, and roasting pork filled the air.

Alerio picked up his swords in one hand and the sentry's two javelins in the other. Once armed, he strolled back into the dark and the rain to wait.

***

Food in the morning was an individual choice. Some men woke up hungry and the slightest smell of food would bring them charging out like a post hibernating bear. Others enjoyed the aroma of food in the morning but often preferred sleep to eating. And a segment of men always chose a warm blanket and their dreams over morning food. Alerio waited to see the distribution of choices among the Syracusan soldier.

***

"What is that smell?" a soldier whispered as he crawled out of his tent. "Praise Hestia, it's a feast."

Before he could rise to his feet, a javelin shaft appeared in his open mouth. The iron head imbedded deep in his gut.

The hungry soldier fell face down in the wet grass. Alerio's stomach growled, and his mouth watered as he waited with the final javelin for another of the three remaining Syracusans.

He didn't have to wait long. Another soldier's head appeared in the entrance to a tent. The javelin entered the top of his shoulder, speared his heart before splitting his hip bone. Although he didn't cry out, the loud grunt woke the final two soldiers.

At the sounds of confused questioning coming from that tent and the one on the right, Alerio knew the locations of the last two men. Swinging his swords to loosen up his shoulders, Alerio ran to the first tent.

Sword clutched in hand, the man scrambled over the body of his tent mate. He made it to the entrance and caught a glimpse of the flat side of a sword before he fell unconscious on top of the dead soldier.

Alerio leaped to the next tent and used his foot to slam the man's sword to the grass. Then as he did before, he knocked the soldier out.

Chapter 41 - Unkind Years and Rust

The rain slackened to a light drizzle and the sky lightened. Someone was chewing loudly, and the smell of roasted pork hung in the air. Normally, the aroma would make the soldier hungry. But a throbbing headache and a sour stomach gave him the opposite reaction. He puked up last night's dinner on his thighs.

Lifting his head, he saw the Latin from yesterday evening sitting by the campfire spooning boiled oats into his mouth with the ladle. In his other hand, he held a slice of pig on the tip of a long knife. Looking around, he noted his Lieutenant across from him. The officer was slumped over and tied to a tree. After attempting to move his arms, the soldier realized he was tied up.

"Good morning," the Latin greeted the soldier. "Sorry about the rude treatment but you took my horse and my gear."

"You'll be stoned to death for this, Son of Mars," sneered the soldier.

"About that Son of Mars thing," Alerio responded between shoving food into his mouth. "I'm a Legionary with the Republic. And, like I said before, I've never been to Messina."

"Your death will be painful," the cavalryman warned.

"You and your officer are alive because I need to complete my report," Alerio informed the man. "I just need the size of your advance force."

"For what purpose? We own Sicilia and the Sons of Mars will be put to death and cast into the sea," the soldier promised.

"Maybe it's the rap on the head. Let's try this again," Alerio said as he stood and walked to where the soldier was sitting. "All I need is the size of the Syracusan advance force. It's a simple question."

"Five phalanxes of Hoplites, one hundred mounted, and six hundred soldiers," responded the soldier.

"Nine hundred soldiers or so," observed Alerio. "That's not a lot of men to take a city."

The soldier laughed and shook his head. "You really have never been to Messina," he stated. "The walls are low. The original Sons of Mars are old, and their equipment is rusty. It'll be a miracle from Ares if they hold out a full day."

"Then why is your King marching with an army in four weeks?" inquired Alerio.

"To claim the city and all the lands between Syracuse and Messina," the soldier reported. "Now cut me loose."

"Cut you lose?" asked Alerio.

"You said that's all you needed," replied the soldier.

"And it is," Alerio agreed as he reached out and sliced through the soldier's throat. Turning to the officer, he performed the same surgery. Then he walked back to the campfire to finish his breakfast.

Alerio had been taught by veterans of the Legion. One of the first lessons was never give an enemy a chance to counterattack or retaliate. The mounted unit of Syracusan Cavalry wouldn't be doing either.

***

The clouds cleared, the sun came out, birds sang, and the road began to dry. It was a beautiful day and Alerio would have appreciated it. But his eyes were closed. Lulled to sleep by the rocking of a walking horse, he dozed. Behind the horse, six more followed in the napping Legionary's wake. Although tied to lines, the slow pace and the calm morning had the horses following without putting tension on the lead line.

The line hung slack until two horses in the back tossed back their heads and danced to the side. Then the line tightened, cutting into Alerio's thigh and the Legionary woke up.

Four horsemen rode at him from the north. As they closed, Alerio tugged the line and the horse carrying the javelins, swords, and extra Syracusan armor moved beside him. Without stopping, he extracted two javelins from the holder, placed them across his horse's neck, and let his horse continue forward.

Act 7

Chapter 42 - The Sons of the Sons of Mars

The riders came up fast but instead of forming an arc where each could employ their weapons, they remained bunched up. Alerio noticed they were young maybe fifteen to sixteen years old. Just a few years younger than him. Despite their youth, their arms and shoulders were heavily muscled. Their legs, however, were those of a normal youth.

One nudged his horse forward leaving the other three in the center of the road.

"The road is closed, Syracusan," the youth announced. "Turn around. Go back to King Heiros and tell him the Sons of Mars are ready to fight."

"How far is it to Messina?" Alerio asked as he used a thumb to shove the petasos back on his head.

"Are you deaf?" the young rider spit out. He kneed his horse forward as if to intimidate the man under the hat. "This road is closed."

"How far is it to Messina?" repeated Alerio while placing a hand over his mouth to stifle a yawn. All four of the youths watched the hand move over his mouth. They missed Alerio's other hand as it untied the lead line from his horse.

Between the yawn, the fancy felt hat, and the man's dismissive attitude, the youth exploded.

"Do you have a death wish?" he screamed kneeing his horse closer. "We'll cut you down. Soak the earth with your blood and leave your corpse for the beetles."

Alerio smiled and asked, "How far is it to Messina?"

The youth drew back his javelin, kicked his horse forward, and jabbed with the weapon.

Alerio leaned to the side, snatched up the two javelins in one hand, and struck the side of the youth's head. As he toppled off his horse, Alerio kneed his mount forward. With a javelin in each hand, he charged the other three.

They hesitated. Holding the tips of their javelins forward, as if to ward off the attacking horseman, the three sat unmoving.

Alerio drove his horse among them sweeping right and left with the shafts of his javelins. All three were quickly unseated. Before they could recover, the Legionary dismounted and walked to each smacking them in the head.

***

The walls were low, the sun was low, and the guard at the gate was bored. At least he was until a rider came into view. From far down the road, he sighted a single rider leading a herd of horses. Most of the mounts had packs, he assumed, slung over their backs.

"Sergeant of the Guard," he called out. "Rider coming. Looks like a trader."

A middle-aged man strolled to the gate. His armor, like the guard's, showed years of patching, and miss matched replacement pieces. The Sergeant squinted as he peered down the road at the rider.

"Your eyes are terrible," the Sergeant exclaimed. Then, without explaining, he hurried back through the gate shouting, "Call out the guard! Call out the guard!"

The cry was picked up by other voices and the Sergeant stood waiting for his duty squad. Meanwhile, the guard at the gate held up his hand, curled his fingers, and looked through the tunnel trying to bring the rider into focus. When he did, he understood the Sergeant's reaction. The rider was armored and four of the packs on the horses' backs were actually bodies.

Long moments later, enough time for the rider to come closer and details to be visible, ten young men appeared. They wore armor and carried shields from the Republic, different Greek States, the Qart Hadasht Empire, and some locally made but of poor construction. As they arrived at the gate, some were still pulling on their armor.

"In our day, we would have been dressed for battle and challenging the rider by now," the guard called from outside the gate.

"You would have been hungover," replied the Sergeant as the squad formed ranks. "But you would have been standing in the shield wall, long before this lot got dressed."

"What's up, Sergeant?" one of the squad members asked.

"An armored rider. Syracusan by the looks of him," the Sergeant reported.

"You called us for a single rider?" another commented.

"It's a good drill," the guard outside the gate observed. Then to himself, he mumbled, "The Sons of the Sons of Mars are not their fathers."

Chapter 43 - Messina

Alerio gently pulled the reins bringing his horse to a stop. It didn't stop the nine horses on the lead line to halt. Six were cavalry mounts. They came forward flanking Alerio with the other three dragged along by their lines. If the horses had riders, it would have resembled a cavalry charge.

A twelve-man squad stretched across the road with a Sergeant standing in front of them. To the Legionary, they looked no better than barbarian tribesmen. Large shields, not as massive as Legion shields, were held in haphazard manners. Some rested on the ground, others held off to the side. Only a few were forward and touching the neighboring shields. Behind the shields, the troops were relaxed to the point several had their legs crossed at the ankles.

Jumping off his horse, Alerio pulled his knife and walked down the ranks of horses to the first one with a young man tied over the horse's back. He slit the cord and the body slid off the horse and crashed onto the dirt road. Following quickly, the other thee joined the first one in the dirt. After cutting them free, Alerio marched up to the Sergeant.

"I am Lance Corporal Alerio Sisera of the Republic's Southern Legion," he announced.

The Sergeant looked around the Legionary's shoulders before asking, "Are they dead?"

"A little beat down. And they'll have headaches when they wake up," explained Alerio. "The blood rushes to the head when you're slung over a mount's back. If I can get your men to take them and their horses, I need to get to the market and sell the other horses and the Syracusan gear."

"Where did you steal the horses?" the old Sergeant sneered.

"I didn't steal them," explained Alerio. "The Syracusan riders had no further use for them. A Sergeant once told me never to let a resource go to waste."

"And I suppose they won't need their armor, shields, javelins or swords?" inquired the Sergeant. "Are you sure about that?"

"You could ride to Naxos and ask them," advised Alerio. "But you'll need to read their entrails as they aren't able to speak."

"And suppose we decided to take the horses and gear. Say as, a tax to enter Messina?" challenged the Sergeant.

This time it was Alerio who looked around the Sergeant's shoulders. He made a show of examining each of the twelve members of the sloppy squad.

"Four dead, five wounded, and three crippled for life," responded Alerio. "And you'll die with your guts in your hands. Interested in a demonstration?"

"What makes you think you can take on the Sons of Mars?" demanded the Sergeant.

"I'm a weapon's instructor for the Legion. It's my job to size up men's fighting ability," Alerio stated. "But I don't have to do anything. If these undisciplined children are the Sons of Mars, the advance force for the Syracuse army will kill them for me."

"Go collect your comrades," the Sergeant ordered the squad.

"But he has insulted my unit," one of the squad members whined.

The Sergeant glared at the man.

"The offer of a demonstration is still on the table," Alerio promised.

"As tempting as it is, I need to get you to the Citadel. Not embarrassing my Sons of the Sons of Mars," the Sergeant said as if he were tempted to take the Legionary up on his offer. "Bring your spoils and come with me."

***

They passed through the gate and entered an old town of narrow streets. Rough bricks and wood covered in peeling layers of clay were the most significant architectural feature. At a center street that ran to the docks, they turned in the opposite direction of the harbor, and started climbing a steep incline.

The residential and commercial buildings ended halfway up to the hilltop fort. On the uphill side of the buildings, merchants had built walls to enclose their compounds. Passed the walls, the hill steepened considerably.

Alerio looked back and, from this height, he could see the blue water of the harbor. Further south and across the strait, the top of the Legion's tower at Rhégion was visible.

"This hill would make for a hard run," commented Alerio. "Your troops must hate it."

"You are assuming we train like Legionaries," the Sergeant said as he breathed hard and continued to climb.

A low wall surrounded the fortified position. Beyond a heavy gate, the Citadel itself was a two-story brick building with wide portals on the second floor. From Alerio's point of view, the fort's purpose was to protect the soldiers stationed inside, not the citizens living in Messina.

Chapter 44 - The Citadel

Captain Crius Nereus sat at a table with six other middle-aged men. On the table were seven platters of food which they nibbled on while discussing business. Adorning the walls around them were old shields, javelins with rusty tips, chipped swords and worn leather gear. The men seemed more interested on discussing trade routes of other cities than in caring for the tools of war. They were, after all, pirates, thought Alerio.

"Captain Nereus. I've got something you'll be interested in," the Sergeant announced as he marched into the great room of the Citadel.

Alerio stepped up beside the NCO. Instead of looking at the table and the men, he gazed around at the old, unmaintained weapons.

"And who are you?" demanded the Captain. He pushed back his chair and stood. "I asked. Who you are?"

After pulling his eyes off the sad display of weapons, he snapped to attention.

"Lance Corporal Alerio Sisera, Southern Legion," Alerio said with a crossed chest salute.

"He's a Legion weapon's instructor," the Sergeant added. "And he has information."

"If it doesn't concern shipping," Captain Nereus exclaimed. "I'm not interested."

"How about five phalanxes, six hundred soldiers," reported Alerio. "and one hundred, no, make that ninety-four cavalry troops?"

"What does that mean?" inquired Nereus.

"It's the composition of the advance force heading your way from Syracuse," explained Alerio. "And the King is headed here in a month to hold a victory parade in Messina."

The six men at the table jumped to their feet and began talking over each other.

"Silence," Nereus shouted. "Where is this advance unit?"

"Two- or three-days march from here," Alerio stated. "Maybe more if the rain held them up."

Captain Nereus began shouting orders to the men. They were directed to get a head count of what forces they had in town. How many ships were due back and how many ships were available to block the harbor. Alerio stood waiting as everyone except he and Nereus ran from the great room.

"Lance Corporal Sisera. Come dine with me," Nereus invited. "Take your pick, there seems to be a selection of empty chairs."

***

"The Sergeant said you're a Legion weapon's instructor," Nereus commented once they were seated. "Are you any good?"

"I've never been laughed off a drill field, Captain," Alerio replied as he speared a slice of beef with his knife.

"Captain is an honorary title," Nereus explained. "Fifty-three years ago, King Agathocles hired tribesmen from the central and western parts of the Republic. They called themselves the Sons of Mars. King Agathocles, that also was an honorary title, declared himself King of Sicilia. The citizens of Syracuse and the Qart Hadasht Empire didn't recognize the title. With the Sons of Mars and mercenaries from Greek cities, the King built an army. They followed Agathocles all around Sicilia and to the coast of the Qart

Hadasht Empire. That's where I joined the army. We didn't do too well there."

Nereus picked up a clay mug of vino and took a sip. Then he continued, "Agathocles treated his mercenary army well. He shared spoils and didn't waste lives needlessly. He was a good General. Despite his tactical skills, the Empire handed Agathocles a good old-fashioned kick in the cōleī. He sailed his army back to Syracuse. By then, the King was old. He used the army a few more times but the old General didn't have the heart. Plus, the Empire was always there when we attacked."

Selecting a piece of meat, Nereus held it up on the point of his knife.

"When Agathocles, died the leadership of Syracuse was in turmoil," he stated still staring at the hunk of meat. "Somehow, they got themselves together and decided to pay off the army. They even offered to row the soldiers home. A lot of soldiers took them up on the offer. But my Captain suggested we stay and have a little adventure. Besides, the climate was nice, and we were young."

He bit the meat off the knife and chewed it slowly. Alerio figured the Captain had more to tell so he ate quietly and waited.

"We took what we needed, did some trading with the spoils, and generally traveled where we wanted. But we kept going back to Syracuse and the easy prey outside the walls. In time, the new leadership got tired of us. They called on the Greek King Pyrrhus for help. Luckily for some of us, Pyrrhus had his sights set on a bigger prize," Nereus reported with a sour look on his face as if the memory of Pyrrhus was unsettling. "He unloaded his army, chased us down, turned his army around, boarded his ships and sailed away. I say lucky, because if Pyrrhus had the time or the inclination, the Sons of Mars would have been wiped out. As it was, over half the Sons were dead. Our equipment in tatters and the wounded dying daily. The survivors marched north seeking a place to rest and heal."

He picked up his mug and took a long pull of vino.

"We arrived at the gates of Messina in poor shape," Nereus described. "My Captain begged the Greeks of the city to at least grant us the protection of their walls while we regrouped. After a full day of negotiations, they threw open the city gates and we shuffled into Messina."

Nereus stabbed another slice of meat and shoved it into his mouth like a predator. He continued his tale while he chewed.

"The remaining Sons limped into the city and around to an unoccupied area. With open ground, access to the water for fishing, and a safe space, we relaxed and tended our wounded."

The Captain stood and began to pace in front of the table.

"And we did relax, for five days. A few Sons got caught stealing and they were brought in by the city guards. My Captain got them out of it by paying the merchants for their troubles," Nereus related. "But events were set in motion. The Messina city guards began to harass us whenever we left our camp. Then, a pair of Sons got accused of assaulting a couple of Greek women. Another three killed some locals in a fight. All five were arrested. The guardsmen dragged them to the Citadel and staked the Sons in the sun while the city's leaders debated the punishments."

Nereus picked up his mug and drained it. Reaching out, he grabbed a pitcher, refilled the mug, and drained half of it before slamming the mug and pitcher down on the table.

"What did they expect us to do?" he stated, obviously not expecting an answer. "We grabbed our shields and swords and went to get our men back."

He walked to an old set of armor and ran his hand over the cracked leather.

"This is the armor from the first guardsman I killed," he said while dropping his arm. "You see, the city guardsmen were used to collect taxes, break up fights, and restrain thieves. The Sons of Mars were frontline troops fresh off Agathocles' battlefields. It wasn't a fair fight. They died in the streets, alleyways, and in homes where they sought shelter. By early afternoon, the Sons of Mars controlled Messina."

Captain Nereus scrunched up his face and looked as if he had a gut problem or gas pains.

"The Sons, just as we'd done in countless enemy towns, began to sack the city," he explained. "Except, we had no master or King to call us back. A lot of citizens died before our Captain and Lieutenants got us under control. We gathered in the open field camp and the Captain laid down the law. Each man would choose a wife, or two if he wanted. We were told to spare tradesmen and sailors because we needed our city to function. That afternoon and evening, the Sons of Mars went through Messina selecting wives. Their husbands or defenders were cut down and tossed into the streets. By sunrise, the Captain held marriage ceremonies for the Sons. While our brides wept, the citizens were outside the walls digging graves for their dead."

Nereus sat down, stretched out his legs, and placed his hands behind his head.

"That was twenty-four years ago," he admitted. "Since then, the Sons of Mars have become rowers and sailors. Denizens of the sea and no longer soldiers of the battlefield. Our sons are more comfortable with an oar than a sword. And the original Sons of Mars are middle aged, elderly, or dead."

"You control an important harbor on the coast of Sicilia," observed Alerio. "It seems to have worked out just fine. Except for the Syracusan army."

"Do you know why the Qart Hadasht Empire, the Republic and, until recently, the Syracusans, leave Messina to the Sons of Mars?" asked Nereus. Then he answered his own question. "Because we are neutral and without prejudice. We take cargo from everyone. And we don't have the will, or the means, to wage war on our neighbors."

"That's all very interesting, Captain Nereus," Alerio assured him. "But why did you ask about my skill as a weapon's instructor. There isn't enough time to teach your Sons to fight, even if I had the inclination."

"I received a letter a few months back from my nephew," Nereus revealed. "He's with the Southern Legion near the Capital. In the letter, he mentioned a Lance Corporal, a weapon's instructor. A man he was afraid to fight."

"I know Private Nereus. He's not afraid of anyone," Alerio responded.

"He's a Lance Corporal and a squad leader now," Captain Nereus corrected. "And, he is afraid of one Lance Corporal Alerio Sisera."

"I don't understand why that's important?" Alerio inquired. "There isn't time to teach your Sons to be Legionaries."

"I have at my command almost a thousand men," Nereus informed the Legionary. "Most are rowers and sailors. They can swarm and act as irregular skirmishers. What I need are four squads to hold the center of my line. I want you to teach them as much as you can before the Syracusans arrive. Train them to hold the center. You do that, and you'll leave Messina a wealthy man."

"And if I don't?"

"You will never leave Messina," Nereus promised.

Alerio picked up his mug of vino and looked into the cup. As he swirled the contents around, he watched as the wine formed a whirlpool.

"You'll need fifteen-man squads. Ten squads in the best armor with the best shields you have," Alerio advised while still observing the red liquid flowing around the inside of his mug. "Two for each of the Syracusan's phalanxes."

Chapter 45 - Floating Centers

Before the sun rose, five old Sergeants marched one hundred fifty grouchy men out of the city's gate. While the NCOs rode, the men shuffled and complained. Too early, too dark, too hungover, too little sleep - all the woes of men forced from their beds before dawn.

The Sergeants rode silently after the initial shouting to get the swords, shields, and armor distributed. Their destination flickered in the distance. Light from a single brazier acted as a beacon and the line of men angled for the bright spot.

As directed, upon arrival the Sergeants formed the men into a giant circle around the fire. The rising sun revealed a pile of woolen blankets on the ground below the brazier. Boredom set in and if it weren't for the Sergeants, the men would have laid down and gone to sleep. Again, per instructions, the men were forced to stand and wait.

***

The blankets moved. As if a specter from the earth, they rose from the ground to the height of a man.

"Silence," ordered the Sergeants when the men began talking about the strange vision. "Lock shields! Hold your positions!"

Legionaries would have snapped the edges of their shields together forming an impenetrable barrier. Some of the one hundred fifty men managed to touch the side of their neighbor's shield, but most left their shields resting on the ground in front of them.

"What's this?" a voice demanded from under the blankets. "You invade my campsite? I should jump on you all and slay you where you stand."

At the threat, more of the shields lifted. The blankets began traveling around the brazier.

"I'm glad you're here," the blankets stated. "Because back in the city, your best friend is under the covers with your girlfriend. While you stand here like an idiot, she is crying out in passion. Repeating your friend's name again and again and again. It seems, he is a better lover than you."

Several men shouted for the apparition to keep his mouth shut about their girlfriends. The floating blankets stopped and faced in the direction of a man who had protested.

"Is it my fault you have a tiny mentula?" inquired the ghost. "If he has more stamina than you?"

One man tossed his shield aside, drew his sword, and ran from his position. The Sergeants didn't have time to react before the man, with his sword held high for a downward slash, reached the specter.

A sheath, old with gashes in the leather letting the underlying wood show, swung up from under the blankets. The blunt instrument snapped forward as the blankets stepped to the side. It slapped into the charging man's thighs. While he stumbled trying to change the angle of his sword, the sheath whipped around and slammed into the angry man's neck. He sprawled on the ground and the blankets hovered above him before lowering over the prone figure. When the blankets rose, the man lay still on the earth.

"You break your circle over an insult? You are no better than a pack of rats," the blankets ventured. "Small, frightened rodents with funny teeth. Let me look."

The blankets spun slowly around as if examining the men in the circle. "Toothy. It's a wonder you can drink vino between those fangs. And why don't you rinse out your mouth once in a while? Your breath smells like rat merda. Oh, maybe you eat rat merda."

Two men from separate sections charged forward. Whether it was that insult or a combination of insults, and the early morning, wasn't clear. What was for sure, the men were out for blood. They came for the blankets with swords and shields.

With his sword held high overhead, the first kept his shield forward. Five steps from the offender, the blankets sprouted legs and ran at the man before leaping up. Flying horizontally, the specter's feet slammed solidly into the shield. The man and his shield arced back while his legs continued forward. Before he could recover from impacting with the ground, the blankets settled momentarily over him.

The second man charged the motionless blankets. Before he could deliver a blow, a sheath shot out and impacted his shins. Despite the pain, the man swept his sword towards the blankets. But the wraith was no longer there. It was beside the man. The second angry man disappeared inside the blankets. When the ghost moved away, it revealed the man lying motionless on the ground.

***

"You break your line, and you die," the specter shouted as the blankets were tossed to the side. Under them stood a naked man. Streaked in dirt, the man stood glaring around the circle. In his hands were two old sword sheaths and, on his head, rested a beaver felt petasos. "You let your temper control you and you die."

Alerio strutted around the circle. As he walked, flakes of dirt fell from his skin. He stopped at a gap between shields. The sheaths snaked out between the gap and slammed the shield holders painfully in their hips.

"Gaps kill. Leave a hole in a shield wall and it crumbles. And you die," Alerio informed them. When their shields were locked together, he bashed at the shields with both sheaths. The hardwood rang cleanly as they impacted the steadily held wood and metal shields. "These men will not die."

Then, he ran to another gap. One shield he kicked away while hammering the side of the other man's helmet. The man fell limply to the ground and lay there moaning.

"He is dead. That's on you," Alerio spit out at the man trying to bring his shield back to the front. "Gaps kill."

Alerio continued around the circle. But the men had learned the lesson and he found no openings in the shield wall. As he walked and tested the wall, the four men in the center of the circle rolled into sitting positions.

"Get back into the shield wall," growled Alerio.

The men in the circle opened the wall to allow the men to take their places. Two of them neglected to lock in their shields. Men on either side of them slapped their helmets and whispered a few words of warning. Soon the wall was a solid circle of shields.

***

"My name is Lance Corporal Alerio Sisera of the Republic's Legion," he announced. "Answer me. Break the wall and what happens?"

"I die," shouted back the one hundred fifty men.

"Leave the protection of the wall?"

"I die," they responded.

"Leave a gap in the wall?"

"I die," they replied.

"My name is Lance Corporal Alerio Sisera," he said again. "I am a weapon's instructor and it's my job to keep you from dying. Is it worth listening to me?"

"Yes, Corporal," they shouted.

"Break into lines of fifteen men," he instructed ignoring the dropped Lance in Lance Corporal. Figuring he'd just received a promotion in the Sons of Mars organization, he continued. "Keep your shields locked and walk to the city walls and back. Go slow, maintain the line, and keep your shields tight. Go! Sergeants, on me."

As the circle broke up and the squads moved away, the four Sergeants rode to Alerio and dismounted.

***

"You'll never make them Legionaries, Corporal Sisera," one of the Sergeants observed.

"I don't plan to," admitted Alerio as he pulled a wineskin of water from under the blankets. After rinsing off the dirt, he slipped on a tunic. "There are five phalanxes coming. I want to prevent them from busting our line."

"No line can stand against a phalanx," commented another Sergeant.

Alerio sat down and tied on his heavy sandals.

"I agree," he said as he stood and belted on a gladius, he found in the Messina armory. "But you can refuse to fight on their terms. Rather than a solid shield wall, I want to create floating centers."

Chapter 46 - Uniformed Movements

The circle reformed and behind each section of fifteen men, a Sergeant sat on his mount.

"Do not break formation," one ordered.

The men stood braced, angry, and frustrated. In the center of the circle, Alerio strutted around holding the old sheaths.

"Will not one of you children come out and fight me?" he cried. "Are there no men in Messina. Just little lads who want to hide behind their shields."

He repeated the challenge and each time a Sergeant reminded the men to hold their positions. Then, the weapon's instructor upped the challenge. He began to pound on the shields with the sheaths while taunting the men.

"You there. Should we send you back to change into a dress?" Alerio teased as he beat on a shield. "Maybe you'd be happier suckling babies."

One man flinched. "Hold your positions," bellowed the Sergeant. "What happens if you break the wall."

"I die," the section responded.

Alerio moved to another section and began pounding on their shields.

"You two. Should we send you to the animal pens?" he asked between wraps. "You look as if you'd be happier tending the sheep. Holding lambs suits you better than holding a shield."

A man took half a step and his Sergeant yelled, "Maintain the wall. Steady."

Alerio moved to the next section and, as he beat on their shields, he insulted them.

"Pirates? You think of yourselves as freebooters, daring sea going rogues?" he ventured. "I say you are cowards. As soon as a warship from Syracuse comes over the horizon, you must squeal like little lasses and row away as your bowels loosen. Does your ship stink of cowards' merda?"

The Sergeant was yelling, the men were yelling and two of them charged at the weapon's instructor.

Alerio ducked low and put his shoulder on the lower edge of one's shield. The man went up and flipped over the Legionary's back. Alerio emerged from under the shield with a sheath in each hand. The man tumbled over and landed on his neck.

Alerio batted away the second man's sword and leaped into the air. He cracked the other sheath over the man's head. Walking back to the first man who lost his temper, Alerio kicked him in the neck.

"What happens when you break the shield wall?" he screamed while pointing with the broken sheath at the two injured men.

"I die," a shocked murmur ran through the circle.

"What happens when you break the shield wall?" demanded the weapon's instructor.

"I die," this time the circle responded loudly.

"The next man to break the wall will die," Alerio promised. "Sergeants, form them up in rows by squads."

The Sergeants called their squads to line up on their horses. Once there were rows of thirty men facing the NCOs, they were ordered to face forward. Alerio marched to the head of the formation.

"Raise your left hand," he stated.

Most of the shields lifted but a good number of shields remained still while the right arms raised. Left and right were a major issue for military trainers. Given time to think, a person could figure out left from right. But in the heat of battle, the recognition had to be immediate. A thought occurred to the Alerio.

"Raise your Port arm," he shouted. All one hundred shields shot into the air.

Sailors, he thought, as he walked along the front rank. They had to know the sides of their ships in order to row properly.

"Make a partial turn to Starboard," he shouted. All of the formation turned right to face diagonally. "That's a Lateral. Face front. Turnabout and lock shields.

The formation became a jumble as some men turned right and others left. Their shields bumped into the man next to them.

"Starboard Turnabout," he instructed, and they easily did an about face in unison. Not smooth or pretty but they completed the movement without snags.

"One quarter turn to Starboard," he instructed. The formation turned right facing their Sergeants. "That's a Flank."

"Starboard Turnabout." They about faced and stood looking at the walls of Messina in the distance.

Now, if they can do the maneuvers while marching, Alerio thought.

"Start on your Port foot. Forward march," he shouted. "Port, Port. Now, Starboard Flank. Lock shields."

The formation moved forward with a lot of men out of step. He didn't care as long as the shields were tight, and they moved in the same direction.

"Sergeants. Pull your squads out of the formation and work them in ranks of two," yelled Alerio. "I'll come around and inspect their progress."

One of the old Sergeants rode up and looked down on the weapon's instructor.

"I served with the Sons in Agathocles' army," he stated. "You're as good in the field as any of our Captains."

With that compliment, the NCO kneed his horse and rode back to his squads.

Chapter 47 - The Fake Greek Command Staff

Alerio climbed the hill to the Citadel. Inside, he found Captain Crius Nereus sitting with four young men and one of the old Sergeants.

"Corporal Sisera, good evening," Nereus greeted him. Then he indicated the four young men. "These are my messengers. Two will travel to the Senate of the Republic with another plea for military assistance. The other two are my messengers to the Qart Hadasht Empire with the same request."

The messengers picked up satchels and walked out of the Citadel. Alerio watched them leave. Although he hoped the Republic responded first, he didn't hold out much hope.

General Flaccus had marched north with his Legion and the reserves from the Republic's treasury.

"Sit down, Corporal Sisera," Nereus ordered. "Over the last three days, you've done a good job turning rowers into soldiers. But the Sergeants have a problem. So, of course, I have a problem."

"And what is that, Captain?" inquired Alerio as he sat across from the Sergeant.

"Individually the squads respond well to their Sergeants," explained Nereus. "And the Sergeants trust you. Our problem is we have no commander for the heavy infantry at the center of our line."

"I assumed you would have Lieutenants in charge of the Port, Starboard and center," replied Alerio using the naval terms. "You must have experienced leaders to face the Syracusans."

"Ship's Captains I have plenty. Even a few retired infantrymen. But no one with land combat knowledge. I'm barely qualified. As I said before, Captain is an honorary title," he stated. "I was a simple soldier, not a commander."

"And I'm only a Lance Corporal of the Legion," pleaded Alerio. "I have no experience…"

Nereus cut him off, "No one in Messina does. But history has many cases of young men commanding armies. Alexander the Great comes to mind."

"I've heard of him," admitted Alerio. "But wasn't he the son of a king? My father is a farmer."

"All we need is to keep them off our walls until relief comes," Nereus stated. "Be they Legionaries or Qart Hadasht soldiers."

"And keep the phalanxes from chopping our lads into sausage meat," the Sergeant added.

"If I have no choice," Alerio agreed. Then he thought about it and asked, "What rank will I hold?"

"Lieutenant of the Sons of Mars," Nereus announced. "I've got a stallion and shiny Greek armor for you. The men will need to recognize you in the heat of the fight. And the Syracusans may hesitate when they see us in our Greek Commander armor."

"A fake Greek command staff," whispered Alerio.

The Sergeant stood, smiled, and hammered a salute into his chest.

"Captain. Lieutenant. I'd best go check on the men," the old NCO announced. "By your leave sirs?"

For the past few days, Alerio had been in charge of the Sergeants. Without thinking he released the NCO. "Dismissed, Sergeant," Alerio said.

The NCO left and Alerio glanced at the Captain to see if he was offended by having his authority usurped.

"Now Lieutenant Sisera," suggested Nereus without a hint of anger. "Tell me how you plan to deploy my heavy infantry."

Chapter 48 - There are Infantrymen then there are Hoplites

It was two days later that the advanced unit for the Syracusan army arrived at the river Longanus. Alerio, Nereus, and two pirate ship Captains, pressed into the roles of Lieutenants, sat on their horses. From the plain south of Messina, they looked down as a line of wagons and men reached the far bank. Five especially heavy wagons pulled by teams of oxen forded the river. When the wheels sank into the river bottom, men splashed into the water and pushed.

"There's the reason they took so long to get here," Nereus observed. "The road must have been a mess after the rain."

"Why are those wagons so loaded down?" Lieutenant Frigian, one of the pirate Captains, wondered.

"Hoplite armor, big shields and long, really long spears," Nereus reported. "We'll out number their soldiers, almost match their cavalry but, we can't duplicate their heavy infantry."

"I thought Lieutenant Sisera built us ten heavy infantry squads," the other Lieutenant ventured.

"It takes years to train a Hoplite or a Legionary," Nereus explained. "Lieutenant Sisera trained our men to move as a unit. If we wanted to match a phalanx, we should have started three years ago."

A Syracusan cavalry patrol crossed the river and trotted towards the Sons of Mars' command staff.

"Back to Messina," advised Nereus.

The four men reined their horses around and kneed them into a fast trot. Behind them, the advance units continued to push wagons and march soldiers through the river and up onto the plain. Tomorrow, the two forces would clash for the right to rule Messina.

***

"Rowers are strong, and they can fight," commented Lieutenant Frigian. "But that's from a warship. I'm not sure about a pitched battle on a grassy plain."

"If you remove the Hoplites, it would be just another brawl," replied Alerio.

"If you remove the phalanxes, I wouldn't be worried," Frigian informed him.

Nereus and the other Lieutenant were dining and drinking. After eating, Alerio and Frigian decided to visit with the men assigned to the heavy infantry.

"Since I became Captain of my own ship, I've found it's good for morale to check on the crew," Frigian stated as they walked to the staging area where the men were camped. "It's one thing to attack a merchant ship. There's no rowing away from this fight."

"I could tell you we'll all survive," Alerio replied as they reached the staging area. "But that would be lying. And I promised my mother, I wouldn't tell lies."

"How about you break that oath," Frigian suggested as they entered the campsites. "At least for tonight."

***

Messina's militia, as Alerio thought of them, resembled a tiny army of units from around the known world. Dressed in armor from ships captured, or stripped and sunk by the Sons of Mars, the arms, armor, helmets, and shields were from Greek city states, Macedonia, the Qart Hadasht Empire, Egypt, and even, the Republic.

Alerio would have preferred Republic armor, shield, helmet, javelin, and a gladius. Instead, he glowed in the morning sun like a golden statue in the polished Athenian armor and unfamiliar helmet. Adding to his discomfort, he rode a big horse and wore a long sword. As a trained heavy infantryman, he would be more comfortable on the ground standing in a shield wall.

"Lieutenant Sisera. Enlighten me," requested Frigian. "Shouldn't our heavy infantry be up front or even standing up?"

Alerio glanced at the men he had trained. They were sitting in two ranks of seventy-five men. In front of the heavy infantrymen stood groups of their eight hundred irregulars. All oarsmen pressed into the militia to face the Syracusan soldiers.

"Why is that?" asked Alerio.

"Maybe to intimidate the Syracusans?" he suggested. "Or at least make a show of force."

Frigian, Nereus and the right-side Lieutenant also wore polished Athenian armor.

"You cut a dashing figure, Lieutenant Frigian," Alerio teased with a smile. "If we display our undertrained heavy infantry too soon, the Hoplites will target our men and bunch up their phalanxes. I'd rather we take their formations on individually. Let's see how the Syracusan commander plans his attack."

Across the grassy battlefield, six hundred soldiers stood milling around. They were waiting, as was Alerio, for the Hoplites to form up in their phalanxes. They were the warships of land battles and like a battering ram, the phalanx could break any shield wall.

The Hoplites, with long spears and big shields, began to fall into formations. Evenly spaced across the battlefield, their placement showed the attack plan. The Messina militia would be broken at five separate places. Syracuse soldiers would follow the phalanxes through each breach allowing them to attack the Messina defensive force from the rear.

It was a good plan against a barbarian horde or an unprepared militia.

"Get to your post, Lieutenant Frigian," Alerio ordered. "I'll send your squads when it's time."

Frigian took a long look at the Hoplites, shook his head, and urged his mount forward.

Chapter 49 - Militia Shuffle

Captain Nereus watched as the phalanxes formed. He divided his attention between the enemy forces and Lieutenant Sisera. The Syracusans moved but Sisera sat quietly on his mount.

Soon, the tightly packed formations had soldiers spread out between them. While the phalanxes were powerful towards the front, its sides and rear lacked the long spears to fend off attackers. To protect the integrity of the formations, soldiers were required.

The Syracusan elements crept across the grass and Captain Nereus grew nervous. A few spears sailed through the air, but they landed short of the Messina irregulars. In a couple more yards, the missiles would fall among his boat crews. Still, Lieutenant Sisera sat calmly on his horse.

The phalanxes snapped down their long spears and locked their shields together. Like armored animals, the compact formations, of thirty-four Hoplites each, moved forward with the soldiers keeping pace. Nereus waffled between signaling his men into action or riding to the young Legionary and waking him up.

A flight of spears rose from the Syracusan lines and despite their shields, ten of his rowers fell screaming to the ground. Sisera seemed oblivious to the agony along the Messina defensive line.

Nereus was proud of his boat crews for standing as the enemy advanced. Another flight rose into the air but only five men fell from the barrage of spears. Mumbling rose from his men and a few heads turned to look in his direction.

Then Lieutenant Sisera leaned forward and spoke to the five Sergeants behind him. Once the NCOs had time to ride to where their men sat, Sisera twisted around and pointed a hand at Nereus. His fingers formed a fist before the arm jerked into the air.

Captain Nereus looked down at his trumpeter. "Sound the charge!"

***

Half of the Messina irregulars shouted a war cry and ran at the Syracusans. They angled away from the five phalanxes and hit the Syracusan soldiers. Shields clashed, swords fell, and men died. Ever relentless, the phalanxes continued their march and the Syracusan soldiers pushed as much as they fought to maintain their place beside the Hoplite formations.

As half of Messina's irregulars engaged with the enemy, the other four hundred irregulars stayed in place. Behind them, the squads of heavy infantrymen stood up and jogged to places where the phalanxes would break through Messina's defenses.

Nereus ignored the carnage as he, again, waited for Sisera. The Legionary also disregarded the fighting. His focus was the locations of the heavy infantry squads. Not until all ten squads were in place, did he raise an arm over his head and circle it in the air.

"Sound the retreat!" instructed Nereus.

***

At the sound of the trumpet, Messina's fighters turned and ran. Several were cut down as a cry of victory rose from the Syracusan soldiers. Seeing the enemy routed, they wanted to give chase, but they were held to the steady pace of the five phalanxes.

Like a mob, the irregulars ran to the stationary line. To give authenticity to the defeat, the retreating men broke through Messina's defensive line and continued to run. It wasn't until they reached Captain Nereus' position that they stopped, turned, and formed a new defensive line.

During the rout, the phalanxes approached the original Messina line.

"Sergeants. Prepare to split them and kill their soldiers," shouted Alerio as he held out his arms and pointed at the Lieutenants at the far ends of Messina's line. When he brought both hands together pointing towards the Syracusans, he ordered, "Execute!"

Alerio's squads were stacked in two ranks. With orders from the Sergeants, the squads faced in opposite directions and marched out of the way of the phalanxes. The irregulars stepped back and reformed behind the moving heavy infantrymen. At the ends of the Messina battle line, the other squads also performed the maneuver. As the phalanxes braced to punch their way through the irregulars manning Messina's defensive line, the line dissolved.

***

On the sides of the phalanxes, Syracusan soldiers went from facing irregulars to battling heavy infantrymen. While they weren't as efficient as Legionaries, Messina's infantry kept their ranks straight and their shields tight. Over their shoulders, the irregulars jabbed with their spears. Syracusan soldiers fell under the coordinated attack of the well-formed shield walls. Despite the discipline of the Massina militia, men from both sides of the brutal fighting fell bleeding and wounded to the ground.

The commanders of the phalanxes noticed the concentrated assault on their soldiers. One by one the Hoplite formations stopped. Before they could break formation and attack individually, Alerio raised his arms and circled it in the air.

The Messina trumpet blared.

At the sounding of the retreat, Messina's heavy infantrymen stepped back. They continued to step until they could safely turnabout and jog away from the Hoplites emerging from the phalanxes. A cheer went up from the Messina fighters.

After losing soldiers, their momentum, and the integrity of their formations, the Syracusan advance faltered.

"Lieutenant Sisera. We should go back and finish them," an infantryman yelled as his squad passed Alerio.

"Keep moving with your squad," ordered Alerio. Then he asked, "Break the wall?"

"I die," the man said as he checked to both sides to be sure he was aligned with his squad mates.

Alerio kneed his horse and headed for Nereus. The Captain waited with the survivors of the initial attack at the new defensive line.

***

"We broke their charge," Nereus announced as Alerio, Frigian and the other Lieutenant reined in their horses.

Frigian studied the ragged line of Syracusan soldiers interspersed between the solid ranks of Hoplites. "Why don't they attack?" he asked.

"They aren't sure about the skills of our heavy infantry," Nereus replied. "Our men look professional and move like experienced troops. Even if they aren't."

"Let's hope they never find out," Frigian ventured.

Then a cry came from the battlefield behind the Syracusans. Soldiers were walking among the wounded pulling off helmets and cutting the throats of any living Messina man. Shouting rose from the heavy infantrymen, and a few took a step forward.

"Stay in your ranks," shouted the Sergeants. "Hold your positions."

From the Hoplite ranks in the center, a Greek warrior stepped forward. The Hoplite banged his sword on his shield.

"Come fight me, pirates," he challenged. "Is there no one man enough to face me?"

"Hold! Stay in your ranks," the Sergeants called as several men began to move.

"It's a trick," Nereus advised his Lieutenants. "When our men are watching the fight, the Syracusans will attack."

"And if we don't do something," Frigian advised. "Morale will fall, and our forces will lose heart."

A pair of Syracusan soldiers carried a Messina heavy infantryman to the front of their formation. Once they were in full view of both sides, one held the infantryman while the other ran a blade into the wounded man's chest. His cry of pain, as the blade was twisted, carried across the battlefield.

"Stay in your ranks," bellowed the Sergeants as infantrymen and irregulars shouted out in anger. "Hold your positions!"

"We're going to lose them," suggested Frigian. "Either we retreat behind the city walls, or we attack. Simply standing here and waiting for the storm to break will get us all killed."

"You know the wall is too short and we don't have enough men to guard the city," Nereus responded. "We hold them here or we take to our ships and leave. I, for one, am not ready to surrender Messina."

"Then we need to attack," stated Frigian.

"Maybe not, Captain," Alerio said to Nereus. "They want a distraction. I'll give them one, but I need a moment to prepare."

"Whatever you need, Lieutenant Sisera," Nereus assured him.

***

Alerio rode to his two Sergeants, spoke with them before trotting to the squads' NCO on the right. There he had words with the Sergeant before turning back. He galloped along the space between the two battle lines. All the combatants' eyes followed the rider in the shiny Greek armor. At the far-left side, he pulled up and spoke with that Sergeant.

"No matter what happens, watch the Hoplites in front of you," he advised. "If they attack, do not advance on them. Let your shields break their charge. If they think you're not paying attention, they'll come at you."

"We'll be watching, Lieutenant," the NCO assured him.

Alerio kneed the horse and at a fast canter, he rode back towards the center of the line. Before reaching Nereus and the other Lieutenants, he pulled the horse up sharply and dismounted.

"Can you ride a horse?" he inquired of a Massina irregular.

"Yes, sir," replied the man in Legionary equipment.

"Come with me," Alerio said leading the man to a spot behind their line. Then to the men on either side ordered, "Form a barrier with your shields and give us some privacy."

The shields closed and blocked the view of the two men. When they opened, the Lieutenant in the shiny armor climbed onto his horse and rode to Nereus.

"What was that about?" inquired Nereus.

"I don't know, Captain," an oarsman replied from under the Greek helmet. "The Lieutenant said he wanted my equipment."

While Nereus and his two real Lieutenants exchanged questioning glances, a Legionary pushed through the Massina ranks. As he strutted forward, he thumped his short sword on his Legion shield. The Hoplite replied by banging his Greek shield.

Chapter 50 - Legionary versus Hoplites

Alerio had fast walked to the center of the Messina line. While Nereus questioned the man in the Lieutenant's armor and helmet, the Legionary forced his way between two irregulars.

About halfway across the no man's land, Alerio stopped and pointed his gladius at the belligerent Hoplite. Then to the surprise of the Massina Militia and the Syracusans, he swung the blade and indicated a second Hoplite. There was no question in anyone's mind, the Legionary had challenged two Hoplites.

The Syracusans had wanted a spectacle that would draw the attention of Messina's defenders. While the enemy was distracted, the Hoplites and soldiers would attack. But with two of their best stepping forward for individual combat, the plan dissolved as the distraction worked too well. Men from both sides leaned forward, or stepped out of their ranks, to watch the fight.

***

Alerio's one consolation was the last time he watched Hoplites in individual combat, the Greeks had used their shields to toss Illyrian pirates over their shoulders. Then, they spun on the disoriented pirates before butchering them. Hoping the maneuver was a standard tactic, the Legionary ran at the second Hoplite.

With the large Legion shield powering towards him, the Hoplite stopped and braced. He bent his forward knee and angled the bottom of his shield ready to catch the Legionary's shield. Once they collided, he'd flip the man over his shoulder.

When Alerio saw the bottom edge of the Greek's shield, he leaped. The two shields slammed together, and the surfaces slid against each other. While the Greek rose, he flipped his shield to throw the Legionary over his shoulder. But Alerio was compensating.

The leap was higher than it needed to be. In fact, the leap was high enough, so Alerio had to extend his arm to keep the shields in contact. As he vaulted up and over the Hoplite's shield, he kicked his legs hard. In the air, he rotated a half turn.

Landing sideways on bent knees, Alerio thrust his gladius up into the Greek's groin. The initial stab severely injured the man. But the Hoplite was turning, and his own momentum caused the blade to rip open his gut. As he fell to his knees in the bloody puddle and sausage like lengths of his intestines, Alerio rolled away from the first Hoplite's sword.

***

"Try that on me, pirate," the Hoplite spit out as he stalked by his dying comrade.

"Correction, I'm not a pirate," Alerio informed the Greek. "I'm Lance Corporal Alerio Sisera of the Republic's Southern Legion. But that shouldn't matter to you."

"It doesn't. Why should it?" the Greek asked as he shifted trying to get between Alerio and the Messina defenders.

Alerio noted a few Syracusan soldiers raise their spears. Only a little but sufficient to make him leery of a spear tip in the back.

"I just thought you'd like to know the name of your slayer," the Legionary stated as he shuffled around the Hoplite. His shifting placed him in front of the Greek with his back towards Messina. If he was going to catch a spear, at least he'd see it coming.

Personal combat came in two ways. Immediately, with the combatants clashing moments after meeting. Or delayed, as the fighters felt each other out for a weakness. But with heavy infantry shields, armor, helmets, and preferred swords, there wasn't a lot to test.

Alerio rushed forward and bashed the Hoplite's shield. Not too hard, he didn't want to reveal his strength or over commit. The Greek easily withstood the strike, spun around the Legion shield, and swung his sword. The blade hacked at the overextended Legionary's position. But Alerio had rolled in the opposite direction and, instead of using his blade, he kicked the edge of the Hoplite's shield.

The shield jerked away leaving the Greek momentarily open. Instantly, the Hoplite jumped back. Expecting a sword strike, he brought his sword down and across in a defensive move. Alerio let him retreat.

"You're strong," Alerio complimented the Hoplite.

"That was a lucky kick," replied the Greek as he stomped forward.

They clashed again. This time Alerio bent his knees, gathered his strength, and powered his shield forward. Caught by surprise, Greek was driven back two steps. But they ended up in a stalemate once the Hoplite dug in his feet. Hacking and grunting, both men fought for an advantage or the first cut. The grass churned and dirt piled up around their small battle, but neither could gain an advantage.

It was the Greek who stepped away to catch his breath.

"This is getting us nowhere," Alerio observed. "Why don't you pack up and go back to Syracuse. It'll save me from killing you."

"You kill me?" the Hoplite replied between deep breaths. "You'll see Hades while I'm drinking my wine this evening."

Alerio chanced looking down the battle lines. Both sides were losing interest in the shoving match. He needed to do something to increase the entertainment level. Moving to the dead Hoplite, he reached down and snatched up the Greek sword. It was longer than his gladius and while he moved back to face the gasping Hoplite, he tried the sword in both hands to see which felt better.

"Are you ready to die?" Alerio asked.

The Hoplite charged, his fatigue suddenly gone. Alerio slipped his arm out of the brace and when the Greek smashed into it, the Legion shield sailed for a few feet before tumbling to the ground.

"Nice charge," Alerio commented as he stepped forward ending up beside the charging Greek.

In panic, the Hoplite swung his shield around. Before he could get it into position, Alerio's blade snapped out. Blood ran down the Greek's leg from a cut across the left thigh. While he backed off, the Legionary cut circles with the gladius and the sword in the air. Looking left and right along the battle lines, he noted all eyes were once again on the personal fight.

***

"Maybe you'd like to run down to your camp and take a nap," teased Alerio as he paced back and forth while crossing and uncrossing the swords in front of him. "Oh, that's right, you can't run. There's a cut on your leg."

"I'm going to cut your heart out," the Hoplite threatened. But he remained where he stood on one leg while probing the wound on his thigh.

Alerio widened the sword swings and lengthened the distance he paced.

"I'm waiting, Greek," he shouted so his voice carried along the battle lines. "Are you a coward? Or worried about a little blood? Come forward and fight me!"

The Syracusans behind the Hoplite bristled and called for their champion to kill the pirate. On the other side, the Messina militia shouted encouraging words for Alerio.

Spectatorship was intoxicating. To build up the courage to participate in a sword fight, or to charge an enemy, took momentum, energy, and compulsion. But watching a blood duel was freeing. The troops on both sides were in full voice with passion for their champion. If they weren't divided by a no man's land, the opposing forces would probably mix and bet on the outcome.

Alerio took in the sporting mood on the battlefield. He doubted the Syracusan commanders could rally their Hoplites and soldiers from this atmosphere to mount an attack. With that thought in mind, he extended his arms out as if crucified, raised the tips of his swords, and turned his back on the Greek.

***

The unprotected back proved too tempting for the Hoplite. His first step was powerful but the second, on the injured leg, caused him to break stride. Still, the Legionary stood in the ridiculous victory pose unmoving. Gritting his teeth against the pain from the cramps caused by the wound, he hopped forward while raising his sword.

Alerio prayed to Mars that the idle time had cooled the muscles of the Hoplite's thigh. Listening to the shuffling let him know two things - where the Hoplite was located and that he was favoring the stiff, injured leg.

To compensate for the lack of mobility, the Hoplite took a longer final step in order to deliver the killing blow. Just a little beyond his normal stance. But still in his comfort zone, even if it the extension forced his shield from in front of his body. He wanted a drink. He wanted to bandage the leg. He wanted to sit down. But mostly, he wanted to kill this Legionary.

Alerio heard the Greek's foot slam down on the dirt. Rotating to his left, he brought his swords together and hooked the blades on the back edge of the Hoplite's shield. Using the hooked blades to increase his spin and speed of two steps, the Legionary pulled himself around the shield and away from the falling sword.

The Hoplite changed the angle of his blade, attempting to reach the moving Legionary. But his shield cocked to the right limiting the reach. Suddenly the Legionary was beside him, moving and still turning. Hoping to duck away, the Greek leaned to his right.

Alerio's spinning steps carried him around the shield and momentarily, he faced the Greek. But he was over rotating, his momentum pulling him passed his foe. As he fell behind the Hoplite, Alerio jerked both swords from the shield and in a sweeping motion raked them across the Greek.

As the Legionary fell behind him, the Hoplite started to turn. Then he felt a burning sensation on his upper arm. Glancing down, he convulsed at the sight of the peeled skin and the exposed bone. But there was too much blood. Separate from his arm, blood ran over his shoulder and down his chest. While still holding his sword, he raised the back of his hand to his neck. His knuckles sank into a deep wound, and his knees buckled. The Hoplite fell face down on his shield.

"This was a brave warrior," announced Alerio to the Hoplites and soldiers. "Take his body to your camp. Give him the funeral rites he deserves!"

The Legionary stood waiting to see of another Hoplite stepped forward to fight or if his suggestion worked. When two Hoplites marched from the line, he set his shoulders readying for another battle. Then he noticed their swords were sheathed. Relieved, Alerio backed off so they could pick up the body and carry the Hoplite from the battlefield.

Alerio tossed down the Greek sword and gave the Syracusans a cross chest salute. Then he slammed his gladius into its sheath, about faced, and marched towards the Messina defensive line.

"What happens when Hoplites break their shield wall?" one of the infantrymen asked.

Another infantryman looked around from his place in the defensive line. "They die," he replied.

Another pointed at Alerio and added, "Because the weapon's instructor kept his promise. He kills them."

Chapter 51 - A Night to Plan a Day to Die

"Lieutenant Sisera, what's our plan for tomorrow?" inquired Nereus.

Unlike the Legion, where meals were cooked by individual squads, the Captain had ordered food from the community kitchens in Messina. The infantrymen and irregulars ate at tightly packed camps along the defensive line. The only open space was the circle around the command staff's campfire. Alerio and Nereus sat and talked while the other Lieutenants were off setting up guard rotations for the night.

"In the morning, the phalanxes will come straight through our center and stab us in the heart, Captain," Alerio answered. Then he thought for a moment and asked, "What would you do if this was a sea battle?"

"Facing five Greek triremes?" replied Nereus. "Row away as fast as the oarsmen could stroke. Unless…"

Alerio waited while Nereus turned his face upward and stared at the darkening sky.

"Unless it was twilight. We're pirates and not always bound by the fears of our crews," Nereus explained. "We might lay off until dark, before rowing in and doing a little damage to the beached warships. Then, we'd run for open water. Our ships would be long gone before sunrise."

"You described two actions. One to wound the enemy and the other to avoid them," pondered Alerio. "They might get us killed, but I have a couple of ideas."

"Run away?" inquired Captain Nereus.

"In a manner of speaking," Alerio admitted. "I need sailors from two boats. Oarsmen from your most tightly knit boat crews. The mounted Sons and two of our heavy infantry squads."

"The river Longanus isn't navigable, and horses don't fit on biremes," explained Nereus. "If you're thinking about rowing up behind the Syracusans."

"The crews aren't for rowing," replied Alerio. "But they know each other and can work in unison under extreme conditions. And we'll need more firewood."

"Extreme conditions and firewood?" a confused Nereus asked. "I don't follow."

***

Deep into the night, Alerio reached out and, by feel, placed the squads of infantrymen online. Once the shields were locked, he separated two and sneaked between the gap. To the rear, he located the first oar of a boat crew. Leading the man and his rowers, they moved to the gap and he placed a hand on the man's shoulder. The boat crew waited.

Alerio moved down the line and separated another pair of shields. Again, he crept through and brought up another crew's first oar and the rowers. Taking the first oar's hand, he tapped out a ten count before moving back to the other first oar. There, he grabbed the man's arm and propelled him forward.

Both boat crews filtered silently between the shields heading for the sleeping camp. They didn't see the guards that Alerio had killed to make their passage unobserved by the Syracusans.

One crew angled for the horses, oxen, and supply wagons while the other moved to where the Hoplites stored their long spears and shields. Because they entered the camp at the same time, the exterior guards were confused when the wagons flared up, the horses broke from their tethers, and oxen fell from sword strikes. Part of the confusion was the line of men calmly carrying spears and shields through the camp. Until the spears and shields were tossed into the burning wagons, the guards didn't have a target. Then they did.

Cries of alarm rose throughout the Syracusans' camp and soon soldiers, and Hoplites were up and arming themselves. In the lanes between their tents, they searched for infiltrators. A few noticed the bodies running for the night. They gave chase until a shield wall and swords leaped from the darkness and stopped the pursuit. While the camp was in chaos, the boat crews vanished into the night.

The horses stampeded until they were rounded up by the mounted Sons. Soon the cavalrymen's horses were herded towards Messina.

The Syracusan command staff gathered at the edge of their camp. Across the grassy plain, Massina militia troops, backlit by roaring campfires, moved back and forth. None of them appeared to be coming forward to further assault their camp.

***

In the predawn, when the Messina campfires were low and movement settled down, the soldiers and Hoplites came abreast and marched across the grassy plain. Seeking revenge for the night raid, they planned to catch the pirates unaware. Secure in the knowledge the Messina defenders lacked discipline, they began to jog in order to cover the ground and complete the surprise attack.

They broke into a run and their lines spread as faster men outdistanced the slower or less enthusiastic among them. At the first campfires, they hacked blankets covering the lazy pirates as they raced deeper into the enemy's camp. Soon the Syracusan force was spread from the middle of the grassy plan to the center of the Messina camp. A few stopped, puzzled by the lack of response. Some used their swords to toss back blankets only to find sticks and sod rather than an enemy.

***

Alerio rose and waved his five squads of heavy infantry forward. In front of them, stragglers and disjointed Syracusan units strolled to catch up with their braver comrades. They didn't see Alerio's infantrymen or those closing from the other side of the plain - oblivious to the danger, until the first of them were struck down.

The infantry squads joined up in the center and turned to face Messina. Finally locating an enemy, the Syracusan commanders began to push the Hoplites and soldiers into a battle line. At last, an enemy to challenge, they screamed.

Then, the Messina irregulars and horsemen poured from the gates of the city. They attacked the Syracusans from the rear.

***

Alerio was tiring. All morning, he took a place stabbing over the infantrymen's shoulders with a javelin, screaming orders to reinforce weak places in his line, and choosing squads to rotate from the battle line to a resting place behind the fighting. Even though his infantry was maintaining their shield integrity, they faced an experienced fighting force. Slowly, they gave ground as the Hoplites and soldiers hammered the Messina militia backwards.

Messina' cavalry and the irregulars were the only reason the infantry wasn't overpowered. Caught between two attacking forces, the Syracusans had to divide their men to fight on two fronts. On the sides, the Messina horsemen kept them boxed in with savage charges.

Despite the success, Alerio realized his infantrymen were exhausted. It was time to cut the Syracusans loose.

"Sergeants, wheel your center squads back," he yelled, "Break the dam and let the Syracusans flow."

Two Sergeants ran up behind the squads holding the center of their line. After calling up another squad, they peeled back the two men in the center. Seeing a gap, the soldiers and Hoplites ran for the open field. The wider the gap, the more Syracusans escaped. None of them thought to turn around and continue the fight. They were as fatigued as the defenders of Messina.

Act 8

Chapter 52 - The Commander and the Captain

"Lieutenant Sisera. Another day, another victory," Nereus exclaimed as Alerio staggered into the meeting with the Captain and the two Lieutenants. "The original Sons of Mars would be proud."

"What are we going to do to them tomorrow?" asked Frigian with enthusiasm. He pointed to the cookfires blazing in the Syracusans camp. "I'd say, they're done for today."

"Sorry, Lieutenant, Captain but I'm all out of ideas," admitted Alerio. "I'd just like to sit down."

Crossing his legs, the Legionary sank to the ground. Frigian handed him a wineskin and sat beside the Legionary.

"Truth be told, we lasted longer than I thought we would," Frigian exclaimed. "It was a grand adventure, but I'd rather be at sea in a typhoon with a green crew than here."

"And I'd rather be at my father's farm," added Alerio as he handed the wineskin back to Frigian.

A silence fell on the Sons of Mars command staff as they sat and thought about another day of field combat. None were thinking positive thoughts.

"Lieutenants. I believe I see a solution to our problem," announced Nereus while climbing to his feet.

Alerio, Frigian and the other Lieutenant stared up at the Captain expecting him to voice a plan. But, Nereus wasn't looking down at them. His eyes were locked on the gates of Messina.

Through the portals marched columns of armed and armored troops. Their shields flashing in the midday sun, they marched out and began spreading across the grassy plain as they moved closer. Soon units of the newly arrived troops stood between the militia and Messina.

"Are they from Syracuse?" asked Alerio.

"No, Lieutenant Sisera," replied Frigian as he stood up. "Those are Qart Hadasht mercenaries."

A man in a yellow cape with polished armor strutted from the Empire's lines. He stopped at a group of infantrymen, and they pointed towards the command camp.

"The officer must be looking for me," guessed Nereus as he looked down at his blood-stained armor then back at the approaching man in the spotless armor and cape.

The Empire officer marched to the camp and looked at the three standing men with disdain. Although his knees were inches from Alerio's face, the officer ignored the sitting Legionary.

"I seek Crius Nereus," the Qart Hadasht officer demanded.

"I'm Captain Nereus. Let me introduce my staff," Crius greeted the man. "This is…"

"You are to report to Admiral Hanno at the Citadel," the Empire officer ordered cutting Nereus off. "Whom you drag along with you is none of my business. The Admiral waits."

Crius blushed and he formed fists with his hands. Before he could respond to the disrespect, Frigian reached out and placed a hand on his arm.

"Go see the Admiral," Frigian advised. "We'll see to our wounded. Take Sisera with you."

"I'll go speak with this Hanno," growled the leader of the Sons of Mars. "Lieutenant Sisera, come with me."

Alerio pushed off the ground and did a quarter turn as he rose. With his face only inches from the Qart Hadasht officer, he replied directly into the officer's face.

"Yes, Captain," Alerio emphasized the words as he smirked at the officer.

"Now! Lieutenant," Nereus ordered when he realized Sisera's hand clenched the bloody hilt of his gladius. "Come with me!"

Nereus walked off hoping the Legionary would follow and not start trouble by killing the Qart Hadasht officer. He relaxed when Sisera immediately fell in beside him.

"Arrogant mentula, isn't he?" ventured Nereus.

"Qart Hadasht cūlus," Alerio agreed.

***

Nereus and Alerio passed patrols of Qart Hadasht soldiers as they threaded through the narrow streets of

Messina. On the road running from the harbor, the two men turned west and continued towards the Citadel.

Alerio glanced over his shoulder. Beached ships deposited more armored troops and other ships rowed into the harbor. All the new ships were Empire design. The Legionary began to count the number of Qart Hadasht soldiers entering Messina.

They began the hike up to the Citadel. Three officers in Empire armor stood glaring down at them as they climbed the hill.

"A Republic Legionary?" one commented as Nereus and Alerio reached the flat at the top of the hill. "I didn't know the Republic had troops here."

"They don't. This is Lieutenant Sisera who is on my staff," Nereus responded.

"And who are you?" demanded another.

"Captain Crius Nereus, commander of the Sons of Mars," Crius proclaimed. "and governor of Messina."

A tall officer holding an elaborate helmet under his arm appeared in the doorway of the Citadel. His shaved head reflected sunlight, causing the dark and fierce looking man to glow. He approached with a scowl on his face.

"Not anymore," he announced. "I am Admiral Hanno of the Qart Hadasht Empire. As of now, you are the Civilian Magistrate for Messina. Unless you prove unworthy. Then I'll replace you."

"I am the Captain of the Sons of Mars. That's my authority," Crius informed Hanno. "You are simply a guest in my city. If you don't act civil, we'll expel you."

Hanno didn't respond. He raised an arm and pointed to the grassy plain. Far below and over the city's defensive walls, the heavy infantry and irregulars of the militia were lined up. Under the eye of an Empire officer and his troops, the Messina defenders were tossing their armor, swords, and shields on a pile before being allowed to enter the city.

"You have no need of an armed force," Hanno explained. "but I need rowers for your ships to continue the business of Messina. For now, I allow them to live. As I do you, Crius Nereus. Do not try me. I can change my mind."

With those words, the Qart Hadasht Admiral spun around and strutted back into the Citadel. For a moment, Nereus glared at the empty doorway then he turned away and marched stiffly down the hill.

Alerio took longer as he ran his eyes up and down the three Empire officers as if appraising livestock. Finally, he smiled and nodded at the officers before following Crius Nereus off the hill.

Chapter 53 - Captain Frigian

Alerio staggered up the ramp. It wasn't the drink from the celebration last night that made him off balance. It was the heavy pack, the stack of Legion armor, and the bedroll. Although the beaver felt petasos prevented the morning sun from directly reaching his eyes, the light reflecting off the water blinded him. So, the Legionary staggered before an arm reached out and pulled him onto the warship.

"Good morning, Lieutenant Sisera," the owner of the helping hand said.

"It's Lance Corporal Sisera, Lieutenant Frigian," Alerio informed him. "My days as a Lieutenant in the Sons of Mars are over."

"As are my days as a Lieutenant," Frigian replied. "I'm back to Captain Frigian where I belong. Go astern and find a place to drop your load. But don't get too comfortable. It's a short row to Rhégion. Handlers, push her off! First oar, prepare to drop oars!"

"Launching," announced the crewmen on the beach as they put their shoulders against the bow of the bireme.

The warship slid off the sand, floated free and the four pushers climbed aboard. As soon as they took their oar positions, another voice called out.

"Blades down," and one hundred twenty oars splashed into the water.

"Back her down!"

The oarsmen rowed in reverse and Captain Frigian's ship powered away from the beach. Once in deep water with room to turn, the ship swung about and rowed out of Messina harbor.

***

A short while later, the ship ground onto the beach at Rhégion. Alerio stood at the bow rail and prepared to toss his pack, bedroll, and armor over the side.

"Hold on Lieutenant," one of the oarsmen called out.

Before Alerio could protest, a ramp was dropped to the beach and the Legionary marched off the pirate ship. He got a few questioning-looks from Legionaries on the shore, but he ignored them. His mission completed, he needed to make his report to the old Tribune.

***

"Lance Corporal Alerio Sisera, reporting for Tribune Velius," Alerio stated to the clerk at Southern Legion headquarters.

Other than the clerk, the offices in the Legion Post at Rhégion were deserted.

"He left but said he'd be back before midday," the clerk responded. "First Sergeant Gerontius is off with the recruit training unit. You can go store your gear or wait."

"I'll wait," declared Alerio as he moved to a wall and dropped his bags. Then he leaned against the clay brick wall, crossed his arms over his chest, and fell asleep while standing up.

Chapter 54 - Report from Syracuse

"Lance Corporal Sisera, the Tribune asked that you meet him in his garden," the clerk said as he reentered the office. "You can leave your equipment."

Alerio's eyes opened. He hadn't seen the clerk leave and had no idea how long he'd been asleep. Rather than take the hallway to the Planning and Strategies room, he went out the front door and took the path around the rear entrance.

"Lance Corporal Sisera, reporting," Alerio announced when he got to the back of the building.

On his knees, the Tribune, who seemed to be digging a hole to plant a rooted flower laid out beside him, replied, "Just let me finish with this specimen. It's from up on the mountain and I want to see if it'll grow here. I saw something interesting from up there. It seems the troops from Syracuse have packed up and moved south of the river Longanus. No doubt due to the arrival of Empire troops."

"About three hundred heavy infantrymen and four hundred irregulars," Alerio added. "and seven hundred plus oarsmen from four Qart Hadasht triremes. But that number could very."

"From a mission to Syracuse, you seem to be well informed about the situation in Messina," observed Tribune Velius as he lightly tamped dirt around the stem of the mountain flower.

"The Syracusan army is marching on Messina," Alerio explained. "I traveled to Messina and got drafted into the Sons of Mars. What I don't understand is why did they asked the Empire to come into their city. What difference does it make which pack of wolves you let into your hen house?"

"The Sons of Mars have been raiding Syracuse farms and outlaying towns. Hiero the Second defeated the Sons at the river Longanus years ago. He left after a promise that the Sons would stop raiding his people," Velius related as he placed his hands on his knees to help him stand. "They broke the promise. So, the Sons allowed the Empire to come in and protect them. The Qart Hadasht may claim sovereignty and declare Messina part of the Empire. But, unlike the King of Syracuse, they won't begin by crucifying the Sons of Mars."

"The Empire sent Admiral Hanno to command Messina," Alerio explained as he followed Velius into the Planning and Strategies room. "He does seem to have taken over."

"I don't know the Admiral," the Tribune admitted as he shuffled to the tabletop relief map. "But I do know the Republic has a problem."

Alerio reached into a box. He pulled out a yellow Qart Hadasht block and placed it on the section of the map occupied by Messina. Not to be out done by the young Legionary, the Tribune pulled a blue Syracuse marker and placed it beside Messina.

"The Empire is on our threshold," Velius stated. "I hope you're ready to travel. We've got to inform the Senate."

"After we report, do you think I can take my leave and visit my family?" Alerio asked as he headed for the internal doorway.

"Like ocean tides, the debate will ebb and flow," Velius answered. "But unlike the cycle of the seas, the Senate takes more than a day to reach a high-water mark."

"Is that a yes or a no, Tribune?" Alerio inquired before entering the long hallway leading to the Legion offices and his gear.

"We shall see, Lance Corporal, we shall see," mumbled the Tribune as he studied the map. With the Empire not much farther than a bow shot from Republic soil, the head of Planning and Strategies for the Southern Legion had other things on his mind. A vacation for Alerio was low on the list.

Chapter 55 - Arriving and Leaving the Capital

Consul Appease Clodus Codex was livid. Not so much at Tribune Velius' news about the Empire being in Messina but at his analogy.

"If we had Qart Hadasht forces that close to the Capital, it would be a siege," Velius explained once he and Alerio had been granted an appointment to see the Consul. "I understand your reluctance, but we need more resources for the Southern Legion."

"Your understanding is merda," burst out Consul Codex. "Flaccus emptied the Republic's coffers to seek revenge on the Etruscanons at Volsinii. The citizens are screaming for infrastructure necessary to expand the Capital. The Senate is divided over funding for a thousand

and one problems. And you promenade in here asking for a Legion to march against the Empire and start a new war."

"No Consul. All I asked for was funding for more Legionaries to protect our southern border," pleaded Velius. "Maybe I could have chosen a better comparison."

"Maybe so. I'll bring it up with the Senate," Codex promised. "Keep yourself available for questioning, Tribune. Now, get out of my office."

***

On the steps of the Capitol building, Alerio turned to the Tribune.

"Does the Consul mean I should keep myself available, as well?" inquired Alerio.

"No Lance Corporal. Go see your family," Velius explained. "But stop at the stockyards and buy a horse. I want you back in four weeks. We have more work to do. King Hiero the Second will delay his march on Messina, so we have time."

"But the Syracusan army is ready to march," advised Alerio.

"That was against the Sons of Mars," Velius informed the young Legionary. "The Empire and Syracuse have a treaty keeping them both from invading the northeast of Sicilia. King Hiero will send protests to the Empire before he marches. If he marches."

"How is it that Hiero was going to capture Messina?" inquire Alerio. "And now he's protesting the Empire's occupation."

"That lad is foreign politics by old nemeses," replied Velius. "Now off you go."

"By your leave, Tribune?" Alerio asked.

"Dismissed, Lance Corporal Sisera."

The End

Reluctant Siege

A note from J. Clifton,

When I started Clay Warrior Stories, I was uncertain if readers would enjoy adventure stories set in the mid Roman Republic. There are many books using the Roman Empire as settings. I went against the trend by writing in an earlier period.

To complicate matters, the Republic before the first Punic War differed from the vast regimented Empire that is familiar to most people. By studying ancient technology, reverse engineering tactics, reading about historical events, searching for Latin curse words, and looking up Gods and Goddesses, I hoped to bring the mid Republic to life.

The result, you like my work and sales are great -a big cross chest salute to you.

I've answered many e-mails from readers discussing the differences between the Empire and the Republic. All taught and challenged me to grow as a writer. Most were positive. Quite a few were informative. And a few were super critical. You can't please everyone.

I appreciate the readers who reached out to me with e-mails expressing their opinions.

The first four books in this series covered the years before the first Punic War. In book five, we'll follow the first Legion units to cross a body of water to fight an established Empire, and a Kingdom, on foreign soil. Hopefully, you'll come along with me for the adventure.

Thank you for reading the Clay Warrior Stories.

To sign up for my newsletter and to read blogs on ancient Rome, go to my website: www.JCliftonSlater.com

E-Mail: GalacticCouncilRealm@gmail.com

I write military adventure both future and ancient.

Other books by J. Clifton Slater

Historical Adventure – *Clay Warrior Stories series*

#1 Clay Legionary   #2 Spilled Blood   #3 Bloody Water

#4 Reluctant Siege   #5 Brutal Diplomacy   #6 Fortune Reigns

#7 Fatal Obligation   #8 Infinite Courage

#9 Deceptive Valor   #10 Neptune's Fury

#11 Unjust Sacrifice   #12 Muted Implications

#13 Death Caller   #14 Rome's Tribune

#15 Deranged Sovereignty

#16 Uncertain Honor   #17 Tribune's Oath

#18 Savage Birthright   #19 Abject Authority

Novels of the 2nd Punic War – *A Legion Archer series*

#1 Journey from Exile   #2 Pity the Rebellious

#3 Heritage of Threat   #4 A Legion Legacy

Military Science Fiction – *Call Sign Warlock series*

#1 Op File Revenge   #2 Op File Treason

#3 Op File Sanction

Military Science Fiction – *Galactic Council Realm series*

#1 On Station   #2 On Duty

#3 On Guard   #4 On Point

Printed in Great Britain
by Amazon